The Birch Grove
and Other Stories

OTHER TITLES IN THIS SERIES
(General Editor: Timothy Garton Ash)

The Birch Grove and Other Stories

Jarosław Iwaszkiewicz

Translated by Antonia Lloyd-Jones
With an Introduction by Leszek Kołakowski

CENTRAL EUROPEAN UNIVERSITY PRESS

Budapest London New York

These stories were first published in various editions in Polish in the
1930s.

First published in this English edition in 2002 by
Central European University Press

An imprint of the
Central European University Share Company
Nádor utca 11, H-1015 Budapest, Hungary
Tel: +36-1-327-3138 or 327-3000
Fax: +36-1-327-3183
E-mail: ceupress@ceu.hu
Website: www.ceupress.com

400 West 59th Street, New York NY 10019, USA
Tel: +1-212-547-6932
Fax: +1-212-548-4607
E-mail: mgreenwald@sorosny.org

ISBN 963 9241 45 8 Paperback
ISSN 1418-0162

Library of Congress Cataloging-in-Publication Data

Iwaszkiewicz, Jarosław, 1894–1980
  [Short stories. English. Selections]
  The birch grove and other stories / Jarosław Iwaszkiewicz ; translated
by Antonia Lloyd-Jones ; with an introduction by Leszek Kołakowski.
    p. cm. – (Central european classics, ISSN 1418-0162)
  ISBN
  1. Iwaszkiewicz, Jarosław, 1984—Translations into English. I.
Lloyd-Jones, Antonia. II. Title. III. Central European classics
(Budapest, Hungary)
  PG7158.I8 A25 2002
  891.8'5373–dc21

                                         2002003353

Printed and bound in Hungary by
Akadémiai Nyomda Kft., Martonvásár

Contents

Introduction

To read Jarosław Iwaszkiewicz's stories demands some time and effort – not because they are complicated, or assume that the reader has some special knowledge of history or philosophy, nor because the sense and flow of the events recounted cast the reader into confusion. The narrative itself is, or seems to be, simple. In it we find all the usual events of human life: love and falling in love, death and dying, partings and journeys, things coming to an end, the concerns of youth and old age, of town and countryside, of day and night, wealth and poverty, music and landscapes. If, however, I say that reading these texts demands time and effort, I mean it in the sense in which this is true of most traditional novels and stories.

In our day and age, being in a hurry is a rule of life and an effective tool in the rat race, while taking short cuts to achieve one's aims is an essential rule of all reasonable activity. But what is the goal of reading novels or stories? If it is simply to take in the main events of the story and the fate of the heroes, then there is no point in reading the works of Tolstoy, Mann or Proust in detail. A quick glance at the pages will suffice, leaving out, for example, descriptions of nature or scenery, or sub-plots, if one merely wants to know 'what happened', who killed whom, who loved and left whom, in what war they took part etc. Every experienced reader is capable of doing this, and thus of speeding up their reading by taking a short cut to their 'goal'. But if this is how one goes about it, one is not actually reading anything.

So, too, with Iwaszkiewicz's stories. In terms of events, their content is for the most part not very exciting; they tell of everyday human concerns, including love affairs, of course (homosexual as well as heterosexual), but never the coarsely exposed details of sexual encounters. There are practically no shocking events, no explosions, hideous crimes or monstrosities, no characters from Dostoevsky, nor is there any satire or mockery. Yet if one reads them properly, these are wise, moving stories. Reading them properly means reading every word, leaving nothing out, including numerous descriptions of rural buildings and manor houses, trees, plants, animals, landscapes and moonrises. (It is generally the case that writers from Poland's eastern borderlands, nowadays Ukraine, are on especially intimate terms with nature.) On careful reading, these stories will render a sad endorsement of life. Iwaszkiewicz knows the world's evil, of course, as well as its good, yet he is aware that wisdom demands affirmation of what is real, and that in the most important human concerns far less changes than the observer, excited by the novelties of the era, might imagine. (We should remember that Iwaszkiewicz was born in a world where there were no cars or radio, but I do not think that the astounding technological changes that occurred in the twentieth century altered his attitude to life.) In the diaries of Anna Iwaszkiewicz, his wife, who was by no means an uncritical admirer of all her husband's works, we find a comment written in 1933. She notes that neither *The Wilko Girls* nor *The Birch Grove* include any special effects, that both stories are 'deep in an inconspicuous way', and that in them we may feel the sadness of hopes that can never be realised, the impossibility of going back in life, and a yearning for future prospects that no longer exist. But as such matters are of little concern to the reading public, Anna, like some of Iwaszkiewicz's fellow writers, though enchanted by these stories, does not predict a wide readership for them.

In *The Wilko Girls* we follow an unsuccessful attempt to return to the past and some ambiguous encounters with bygone days. The hero of the story stays at the same manor house, in the company of the same women that he knew many years ago. The main difference between these encounters is not that everyone has inevitably grown older, but that in the bygone era he had ahead of him a future that he now knows will never happen. He is not old, he is not yet forty, but he knows that life has already passed him by. He remembers that he and the woman with whom he was once in love promised each other that later on, in time, they would 'explain' it all to each other, but now it turns out that there is nothing to explain.

The Birch Grove tells of two brothers meeting after many years apart. An inability to understand each other has grown up like a wall between them. The younger brother is an elegant man of the world, who comes back from 'Europe' with a fatal illness. The elder brother is a forester, recently widowed and consumed by work. Each of them becomes aware, in a different way but with just as much force, of the bitter emptiness of life.

In *The Mill on the River Utrata* we find all the elements that fill Iwaszkiewicz's writing: love that starts badly and ends badly; religious faith, first as a support in life and a source of happiness, then lost; a feverish, desperate search for some meaning amid life's adversities. And when that meaning finally reveals itself, on the point of death, it can no longer be expressed.

Despite having entirely different narrative material the stories do present the reader with similar landscapes, suffused with the irremovable sadness of life: love, even when 'consummated', leaves behind an unidentifiable longing for yet another consummation that never comes; returning to a time gone by is always branded with the impossibility of understanding what has happened. Death is ever present, ordinary, and accepted as an ordinary thing, yet impossible to comprehend.

Jarosław Iwaszkiewicz was born on 20 February 1884 in the Ukrainian village of Kalnik and died in March 1980 in Warsaw. He studied music and law in Kiev, and in 1918 moved to Warsaw for good. There he worked on various literary periodicals and was a member of the Skamander group of poets.

The generation that entered the Polish literary scene immediately after the First World War produced many extremely talented poets, whose voice was dominant in the inter-war period and after. Among them the Skamander group stood out – the name comes from the title of the periodical *Skamander*, in which they published their manifesto in 1920. Besides Iwaszkiewicz, the group included Julian Tuwim, Antoni Słonimski, Jan Lechoń, Kazimierz Wierzyński and Maria Jasnorzewska-Pawlikowska. The Skamander writers used mainly poetic forms inherited from tradition, yet they spoke in the language of their time, avoiding artificiality, pathos and abstraction; they wanted their writing to have relevance for their contemporaries. They rejoiced at Poland's regained independence, but they loathed nationalism, militarism and the conceited prolixity of the right wing. Each of them was an outstanding individual who developed his own writing style. Tuwim, more than the others, indulged in various experiments with language. Within this group, Iwaszkiewicz was the only prose writer in the full sense of the word. In his pre-war poetry he was perhaps the strongest exponent of classical forms.

For some years Iwaszkiewicz was employed at the Ministry of Foreign Affairs, and from 1932 to 1936 he was in the diplomatic service in Copenhagen and Brussels. His work is extremely rich, including many collections of poetry, lengthy novels (such as *The Red Shields*, 1934, and *Fame and Glory*, 1956–62), short stories, plays (including *Summer in Nohant*, based on the life of Chopin in France) and translations from the French (including Rimbaud and Gide), Danish (Andersen and Kierkegaard) and Russian (Chekhov and Tolstoy). He also wrote libretti for the works of his close friend Karol Szymanowski, as well as literary criticism, essays and memoirs.

I knew Iwaszkiewicz. I could not say that we were close friends (the fact that we were on first-name terms is no indication, as that was customary at the time within literary circles, even among people of different generations). We used to meet and talk mainly in his office at the periodical *Twórczość*, which he edited for many years from 1955, sometimes in a neighbouring café, and sometimes at meetings of the Writers' Union, but never in anyone's private home. Our conversations were always friendly, without a hint of mistrust.

Introduction

Iwaszkiewicz was highly and thoroughly educated – not only in music and world literature, but also in history and religion. He knew many languages well, including a language as exotic for a Pole as Danish. Throughout his life he read books properly and carefully – not in order to write reviews of them, but to learn from them. I myself can boast that Iwaszkiewicz read a very stout work of mine on some quite obscure sectarians and mystics active in seventeenth-century Holland, Germany, Italy and France. I know that he read it, because I received a letter from him with comments; he also wrote some poems related to this reading matter.

A melancholy affirmation of the world as it is – that is the hidden message, never directly expressed, of Iwaszkiewicz's prose, and also of his poetry and plays. Whether he acquired this view of the world from Christian traditions or not, I don't know. Coming to terms with reality is, however, in his account, a sign of spiritual maturity. This does not mean that we should passively put up with everything that happens, without distinction. During the German occupation in Poland such a recommendation would have meant running away from a basic sense of decency. One had to be on this side, not the other, take part in the underground fight, support the resistance army, harbour Jews and help conspirators in hiding, exposing oneself to the risk of death. Jarosław and Anna Iwaszkiewicz did all these things. But the German occupation was an unusual, unprecedented concentration of evil, with no room for compromise, hesitation, or half-measures.

What if behind this sad affirmation of life there lies hidden a metaphysical or religious outlook? The careful reader often feels this to be the case, though it is certainly hard to prove. The careful reader will notice this in almost all the stories and in many of the poems. Maybe the beautiful, moving novella, *Mother Joan of the Angels*, written during the war (and later made into a film by Jerzy Kawalerowicz), illustrates this better than any other of his works. It is a version, transposed to eastern Poland, of the famous story of the collective possession by the devil of nuns at the convent of Loudun in the seventeenth century. In it, some complex theological issues are interwoven with an equally complex analysis of some dark human souls, especially those of the exorcist and the bedevilled nun.

Yet coming to terms with reality, as Iwaszkiewicz understood it, was certainly the reason – or one of the reasons or pretexts perhaps – for his loyalty to the authorities in Poland, both in the inter-war years and in the communist era. Reflecting on this shortly after the First World War, Anna Iwaszkiewicz saw in it the writer's patriotism but also, maybe to an even greater degree, a certain snobbery and weakness for 'the court'. Iwaszkiewicz, as his acquaintances often commented, had a quasi-instinctive reverence for authority. In communist Poland, one's loyalty or refusal to be loyal to the ruling powers was, at least from the mid 1950s, in the years of the so-called thaw and beyond, the main dividing line among writers and artists. For a writer, being loyal to the authorities meant, of course, that the rigours of censorship were less severe, but it was not a total guarantee against being censored. Iwaszkiewicz's greatest, three-volume work, *Fame and Glory*, was published after several years' delay. Irena Szymańska, who worked at the Czytelnik publishing house in those days, recalled in her memoirs that this was because he had failed to describe the Russian revolution through the eyes of a Bolshevik. Iwaszkiewicz's loyalty to the communist authorities expressed itself in occasional panegyrics that could be found in his magazine *Twórczość*, and sometimes in his participation in showcase public bodies. As far as I remember, however, there were no explicitly political concessions in his writing, if one ignores a couple of second-rate poems on the subject of peace – when 'peace', as in Orwell's Ministry of Truth, was the great ideological catchword of the communist world. Iwaszkiewicz undoubtedly thought his poetry, novels, stories and plays would occupy a permanent place within the canon of Polish literature, and that no one would remember a few flattering remarks addressed to the authorities. Iwaszkiewicz's loyalty was also expressed in his behaviour within the Polish Writers' Union, of which for many years he was chairman. He never persecuted or oppressed anyone, but whenever a storm was brewing with political overtones – and more than one such storm blew up – it generally turned out that at the critical moment Iwaszkiewicz would be away in Sicily or Paris.

One should emphasise that Iwaszkiewicz did on occasion flatter the authorities and was regarded as a loyal subject, the darling of the ruling powers. Yet no one has been able to provide even a single example of him treating anyone badly; on the contrary, he helped many people, even those who had been dismissed from their jobs and endured other difficulties at the hands of the authorities. He was quite simply a very good person in the purest sense of the word, extremely obliging and ready to help his neighbours in all kinds of misfortune and adversity.

There is another fact that should be stressed. Among Polish 'people of culture' as they were known – writers, artists, scholars and film directors – there was a group, maybe not large in numbers but noisy and aggressive, of 'janissaries of the system', informers, oppressors of the 'class enemy', tub-thumpers; as a rule they were mediocrities as writers or artists. There was also a small group of people who expressed their opposition publicly. The resulting unpleasantness was no longer dramatic after 1956, but it was still troublesome. It included being banned from publishing, being sacked from one's job, and being refused a passport. Finally there was the then large population among the officially termed 'creative intelligentsia' of those who fawned upon the authorities and praised the communist system, while telling themselves and others that one must do so in order to save the 'cultural substance' and preserve traditional values from extinction. In most cases what they actually preserved was their own privileges and their own pockets.

· Yet if anyone were truly able to lay claim to such an attitude, it would be Iwaszkiewicz. The monthly *Twórczość* was not, of course, a periodical of the political opposition (such periodicals could not legally exist in the Polish People's Republic), but it was a forum where Polish literary culture really did continue to exist and grow, in poetry, prose, literary criticism and essays. *Twórczość* also published many writers who not only had a scornful, derisory attitude to contemporary socialism, i.e. Sovietism, but who were well known to the authorities for their opinions and were regarded, not without reason, as enemies of the system. (Naturally they were only published if they had not been honoured with a total ban on publication.) One can truly say that *Twórczość* was a cultural oasis in the desert of the Polish People's Republic.

Friends and acquaintances of Iwaszkiewicz, as well as others who read his periodical, were irritated by his conduct on more than one occasion. Yet it is worth mentioning that he was one of the very few who were forgiven this within circles stigmatised by the authorities for hostility and underground warfare against the system. Well into the 1980s the post-Yalta order in Europe was regarded as a permanent reality, and the real question was not how to break up the Soviet empire, regain independence for Poland, and do away with the one-party authorities and the censorship, but how, within the boundaries imposed by such conditions, to preserve intellectual virtues, artistic values and respect for the truth – that is, everything that the regime of the time regarded as a criminal attempt against its monopolistic authority. We did not envisage the destruction of an empire, but within the already weakening and ailing totalitarian system we sought to broaden the range within which the truth could appear as much as possible.

While Iwaszkiewicz may justly have been criticised for his loyalty or compliance towards the ruling powers, one should acknowledge that those who published their work in *Twórczość* were in a way indirectly benefiting from that loyalty. Loud condemnation of Iwaszkiewicz began after the fall of communism in Poland in 1989, voiced as a rule by people whom no one had heard of as having fought against the authorities or run risks in the communist era. Yet they made their condemnation public as soon as they were free to do so without any risk. Such censure will have no effect, however. Just as Iwaszkiewicz undoubtedly anticipated, he will endure among the classics of Polish literature, and his servility towards the authorities will be remembered only by his biographers.

Leszek Kołakowski

A New Love

Everything was ready before the bell rang. On the table stood a huge bouquet of ten pink roses. In full bloom, they looked more like fruits than flowers, or like edible flowers. Each neatly pleated rose resembled a small cream cake, coated in cochineal icing. Their scent floated right across the room, permeating it gently and sweetly. Close to, it was oppressive. If he buried his nose right in the middle of the bunch, he felt dizzy. As he touched these flowers he was reminded of something meaty and over-sensual. He was touching flesh. He took a long, careful look at them: they were already very over-blown. The small, round, wrinkled patches in the centre were going a bit white and had half-opened, revealing a few golden stamens. They were very short and shame-faced for having failed to turn into sweet-scented petals before the rose had reached full bloom. The sight of these golden stamens and the white spots surrounding them gave him the grudging thought that they were only ordinary cabbage roses. Just as this occurred to him, the doorbell rang.

It was a strong, confident ring that immediately reminded him of the look in her eyes yesterday. That first look as often as not encapsulates the entire essence of future impressions. There in the light of a new pair of eyes he had found all his old strengths and hopes. Such a fervent portent of unexpected happiness that at first he had been taken aback and had failed to respond with the same sort of look. He could see that what had come crashing down on him was without question a great love. He felt like a chemist at the moment when an experiment confirms the theoretical calculations he has made earlier. He had known it was bound to happen again one of these days: maybe today, tomorrow, or a week from now. Once more he was destined to be filled with a fresh, new emotion, to get drunk on it and intoxicate others with it too! Greater than ever before. He hadn't had many such loves, but this one would be greater. He had been waiting a bit too long now for it not to be the greatest. It was coming along to sweep him off his feet. So should he once again surrender to that violent wave imbued with a fragrance of roses? Four years of waiting for just such a ring at the door.

At the first jingle of the clapper his eye was caught by something moving among the roses. One flower appeared to have flexed its muscles among the rest; it had shifted to a more comfortable position, drawing itself up a bit by working its way out from under two small green leaves, which were still gently shaking. The flower had unfurled even further, brazenly showing its pale centre, like a wide-open mouth with golden teeth shining inside. For a moment he hesitated, wanting to hear what the parted lips of the flower would say to him.

It doesn't take much talking to reach an understanding. A night of intense certainty stood between him and yesterday. There is nothing sweeter than a sound night's sleep with the thought of something miraculous growing inside us, gradually filling us up. The sort of night slept by mothers when they have just found out they are pregnant. Deep, peaceful sleep had weighed down on him like a golden sepulchre, but the thought of new happiness had remained alert at his bedside, and as soon as he awoke he had immediately, quite naturally, been aware of it. He had dressed quite quickly, revelling in the coolness of the bathtub, the freshness of the eau-de-Cologne and the chill of the autumn morning, fully conscious of fast approaching happiness, soft, deeper than other happinesses. The plural number caused him to stop and wonder. There is only one true happiness, he thought, and that is love. The ashes of a former love, and the sense of a lack of love had been dribbling through his fingers for far too long now, finding no response in him, for they were nothing but ashes. One does a thousand things, travels, walks, thinks and reads, but it takes just this sort of encounter to understand that all this time one has been living on the ash-heap of the past, that the sun looked dead, as if in a haze, the air was steeped in the smog of decay. For all that, there was only one thing he wanted – for her to come and sweep him off his feet at last. She had kindled a new pillar of fire on the ash-heap and had filled the air with easy breathing. The years go by, and the clocks of all cities strike out hour after hour in unison, while there is no one, until along comes just such an evening as yesterday's, and the whole world is revealed anew. Everything that lacked colour takes on a tone, everything that was too hard to disentangle is resolved.

He noticed that the flower, which had recently spread wider among the little green leaves, like a bourgeois lady in a pink dress, had bowed its lower petals downwards as if under the weight of an invisible insect. Instinctively he wanted to stop them from falling and to give it a natural pose. He brushed the tip of his finger against two of the petals from underneath. He felt a velvet touch, but as he let his hand drop, the petals came loose, described a great circle and as gently as two tiny sails, settled nearby on the carpet.

He knew what was coming next. An unexpected discovery, the revelation and devotion of another soul, of an unfamiliar treasure. Something he certainly valued in love was the satisfying of one's curiosity, the boundless world of the human soul and of human life, which gradually throws itself open before a lover, as he grows more accustomed to the presence, existence and memory of his beloved. First there would be that charming novelty of tastes, habits and perceptions. Favourite dishes, one's way of taking one's seat in a carriage, one's way of threading a needle. A thousand little trifles that at first absorb one on the outside, then make their way into conversation and fill one's very voice with a different tone, relating to all sorts of subjects, and taking on a thousand associations. This tone of voice will then colour one's thoughts, which on the surface are abstract and internal, and blend with one's particular philosophical outlook, altering one's entire view of the broad or narrow horizons of the world.

A total change of thought, a new approach to things, to works of art, to ways of working – yes, that was what lay ahead of him. He would have to change his newspaper, his bookshop, his friends, his restaurant, his collars, his philosophy and references. Under her influence he would be sure to start throwing foreign words into his conversation (Italian, or English, perhaps?) and would yearn for travel. They would share reminiscences. The multitude of characters he had encountered in the past would double. Once again new friends would be introduced to his imagination: someone else's childhood would pass before his eyes like an English novel.

The two petals lay at his feet on the green carpet, just by the shiny tip of his unpolished shoe. He gave the pink petal a gentle nudge with his toe, covering a tiny bit of it. The blush of the petal looked pale against the rather commonplace colour of the carpet. He looked up at the bouquet. Another petal was starting to droop, just as slowly, but just as inevitably, turning its washed-out inner face towards him.

How intriguing! Nights spent no longer on endearments, but on telling each other one's life story. One's entire life story. How many such stories he had already heard by now! Of course, each new love pervaded his whole past life with its essence, manipulating it as it fancied. As a rule he had treated all those women with contempt. On each past emotion he had bestowed the label 'not it'. Besides, he only used whatever he regarded as potentially seductive material in his narrative. On the other hand, he drank in, he simply drank in women's confidences about themselves (he could listen to them for nights on end). They nonchalantly opened their hearts to him to the depths of their souls, all their greatness and all their weaknesses. He knew about their adventures in motherhood, in love, about their sweetness and their indifference. He could reach directly into the core of their experience and try to get to the heart of their words, even to the heart of everything they hid from him, right into the essence of things they weren't aware of, just as he was able to find pleasures in their bodies that they had never suspected were there. Besides, there had only been four or five such women who counted as his 'great loves'.

Jarosław Iwaszkiewicz

The doorbell rang a second time. The shudder in the air caused the drooping petal to fall. With an instant reflex he tried to stop it from falling, caught it in mid-air, weighing it for a moment in his cupped hand, then raised it to his lips.

'Love!' he thought. He would have to tell his life story all over again, well, at least sketchily. This time it would be just a summary, of course. Why worry about the past when the task of creating the future lay ahead of them? It would be intensive, exhausting work. Shunting his life onto new tracks, into the rays shining from new eyes, different from any others that had ever cast their sunlight upon him. The stones might be heavy, but he would be building new bridges between what was already possible and the yet-to-be-realised. He would be casting bold arches, capturing infinities of thought, vigorously shaking himself free at last of all the bitterness that had welled up over the past few years of drought. He had torn himself free of the ensnaring net of humdrum days, so much so that he had ceased to feel the passage of time. Suddenly he was looking around himself, wondering how he could have lived like that until now, amazed that he hadn't rebelled. He would have to move out of this flat – he cast a glance around the room – just as one should move out of a building full of preconceived ideas. The sort of cold cynicism he had wallowed in for the past four years isn't appropriate for a man in love. He might even have to rebuild his whole system of beliefs. She seemed to have so much enthusiasm in her eyes. He forced himself to think about packing up his books and sticks of furniture into wooden crates, and all that straw – the place would be full of it! But of course true love asks no questions. He wouldn't confide his entire life story to her, and he wouldn't ask her any questions either. But what if she has another lover?

Several more petals had fallen onto the table, all in a rush, as if jostling one another: tap-tap-tap. The rose had spread its remaining petals even wider, as if attempting to hide the loss, yet all the more plainly revealing its whitish centre, like inelegant underwear.

Taking on a new love, he thought further, without doubt means taking on a massive burden. All one's efforts will have to be geared towards making sure nothing can ruffle the harmony of two bodies merging into one, two souls joining in unison. There must be no little niggles, not even the tiniest point of friction. One should be able to look both oneself and the truth in the eye and adroitly juggle the events of one's life to make sure they don't sully everyday conversation. That's quite a tall order! One must constantly keep oneself up at a certain level, like a swimmer, while at the same time never taking one's eye off one's partner. One must direct events skilfully, conversation too, which demands far greater social tact. Frankly speaking, through clever moves one must seize the initiative from the lady's hands. That's all rather tiring, especially at length. He smiled. It's quite simple, really, but love is just a fight for the initiative.

Still smiling, he prodded the remaining petals; off they fell in such a violent rush that in falling they looked paler, like a flock of sea gulls illuminated by the setting sun. They sent a subtle fragrance floating into the air. Leaning over the wilting vase no longer made him feel dizzy. Yet the scent in the room was becoming more pungent. There were only a few pink featherlets left on the green stem now, wrinkled like silk after rain. Granules of golden dust from the centre had scattered on the petals.

So what? He was still young. He could boldly take up the battle anew. Take her in hand from the start. No, he wouldn't think of moving house, he wouldn't change his flat or his bookshop. Nor his collars either, nor would he go abroad. That's just pretension. Too bad, she'll have to take him as he is, without looking around at the rest of the world. It was she who would have to cast off her usual custom and adapt herself to him. His habits were already set, and it would be hard for him to give them up. However, imposing his will on the woman was bound to involve a fight. That fight would have to be dextrous, in forays. Small but firm remarks at table and in the bedroom. It would mean taking control of her desires, saying no over a few basic points, and making a careful effort to conceal his jealousy.

'Well, I'd better open up then!' he said to himself and set off for the door, but just as he reached the hall he stopped.

Conceal his jealousy? Fight? A heavy burden was already starting to oppress him. But then a great love is a very heavy thing, isn't it? How much there is to overcome, how strong one has to keep on being! The bitterness of the first time she was late, the despair after the first tiff, the aimless wandering with a heavy heart after the first quarrel. Pacing the streets (usually in the dark) that first evening not spent together. Oh, it's beyond my strength, he said to himself and leaned his head against the doorframe. Accumulating mutual bitternesses that burst into a sulphurous, smoky flame for any reason whatsoever, because of a lost ribbon, or a half-smoked cigarette. Terrible hatred at the most painful moments. How can she be like that? She, whom I love like a goddess, is behaving like someone ordinary, she's crying! Ah!

And the burden of tears, which every woman uses to crush, to cast a gloomy, ashen cloud on a bright and cheerful sky, remains for good and all like an indelible shadow, like the dingy, dying pallor of a pearl. This burden of the burnout to come, which would leave nothing but a heap of ashes.

The bell rang for the third time, not so boldly now, but rather uncertainly; its sound dissolved into *mezza voce*, as if the finger pressing it were starting to tremble and withdraw. But he just went on standing in the doorway, listening intently. He thought he could catch the sound of her breathing on the other side of the door. After a long pause, while his mind went blank, fully occupied with listening, he heard reluctant, ponderous footsteps turning away. He tiptoed up to the door. The footsteps were moving off, at first slowly, but as they got further down the stairs they grew faster, as if gladly. He sighed with relief as the downstairs door gently banged shut.

He went back into the living room. As he drew near, the final rose petal fell. The green stalk, reaching down into the fluted grooves of the vase, gave its empty interior a willow-green glow. A few golden stamens still sat in the small brown centre. He stuck his little finger into the cavity and raised the tiny, sticky granules to the light, golden dust colouring his fingertip. He blew it towards the light of the window and off the stamens flew, leaving a tinge of golden dust, so he carefully wiped his fingers on his handkerchief.

1925

The Wilko Girls

The war was long since over. In the daily demands of his job, Wiktor Ruben had forgotten all about it and was fully occupied with mundane, yet engrossing tasks. Nor did he ever think about the time before the war, the daily grind of his indigent youth, and university – to which he had given so much of himself, but hadn't been able to finish – before historical events had thrown him off course. Now it had reached the stage where he was so wrapped up in his work that he never spared a thought for his youth. Meanwhile, the fortieth year of his life had crept up on him. He was very overworked, but all the better, he used to say; he hadn't the time to brood on the past, and anyway he knew from experience that it did no good. But Jurek's death had shaken him badly. He couldn't come to terms with it. He had felt so ill that he had sought the advice of a doctor.

It wasn't a proper medical consultation, of course; he hadn't gone off to the surgery or made a special trip to Warsaw. He had clambered down from the cart that had brought him in from the fields – it was at the start of summer – just as the doctor was getting out of his car to make his usual weekly visit to the institution. For three years Wiktor had been managing a small farm bequeathed to a charity for the blind, where each year they held summer camps for blind children. The doctor came every week, and had just arrived as usual. Wiktor had chatted with him a bit, and then said he was feeling unwell. He couldn't sleep at night, he felt very nervous and he couldn't work at all. And he couldn't stop thinking about his friend who had died of consumption two months earlier. He told his story casually, but he couldn't talk about Jurek without emotion. Jurek was the only close friend he had ever had. He was a seminarist, the nephew of the camp's Mother Superior, not an unusual person, but Christian, quiet and good. Almost from childhood he had worked very hard and rushed about the city; dressed in a threadbare overcoat he caught cold in the rotten Warsaw weather, and then tuberculosis took hold. He died without being fully aware of the dangerous state he was in, as if he had long since passed over to the other side, no longer anchored by anything; even if he did know he was dying, he was past all regret. Wiktor hadn't been there when he died. Jurek had lain dying in hospital, in spring. Wiktor never thought it would happen so quickly. There was so much he had to do at Stokroć, as the farm was called. That year they had installed the first growing frames, two hundred panes of glass at a go; there wasn't enough manure, and nowhere to get it from. He was being pulled in all directions, and had gone over to Błono to see to these matters. On his return he had been told of Jurek's death. That was more or less what he told the doctor, as they sat beneath the chestnut tree by the camp house, waiting for the children to come back from their walk. The doctor was drinking a bowl of cold buttermilk, with great relish, as the day was hot. He didn't speak, just nodded as he smacked his lips with pleasure.

11

Only when he saw the ranks of blind children, huddling together as they came tripping along the dusty road, did he look Wiktor in the eye and say:

'Wiktor, dear boy,' (the doctor addressed everyone in a familiar way), 'it's no use arguing. How long have you been working here?'

'Three years.'

'It's no use arguing. You're going away for three weeks. I'll tell the Mother Superior. Janek will fill in for you, and you'll go away. Any family or friends in the country? Go off and see them.'

And so here he was on a journey. He had been thinking for ages of coming here again, but it was only a vague idea, like the decisions we make to go on distant voyages as we stare at the beautiful pictures in shop windows. No, he never thought about those days, or of actually doing it; he never saw anyone from those holidays and he had had no news of his destination. Of course, nothing much had changed along the way. Only at the station, which had once kept sole company with an abandoned Jewish inn across the way, about a dozen houses had sprung up, buzzing with railway trade. Further on there was a fence around a depot for coal and wood, and then, to the right, began the highway, which was exactly the same, of course. A red-brick mansion, newly built in those days, had aged, and the little garden around it had grown up. But further down the road stood the same white poplars, so gigantic that time could no longer make them taller, but only topple them. There may have been a few less than before; he remembered that there had been some fierce fighting around here during the war. Bullets had evidently slashed these trunks. He hadn't been in these parts; his artillery unit had been stationed further north. They had run out of shells, and he could remember the retreat as clear as day. But he remembered the times he had walked or ridden along this road to his aunt and uncle's even more clearly than the present. He hadn't been here often; his mother had disliked his aunt, but he remembered it very clearly.

Then the road ran downhill. There was a gully and some willow trees, still there today. Then it comes out uphill, and there's a copse. Out he came, but by now it was a wood. Neither memories of the war, nor of the camp near Murmansk, not the final battles in France, nor the attack on Kiev and the retreat, not memories of his garrison years, nor his local government work – nothing from his entire life, that had trickled away in such relentless, meaningless toil, none of it gave Wiktor such a sense of time past as the sight of that wood where the copse had once stood. It was something so odd, so unexpected, instead of small, silvery shoots with yellow rabbit holes among them, to see great black trees against an earthen floor littered in pine needles. He stopped for a while, and sighed. He leaned down and saw a small black post, a boundary marker stuck into a mound at the corner. That hadn't changed; it may have gone black, but it was the same one. He remembered the marker well; they had sat by it then, on that memorable day in July, when he had left at the news of the outbreak of war. This was as far as Jola had come to see him on his way. Here they had sat and eaten the first ripe apples that she had brought him for the journey. Then he had left. The horses had been mobilised at once, so there was no transport to take him to the station. Anyway, he had come and gone on foot so many times before. He started to count. It was fifteen years now, without a backward glance.

› Fela, Julcia and Jola. What on earth had become of them? Unconsciously he quickened his step, to get to the hilltop sooner, but the copse had grown, and he no longer had the same view from there as before. He knew his aunt and uncle were there, still living there, still alive; he had had occasional news of them, although rarely. But not a word about that house. Somehow they had passed each other by, for all this time – so easily done in this world. And he had been neglectful – he hadn't written, he hadn't asked after them! He began his mental arithmetic again, but it wasn't a great success. His pace unconsciously slowed down. They would be old now, they would certainly have got married. Of course, Julcia was twenty, or twenty-one in those days. Kazia was a bit younger. And Jola? She must be over thirty by now too.

He came out of the wood. Straight ahead stood a signpost marking the county border and a statue of St John of Nepomuk.* He cast a glance in that direction. How many times, on the journey to or from his uncle's place, had he turned off the road and taken a two-kilometre detour just to drop in there. It had a funny name – Wilko, that's what the estate was called; there wasn't a village by that name. He used to drop in there so often; once he had even spent the entire holiday there giving Zosia tuition. That was the year before the war. Oh! Zosia must be a grown-up young woman by now. He stood and gazed ahead of him.

In a small hollow, some way off, but clear as day, stood two large barns set at right angles. Between them stood a large green yard, two old poplars, and beyond them the house, which used to have a metal roof that could be seen shining from here, but was now red-tiled. That looks

---

* Bohemian cleric and patron saint of Czechoslovakia, *c.* 1330–93.

14

better, thought Wiktor, as pleased as if it were his own house that had been given a new roof. Beyond the house stood a clump of trees – that was the garden – and then a pair of very tall pines, because they were standing on a rise. Beyond that, a small wood and a meadow, then the white line of the road again – that way led towards his uncle's place. On the horizon on the opposite side of the hollow there should have been a wood, but it wasn't there any more – it must have been cut down. Just one great tree was still standing; that was the way he would go now, as he crossed the road that led down to Wilko.

But he couldn't resist it; almost automatically, just like in the old days, as if by appointment, he turned right, towards the house he hadn't thought of for all these years; he walked along briskly, whistling and swinging his briefcase, which held a couple of shirts and a toothbrush. He couldn't be bothered with any other luggage. As if walking alongside his own youthful self, he passed a grassy mound rising on the right-hand side of the rough road. Here on the left there should have been a large pile of stones, where the best blackberries grew, but it wasn't there; the stones must have been sold. Then the road dipped further downwards, and it occurred to Wiktor that nothing had changed here, nor had anything in him changed either. The fields were sown and tilled, just as fifteen years ago – just as two hundred years ago, perhaps – and here he was again, with his case and his only suit, just beginning to unwind and relax again after the bustle of city life. Until, to his surprise, it all started to go blurry in his memory: Jurek, Stokroć, the blind children walking along in crocodile file but hand in hand – now they were flying by, as fast and as easily as if they were sighted. He was still young, after all – so why the stupid thoughts

15

about old age? It didn't matter how many years had gone by – here he was, on the road to Wilko, whistling as he went; it was summer, it was a warm day, it was June – the end of June, about ten days to go till harvest time – sooner, perhaps, as the weather was all set for it. That's what his uncle always used to say – 'The weather's all set for it.'

⸳ For some time now he had been aware that very often, especially when he was tired or overworked, alongside the normal flow of coherent thoughts running through his head, quite inexplicably, a scene from the distant past would suddenly rise up and rest for a moment on the surface of his consciousness until he had noticed and identified it. Then it would sink back into the depths again. After a while the same scene would float back up again, or more often a different one. And just then, as he was heading along the familiar road towards the familiar hedge, the sun shining as ever, the dogs barking as ever at the cows on their way back from the field through the peaceful meadows, suddenly a familiar scene arose before his eyes, a scene of summer, but a very different one. Burnt fields, hot dust, to one side beneath a pear tree the glint of an abandoned machine gun, and in a patch of stubble a tangle of grey and green rags: it was the corpse of a man who had just been shot. He had identified the scene – yes, it was during the retreat when they were or-dered to shoot deserters or spies; the man had been a small, thin soldier, who had calmly smoked a cigarette before his death.

Then the image sank back again. There was the rough road once more; he recognised the unevenness of the ground beneath his feet, and the pattern made by clumps of green couch grass, its tangled tongues creeping onto the path, heedless of being trampled on. Here was the hedge and here the outhouses. No one had noticed him. Towards evening they're all so busy – everyone has something to do – the cattle, the horses, hens and ducks are settling down for the night, and the people have to see to them, shutting them in the cowshed or the henhouse, feeding and watering them. Down the curve of the drive, Wiktor Ruben entered through the porch. Once inside the hall, the smell of the house enveloped him. It was like approaching the buffet in a dining room: there was a scent of dry tea, and a whiff of something metallic, like a tin; also pine wood, and just the merest hint of dried mushrooms. He stopped and automatically hung up his briefcase, coat and hat on a hook to his right. He noticed that the furniture in the hall was different, but he didn't dwell on it, for further inside, beyond the hall he could hear loud conversation. Several women were talking all at once, and there were children shouting too. The voices were so exactly the same as the ones he had heard here before that he was sure that at any moment little Tunia would appear in the doorway and cry out, 'It's Wiktor!'

And indeed, just then someone did push back a chair, laughing, get up and come running into the hall. There in the doorway Wiktor saw a young and very pretty girl in a brightly coloured dress. She stopped and stared at him inquiringly. Wiktor just bowed, not knowing what to say. The girl hesitated.

'Have you come to see Mr Kawecki?' she asked in a low, warm voice.

'I …' said Wiktor and smiled. The girl recognised him by the smile and burst out with the old formula, 'Heavens above! It's Wiktor!'

17

She took him by the hand into the next room, where a lamp was already burning, although it was still light outside. There he was embraced by a swarm of female arms, warm and naked, and someone even kissed him. 'Where's Mama?' was the general cry, 'Mama, it's Wiktor!' But Mama, as usual, did not appear; nor for that matter was it certain if she would remember who Wiktor was. But the young ladies remembered him perfectly, as one of them was quick to explain. She was a stout, warm, well-dressed lady, very plump, and for a moment or two Wiktor wondered why she was being so familiar with him; from all the evidence she had to be Julcia, the eldest. He recognised her beautiful low-pitched voice, unforgettable across the long years, but the actual person was quite different. Feeling a bit confused, he looked about at the company. The general commotion was heightened by the children, a boy and a girl skipping around him, absurdly excited considering they didn't know what all the fuss was about.

Meanwhile, Julcia was gradually clarifying matters. 'You should know that you're a legend at Wilko. We're always saying, "If only Wiktor were here, he'd deal with it …", "if only Wiktor were here, he'd this and he'd that …" Only the other day I said to Jola, "That would never have happened in Wiktor's day." '

The bewildered Wiktor was starting to feel more relaxed. 'Do you know, that's not at all what I expected. But there you are, that's how history is made – I was convinced I'd passed through Wilko like a shadow. That's why I never made much effort to think of it – I thought no one here would remember me.'

'You thought wrong,' said another woman, whom he recognised at once; it was the lovely Jola, the prettiest sister of all. 'Every time we've been to your uncle and aunt's we've asked about you.'

'But they didn't know anything about me,' said Wiktor, laughing.

'And we're all set for a holiday here, children, bags and baggage and all. We often miss each other when we come here, but this time we're all here together.'

'So where's Fela?' asked Wiktor.

'Fela, Fela, come here,' called Julcia. 'Look what a great big girl she is – come on, Fela!'

From the next room a large, fat, ten-year-old girl came in, ugly, although similar to her mother and aunts in colouring, and greeted Wiktor.

'She's my eldest,' said Julcia, 'and the little girl is my other one, Kicia.'

'Yes, they're huge already,' said Wiktor absently. 'I didn't even know you were married. But I meant the big Fela.'

'But ... don't you know, then?' said Julcia quietly. 'Fela died, er ... more than ten years ago now. Of the Spanish 'flu.'

Wiktor felt very upset, unable in the first instant to take in the fact that Fela was dead, only that he had made a *faux pas*.

'I'll take you to see her grave,' said Jola. Solemn and thin, Kazia, the least pretty, but always the efficient one, got up and said, 'I must see to the supper.' And to Wiktor she added, 'You'll stay for it, won't you?' Then she left the room. The little boy skipped after her; he must be her son. The girls started showering Wiktor with questions again, or rather two of them did – Julcia and Jola. The two youngest, his former pupils, stayed out of it, and just stared wide-eyed at the handsome, dishevelled fellow

Jarosław Iwaszkiewicz

whom they hardly remembered; so this was the legendary
Wiktor. Once they were sitting at supper Wiktor took a
good look at each of them in the bright lamplight. On the
way from the study into the dining room he had had a
closer look at Julcia. No, it was quite another person, so
grave and dignified: her laughter was merry, yet restrained, every gesture suffused with such serenity. It
wasn't the Julcia of old. Wiktor looked at the assembled
company and said, 'So come on, tell me all about your-
selves. It's fifteen years since I …'

'Don't count them, don't!' cried Jola merrily.

'… fifteen years since I've had any news of you at all.
What have you been doing? Where have you been? Tell
me who's married, and who's not, so I don't drop a brick.
Well?'

'I'm married with two children,' said Julcia. 'Kazia's
divorced with one son; Jola's married with no children,
and Zosia's married with one son.'

'Oh no, enough, enough!' said Wiktor and turned to
his former pupil. 'How's the Latin?'

Zosia laughed and said, 'My son's two now. He's called
Henio.'

'Tunia's still single,' Julcia went on, 'and that's all.'

Wiktor smiled and looked at Julcia, then at Tunia.
They were perhaps the most alike, but how very different.
Tunia must now have been about the same age as Julcia
was in the old days. Perhaps she was prettier, less buxom,
with more of an hour-glass figure and large, startled grey
eyes, while Julcia's were blue, pretty but unremarkable.

'What about you, Wiktor?' asked Jola.

Wiktor gave a different sort of smile. Was there really
anything worth saying about himself? 'I've got a job now,
running a charitable farm just outside Warsaw. I used to

be in the army, I was a captain, but I've been decommissioned now. That's it, really …'

Suddenly, in front of the women's faces a whole succession of images floated before his eyes – painful incidents, tortuous efforts and futile endeavours. He thought of his life, all tangled and broken in its prime, and shuddered. 'No, no, really, I'm not doing anything special,' he said. 'There's nothing to say, really; I just go on living, like everyone else.'

That felt truly awful, the idea that he just went on living like everyone else, and that everyone else went on living just like him.

He was starting to remember the times he had spent here. He had always thought his life would be different, fuller, richer and more remarkable than anybody else's. He had only told Kazia about it. Normally they hadn't said much to each other, but once a week or so they had had a really serious conversation, what they used to call 'a milestone'. On the road to what? They had never stopped to consider whether it meant a milestone in their spiritual development, or in the development of their friendship, or simply along the road to the future; they never stopped to ask. All he could remember was that one of these 'milestone' conversations had been devoted to his future prospects. He had just left school, and Kazia had been trying to dissuade him from studying law. She had warned him against thinking it would be easy, or that his life would just fall into place – she had naively expressed some crucial warnings, but none of it had meant much to him at the time. 'That's funny,' he thought, 'in those days I never thought of Poland being independent – that was the easiest way, after all.' And yet she had been right. He wanted to look Kazia straight in the eye and thank her for those 'milestones', but just then she was leaning forward, looking over her sisters' shoulders to see what was going on at the far end of the table where her son, Antoś, was teasing one of his cousins. Even then she had had no illusions, and yet she had been through a marriage and a divorce. Was that all? That he would never know; no one had ever known anything about Kazia. She was very private, reticent and efficient. He remembered being amazed at her intelligence, which seemed a bit misplaced; there was nothing for her to apply it to, apart from a pessimistic view of the future. 'I wonder what sort of future she foresees for Antoś?' thought Wiktor.

Meanwhile Julcia was telling him about his aunt and uncle. His uncle had aged a lot, but his aunt was the same as ever. Halfway through supper, meek and quiet, 'Mama' emerged from the back rooms. Words of greeting failed her; she just kissed Wiktor on the head and sat down in the shadow of the stately Julcia, who was sitting at the head of the table. There was no interruption in the flow of conversation, which was loud, lively and jolly, nor did Mama start her supper from the beginning, but from the second course, the point at which she came to table.

Wiktor was surprised to find how well he was remembered here, and that for fifteen years they had gone on talking about him in this backwood. He had always thought of himself as an obscure, unwanted tutor, a young man who just happened to be on holiday in the neighbourhood; he thought he had glided inconspicuously through the manor house at Wilko, where they wanted for nothing. Yet it seemed he had played an important role here, quite without knowing it for all these years. In those days he had been too young to feel the gaze of these women upon him.

There was a lot to think about, but he had no time for reflection, as he had to answer their questions and listen to
what they were telling him.

He fixed his eyes on Julcia as she talked, and thought
of the old days. If during the war years, or his time in the
garrison, or while working at the local administration, or
finally at Stokroć, if amid all that boring, tedious toil he
had remembered Wilko, it was inseparably linked with
the face, the figure and voice of Julcia. Not this stately
lady, warm, dignified and lovely, sitting here at the end of
the table, recalling other events of those same bygone
years in a low, kindly voice. Oh no, that Julcia was slender, shapely, lively and impetuous, and had some strange
impulses. She was always taking him out on riding expe-
ditions, during which she never said a word to him; they
used to play tennis too. There was no flirtation between
them, no real intimacy. Rather, it was Jola, then a daz-
zling young sixteen-year-old, who had paid him court. He
didn't have conversations with Julcia the way he did with
Kazia; he didn't discuss things with her at all, and it occurred to him that today's conversation, in which Julcia
had so decisively taken the lead, must have been the
longest they had ever had. Another thing that had sometimes occurred to him in passing was that when he and
Julcia met again they would explain it all to each other.
Yet now he realised that things get buried in the abyss of
years gone by, never to be explained. Now, as he watched
Julcia, talking fluently, as he looked at her cold blue eyes
and her beautiful, regular features, at the large diamonds
glittering on her plump white fingers, he realised that
none of it was ever going to be explained.

To understand what 'it' meant would require familiar-
ity with the routine and geography of the house at Wilko.

As they grew more mature, each of the girls had become obsessed with having her own separate room. The three youngest were still packed into the enormous nursery beyond the study. Jola had her own dressing table in there, but slept on a couch in the little parlour on the far side of the drawing room, while Kazia and Julcia slept upstairs. The upper floor consisted of four identical rooms along a corridor. When he had come to stay for the holidays in 1913, Wiktor had been put in the guest room next to Julcia's room. Both rooms had very similar furnishings, and Wiktor was always dropping into Julcia's room for books or photographs – which Julcia used to develop – and knew its layout perfectly.

Once, just before the end of the holidays, Wiktor and Jola had gone for a walk late in the evening and on into the night. Running between the ponds at Wilko and the sizeable lake at Rożki, his uncle's place, ran a stream overgrown with rushes and duckweed, where ducks and kingfishers lay in hiding. Jola and Wiktor had decided to take the little Wilko boat up to his aunt and uncle's for supper. They had set off just after tea, but the journey had been difficult – they had had to drag the boat along a couple of times, and had only got to the Rożki lake just before suppertime. Despite his aunt and uncle's misgivings they had insisted on going back the same way. It was a moonlit night, and the return journey had gone much more smoothly, but they had got back rather late, when the entire household was already asleep and the dogs had been let off their chains. Wiktor was feeling dreamy about his close relationship with Jola, whom he had always found the most attractive of all the sisters; she was the only one who might not be entirely indifferent to his charms and wit. They used to spend hours on end making

24

up silly jokes and teasing each other, and he would end up getting a box on the ear. Sometimes they would have a fight and then go off on a trip together, take the cart into the woods, or into town, perhaps. They used to go bathing together, and riding; they could always be heard from afar talking endless, noisy nonsense. If anyone approached they would fall silent, but only because they were embarrassed by their own meaningless chatter. Everyone was used to seeing them together, and no one regarded it as a flirtation, just a close friendship. Wiktor had even corresponded with Jola for some time after leaving school, but then the whole thing had blown over. That evening, tired and sleepy, they had arrived home walking on air and said goodnight in the drawing room, where iced tea, bread, butter and sausage had been left out for them. They had eaten it up, then Jola had retired to her 'alcove', as she called the little parlour, and Wiktor had gone upstairs to his own room.

Lost in thought, without realising he had opened the door to Julcia's room instead of his own. He often wondered afterwards how it could have happened, and couldn't work it out. But he was sure he would never have allowed himself to do such a thing consciously. He stepped into the darkness, and without lighting a candle sat down in the nearest chair and gazed out of the window at the sky, shining blue in the moonlight. He took off his shoes and socks – his most essential items of clothing, apart from which he was wearing just a few light garments that he discarded by the chair. He went up to the bed and then realised his mistake. He laughed gently and, quite unsure why, started to follow the mistake through, as if playing out a scene for himself. He touched Julcia, who was lying in the bed, but she didn't react. He sat down beside her and saw that she

25

was asleep. Then he lay down next to her and started to feel her luxurious body through the thin sheet. After a while he became aware that she wasn't asleep after all, and he froze on the instant. There they lay for a long time, holding their breath in silence. Little by little, as imperceptibly as the hands of a clock, they performed a whole series of changes of position, to come into a close embrace. For ever after, Wiktor would never forget how he had felt at the touch of her skin. It was extremely beautiful, as warm and tangible as a flower. He didn't know why neither of them had said anything, or why they had put on a comic pretence of totally implausible sleep. What they had been doing couldn't possibly have been done unwittingly. Wiktor felt such an intensity of all the erotic force within him that he was enveloped in a sort of painful rapture; each move of his hand along Julcia's body almost made him faint. It was no surprise that he had never felt anything like it before, as he had had a paltry sex life until then, but he never felt anything like it ever again, and bore the memory of that first night of love, passionate and silent, for the rest of his life. Nothing else, no fruit, no body had ever felt as supple or as silky to his touch as Julcia's young breasts that night at Wilko. They hadn't slept at all, but had pretended to till dawn. Then Wiktor had taken his things and slunk off to his own room, where he slept like a log and woke rather late.

Early that morning Julcia had gone to Warsaw with her mother, so he didn't see her again until two days later, towards evening. He was playing tennis with Jola and Kazia in the yard, where they could see the road from the station. He saw Julcia sitting beside her mother, dressed in an almond-white outfit with a red tie. (Later he had stolen the red tie from her and had kept it among his possessions for a long time, until it all got lost along the way.) With her gaze turned blankly towards the haystacks opposite she never looked around at the players. Only after tea did she come out to play with them, as if nothing had happened. And from then on they had never said a word to each other about it. Of course, they went on chatting as usual and went riding together; he would drop in on her for a book and they very often ended up alone in the room together, or in the forest, or the boat, but they never said a word about that night.

It had happened towards the end of summer, and Wiktor hadn't stayed on at Wilko for long afterwards. Yet he had come to Julcia twice more in the night, and everything had happened just as before, in a silent comedy of impossible sleep. And the experience of those nights remained forever in Wiktor's memory as a contact with something infinitely beautiful and fragrant, as if those nights involved nothing carnal, but a sort of religious ritual. In particular the third night, on the eve of his departure, had left him with a memory of such joy and sweetness as a summer's day at the seaside.

The next year he had stayed at his aunt and uncle's, just dropping in at Wilko from time to time to give the younger girls lessons. He had arrived late, and soon the infamous first of August was calling him back to town. But this time he had had the courage to do a crazy thing. One day, after long reflection and hesitation, he had gone there at night and climbed up on a foundation stone, then onto a ledge and through the window into Julcia's room. Once again not a word passed between them, and the night was just the same, sultry and fragrant.

Now those four nights, the most beautiful nights he had ever experienced, were returning to his memory between one question and the next, over the peas, fried bread and chicken, as he gazed at the beautiful stout stranger beside him, talking a lot and eating a lot, flashing her diamond rings and firing motherly commands in an imperious tone at Fela and Kicia, who were sitting with Antoś and their nursemaids at the bottom of the table. He had always imagined himself and Julcia meeting up in old age and talking it all through, explaining it all to each other; he would tell her he had never been in love with her, but that he owed her more than any other woman in his life, how amazingly beautiful it had been. At the same time he wanted to find out what those nights had meant to her, and whether she still remembered them too.

But now he could see it was hopeless. His questions and would-be conversations were lost for ever; they would never discuss it, and just as at the time they had pretended to be asleep, so now they would have to pretend they didn't remember.

Straight after supper he asked Kazia for horses to take him to Rożki. Before they had finished drinking coffee in the study, from old gilded cups that Mama had managed to keep intact, a carriage rattled up to the porch and stopped. Wiktor hastened to say goodbye, and everyone came out to see him off. There was quite a hubbub. Julcia invited him to lunch the next day to meet her husband, Kawecki. But Wiktor replied that his aunt and uncle would be offended.

'I should have lunch with them tomorrow, but I'll come for afternoon tea, and for lunch the day after tomorrow.'

Still talking excitedly, he leaped youthfully aboard the carriage. It felt good to be liked and remembered here. The ladies, too, were excited and chatty. They all felt fifteen years younger, and everyone was glad of it.

'You still haven't got yourself a wife, but all our young ladies are married now,' said old Antoni, the coachman, sententiously.

'Not all – there's still Miss Tunia,' replied Wiktor.

'Oh, she's just a child,' mumbled Antoni, flicking his whip. It seemed he felt time had stood still for fifteen years too.

Compared with Wilko, Rożki was a very modest little place, and modestly run. His uncle, once the steward of an estate, had done well; his aunt had helped him by running a chicken business. Their farm was tiny, but economical and wisely maintained. The house, too, was small and modest, providing meals from its own resources, that is, poultry, cucumbers and buttermilk. But Wiktor adored this dedicated, homespun modesty.

This time, however, he didn't spend long with his aunt and uncle, only as much as seemed proper; he admitted having dropped in at Wilko, and his aunt nodded knowingly. 'Oh God, the best girls have been snatched from under your nose!' she said, at which his uncle started to chide her. Kasia, the lumpen maid, the image of Walercia who had worked here fifteen years ago, carried the lamp ahead of him into the cold, stuffy room. Wiktor was left alone.

He started pacing the room, just as he did at home in Stokroć, but without thinking of any of the problems that beset him there, or any of the things that usually caused him so much stress and anguish. They had all dissolved into thin air as soon as Wiktor had bridged the gap across to the two summers he had spent at Wilko and Rożki, the most memorable of his youth, even if lacking in incident. He had sometimes heard from his clever friends, from Jurek among others, that people are fascinated by the concept of time, and that there are even whole books about trying to get control of it. That was how it felt – as if he had mastered time, as if he had managed to turn the clock back and were now at exactly the same point as fifteen years ago, and that now he could make his choice!

Only now did he realise what the attraction of those two years had been, and why they were so easy to picture in his memory. It was the subconscious adolescent sexuality that had floated in the air around those six lovely, pretty girls. And that was what had mattered to them in those days too – that was why they remembered him so well. They could recall his most trivial words and deeds – the time he had mended the glockenspiel, or the time he had cleaned his yellow shoes with buttermilk.

, All the events of that time had been unrecognised predictions of things that had never come to fruition. But now that he had bridged the gap and turned back time, everything that had been predicted then could now become reality. At the time it had been nothing but childish high spirits, but now that he was a mature adult he could make what had then been just a sketch, a shaky drawing, into something real. Yes, that was it. So far he hadn't achieved much in life, but there had been extenuating circumstances. And besides, this must have been the reason why he had kept putting off coming here – because subconsciously he knew he would return, that one day he would have afternoon tea at Wilko again, which was something completely different from everything that came before it.

Julcia, sadly, wouldn't come into the reckoning. All connection with her was irretrievably broken; he wouldn't even be able talk to her. She was a closed book. Quite different, unfamiliar, a thing of the past. So the years aren't always so easy to bridge after all. Kazia had never been special, but what about the others? There was Jola, and Zosia, and Tunia. Poor Fela, she would have been the prettiest now, but she was dead.

He opened the door to the adjoining room, where he could hear his aunt and uncle talking. His aunt was at the mirror, dressing her long, grey hair.

'When did Fela die?' he asked abruptly. 'I didn't know about it.'

'When the war was still on, that's why,' said his aunt. 'Just after Julcia's wedding.'

'And what did she die of?'

'Spanish 'flu, they said. She always did have a weak heart.'

'My God, what a girl she was!' mumbled his uncle from beneath the eiderdown.

'Goodnight, then.'

'Goodnight.'

Wiktor retired to his own room. At last he lay down on the high, creaking wooden bed. Sleep was a long time in coming; the smell of freshly laundered sheets and the straw-filled mattress disturbed him. Finally he dozed off, then woke to find it was day. Outside the hens were clucking, a cock was crowing, his aunt was having a discussion with Mrs Kaźmierzowa – in short, life at Rożki was in full swing. He got dressed at a leisurely pace, then went for a wander about the little garden and the enormous farmyard, full of Uncle Robert's innumerable farming tools. Idly he inspected sowing machines and crop sprayers, while impatiently waiting for lunch, which luckily they ate very early, as healthy people are inclined to. He was keen to find out something extra, some confidence about the Wilko girls, as they were called – and his aunt was a chronicler of the entire neighbourhood. She could certainly fill in the information he had deprived himself of all this time.

Unfortunately, over lunch of barley soup and mince, he wasn't able to find out much. His uncle didn't give his aunt a chance to speak, but bombarded Wiktor with questions. What was he doing now, what did he do before that, what about the distant past, such as his time in the Russian army, and in the prison camp, the journeys to France and the retreat from Kiev. Every time his uncle asked a question Wiktor stared at him for a moment in amazement, then had to force himself to bring the past to mind.

'Yes, yes, uncle …' he kept saying, giving curt replies. He couldn't ward off the questions, but he did try to ward off the thought of those past events, and once he even said, 'Yes, yes, that was awful – I'd rather not think about it.'

In fact it was the least awful episode of his past life – namely, his reasonably happy and carefree time in Archangel, but only now did that world without women, which he had battled his way through, seem so very awful. His aunt immediately noticed that Wiktor didn't want to talk about the past, and even less about his present job, which all his relatives regarded as a backward step in his career. But his uncle wouldn't let her get a word in edgeways. Finally, towards the end of the meal, when Wiktor had managed to take control of the questioning, he had to listen to the entire genealogy of the Kawecki family, what Kawecki did for a living, how wonderfully he was running Wilko and its farmland, how well the place was doing, how many cows they had, how many sheep, and how many beets they had planted that year. Then his aunt described the births of Julcia's daughters, one born in

Warsaw and the other at Wilko, and all the fuss there had been. Indeed, he found this less upsetting than his uncle's questions. He got up from the table in a good mood and said: 'If you don't mind, Auntie, I shan't be in for tea. I've already promised to be at Wilko.'

His aunt smiled. 'My dear boy,' she said, 'we're never going to get our fair share of you.'

'What can one do?' sighed his uncle. 'Young people are always the same.'

'Young?' laughed Wiktor. 'Not so young any more, I'm afraid, Uncle.'

His aunt waved dismissively and said: 'You're younger than ever, and even more handsome. I was just saying to your uncle, who'd have thought you'd grow up into such a handsome boy? When you used to come and stay, only Kazia and Jola thought you good-looking, and everyone else laughed at the idea. You were so tall and skinny as a whippet, but now it's a joy to look at you. The Wilko girls will be sorry they didn't wait for you. Anyway, getting married is just a rehearsal these days …'

Wiktor ran whistling to his room, and as he was changing his tie for a darker one (there was more than just a couple of shirts in his case after all), he looked at himself in the mirror. He really was handsome, just a bit dishevelled, with a crevice in his cheek – a brush with a bullet. The points of his forehead were a bit too deeply set into his curly hair; after his daily shave he immediately looked cleaner and better. Recently he had been told he had fine eyes. Someone quite impartial had said it, one of his colleagues – Janek, it was. On the whole he had always thought himself very ugly, which had made him all the more bashful. Over meals at Wilko he had rarely spoken; he had avoided people, arrived unnoticed, and until

33

yesterday he had been convinced he didn't merit any attention. He used to go and read in the garden, on a knoll beyond the pine trees, but he kept quiet about it because the girls were always sneering at his reading matter. Schiller in particular came in for this, Nietzsche too. In fact he didn't really understand much of Nietzsche himself, but he was thrilled by two books which made a deep impression on him – Poincaré's *Science et hypothèse*, and Bergson's *Creative Evolution*. Why these two books in particular, and no others? It was one of those mysterious quirks of youth, which picks out certain odd things for unknown reasons, now turning to Nietzsche, and rejecting Bergson, then favouring the Frenchman again, disliking Nietzsche and failing to understand the simplest concept of Hegel, but keen to study the problems of Kant. Anyway, to hell with it all. He no longer read Kant or Bergson, nor had he ever read them since those days. Not in Archangel, or as under-foreman at Rudki, or as manager of Stokroć had he ever had the time. And he certainly wasn't going to start reading them now.

He put on his hat, took his uncle's riding crop, and slapping it against his thigh went out at the front of the house. The day was warm and bright. A smell of dried grass and wormwood filled the air, and although the sky was brightening, the blue ponds and all the water he passed along the way looked white.

He didn't know why, but he kept on thinking of Fela and her premature death. Fela would have been prettier than Jola, perhaps, firmer and more shapely; she always stood straight and carried her small, budding breasts with childish solemnity, like vases full of water. He had a vivid memory of her. On the other hand, in everything he had heard from his aunt today, and also in his uncle's questions, a certain negative feeling towards Jola had come through. Maybe not so much dislike as a sort of tacit disapproval; his aunt had spoken, with evident sadness in her voice, of Jola's husband who very rarely came to Wilko. Listing the guests who had stayed there she had mentioned several fellows rather vaguely, saying, 'he comes by', 'they became friends'. Wiktor gave this a precise and blunt interpretation as he passed above the pond towards the cut-down wood and the road; he slashed at the hazel with his crop, sending dark green leaves flying and said, 'She's a loose woman, that's all.' This realisation didn't cause him any grief, but it did seem to cut Jola out of his plan. A pity, really – she was still very pretty, but he couldn't define exactly why it was a pity.

Lunch at Wilko took place much later than at Rożki, so quite unintentionally, Wiktor arrived when the table had only just been cleared. All the ladies had retired to their rooms, and when he looked in at the nursery, he saw no one but Fela and Kicia having an after-lunch lie-down on sloping boards specially set up for this purpose; moody and ugly, they didn't respond to his greeting. All the girls were upstairs; those four rooms now served Julcia and her husband, Kazia and Antoś, Zosia and Henio, and Tunia. Jola hadn't moved out of her 'alcove', having entirely transformed it into a bedroom. The upstairs now had a scent of mignonette and eau de Cologne, fresh linen, sheets and powder – in a word, of women. He knocked at Julcia's door, went in and found her lying on a sofa dressed in a pink robe, very shapely and beautiful. Beside her in an armchair, with his legs on the table, sat her husband, Kawecki, handsome and resplendent in a pale, very smart suit. Wiktor at once felt towards him the total aversion of a shabbily dressed man towards an elegant

35

one, besides which Kawecki jabbered endless banalities, full of common sense but entirely obvious. He put into words everything that Wiktor and Julcia took for granted or were already aware of, such as, 'On a fine day it's nice to take a turn in the fresh air.' In vain Wiktor tried to steer him onto agricultural topics, in which he himself was interested. The idea was to find out something worth knowing from the perfect farmer and to put the information to use in his own work at Stokroć. Estimates for dairy farming, for instance, on a property a long way from Warsaw – whether to produce milk or butter, supplies, tariffs, the cost of transport to the nearest station, and so on. But Kawecki wasn't keen to take up these subjects. He preferred to make pointless observations, such as noting that the sky is blue, it's hot, the dust is an awful bore in summer, and 'Flit' is the best thing for killing flies. Wiktor couldn't stand it any longer and asked if Jola was in.

'Jola's got guests today,' said Julcia. 'They came from Warsaw with Edward (Edward was Kawecki's name), so she won't be able to keep you company. If you want to go for a walk after tea Zosia might go with you.'

Wiktor went out into the corridor and wondered how formally he should address Zosia. He thought it best to use her first name, as in the past, and called it out. She answered from next door, his old room; he went in and found her lying on a sofa, contented and lily-white, and thought she too had a tendency towards plumpness. Beside her in a gauze-fronted pram her little son was sleeping.

'You don't have to worry about him, Wiktor,' she said, without lowering her voice. 'He always sleeps a solid couple of hours after lunch – he'd snore through cannon fire. He never wakes up before four. Just like a man!'

'And do you have to keep an eye on him?'

He noticed that without the least ceremony Zosia had addressed him by his first name, just like her older sisters. Of course, that was simplest, but it should really be defined by mutual consent.

'No, I don't, his nanny's just coming.'

'Would you like to walk around the yard or the garden with me?'

'Oh, after tea perhaps. I'm too lazy right now. Tunia will go with you, she's all keen and healthy,' she said, laughing, showing her strong white teeth, the finest ornament in her fresh young face. She had a very sweet smile.

Wiktor felt that the ineradicable memory of their former lessons would always be an obstacle between them; an antipathy had arisen between teacher and pupil, thanks to her idleness and his lack of interest. The trauma of these encounters had left its permanent scars, and in this serene woman now busy digesting and being a mother, Wiktor could still see the little girl who had despised him and made scenes on hot summer afternoons, as he had gone through Latin texts with her, when all she had wanted was to go riding. In those days she called him the steward, his uncle's administrator, and Wiktor, not bothered by such egalitarian notions, had enraged her by failing to be riled. And now in her words, in her excuses for not being able to go for a walk, in the few questions she had put to him, although proof of great social and conversational skills, he was searching for signs of her old contempt. And indeed he found them. The ease with which she had slipped into the familiar form of address, the way she had managed to skate around the subject of his job, and the way she avoided giving the full picture

37

either about her sisters or her husband, who worked at
the Ministry of Foreign Affairs – all this was to some
extent a thinly veiled expression of that old contempt and
antipathy. But at the same time he found little Zosia, so
unbearable in the past and now the most ladylike of all
the sisters, extremely attractive. He was impressed by her
serenity, her carefree manner and her skill at giving light
and shade to her words. Besides, she was young and
pretty, though a bit languid and dozy, as if tired by her
own physical existence. She made him feel a bit like a
farm hand with ignoble intentions towards the lady of the
manor, and he deliberately spoke more coarsely and
brusquely than usual. Zosia pretended not to notice;
instead of going out into the garden they went on
chatting until four, when something started to wriggle
beneath the gauze and Henio's voice rang out, clear and
energetic, with not a hint of sleep in it. The nanny took
the baby and dressed him, a scene that delighted Zosia
but left Wiktor indifferent to his charms; then at last it
was time for tea.

The tea was a disappointment to Wiktor. There were
too many strangers, and everyone seemed embarrassed
about the previous day's high spirits. Besides, yesterday
he had been alone with the girls, whom he knew well,
and now a great crowd of people had turned up who –
unknown to him and without knowing him – had acquired their own roles at Wilko over the past dozen
years or so. Above all, there was Kawecki, reigning beside Julcia and setting the whole tone of the gathering.
It was evident that neither Kazia nor Jola were fond of
him; Wiktor guessed that there must have been some
knotty financial issues in the house over the division of
Wilko's income, especially as the youngest sister had

come of age a year ago and must have come into the legal picture now. Mama didn't come down for tea at all, and Jola was very late in arriving, despite the double clang of the gong, appearing only some time after through the french window from the garden, with two unfamiliar gentlemen, one of them in military uniform. As he chatted with Kawecki, Wiktor could see her coming across the veranda, very happy and smiling. He remembered that Jola was very short-sighted, and now he noticed that this defect had got so much worse that as she crossed the veranda she stooped a bit, and kept staring underfoot. She was holding a long cane, which gave her a strangely elderly look. But as she raised her head to look at one of her companions, the enormous white hat, that a moment before had concealed her like a mushroom, became a sunny halo around her laughing, long and slender face. How pretty she was. In the bright afternoon sunlight it really showed. Once inside, she moved about briskly, shrugging her slender shoulders, left bare under a light white dress. She laughed with everyone, even Kawecki, greeted Wiktor warmly and introduced him to the elegant gentlemen, both very smart and well groomed. Wiktor found the skin above the officer's stiff military collar particularly exasperating – it was white beyond measure, and lined with a gentle plumpness, well fed on top-quality Parma ham. The Captain himself was tall and lean but muscular, with extremely beautiful hands. The conversation at table was animated and amusing, yet very casual and informal. The presence of the unfamiliar gentlemen cast a chill over Wiktor, and the tea he had so looked forward to soon became a bore. He turned to Tunia; thin and wide-eyed, she was virtually sitting among the children.

'I see only Tunia's left to take me around Wilko and show me what has changed,' he said. 'Shall we go for a walk? All right?'

Tunia mumbled a 'yes' and hid her face in a cup of milk. There was still something extremely childlike and girlish in her behaviour, and Wiktor wasn't surprised that Antoni had called her 'just a child'.

Finally, after tea they did go for a walk. Kawecki took Julcia to the growing frames to show her something; Kazia gave Antoś a lesson; Jola, back in the shade of her linen hat, occupied a deckchair on the veranda and sat surrounded by 'her gentlemen'. This time Zosia kept her company.

They went out at the front of the house and stopped to admire the wonderful view that lay spread out before them. At the bottom of the drive there was a narrow canal, running along an avenue of old hornbeams, clear and straight as an arrow for at least a kilometre. At the far end of the avenue stood a large wooden mill which marked the edge of the parochial village.

'Do you like going for walks?' Wiktor asked Tunia.

'What about you, Mr Ruben?' she asked.

'You can't possibly call me "Mr Ruben". All your sisters call me by my first name.'

'It'll be hard for me at first,' she whispered in confusion. 'You're so much older than me, Mr ...' At this she grew even more confused and blushed to the very arches of her eyebrows. 'Oh dear!' she cried, 'I've put my foot in it.'

'No you haven't, not at all – you're right, my child,' said Wiktor, trying to make the best of it, though in reality Tunia's words gave him no cheer. 'I remember when you were a very little girl – you always had terror in your eyes … especially the time you came rushing into the drawing room, all out of breath, crying in absolute terror, "Help! There's a chicken after me!" '

They both laughed. They walked down the drive and along the canal, crossing the main road.

'Fela and I always used to walk down to the mill,' said Wiktor. 'Do you remember Fela?'

'Yes, I do,' said Tunia unemotionally, 'but it's ten years since she died …'

'You know what, let's go to the cemetery.'

'All right,' agreed Tunia. 'It's not far.'

As they walked among the hornbeams Wiktor kept talking about Fela, remembering things she had said, walks he had taken with her, and the games they had played. Fela was always at the ponds, always in the water; she used to go bathing for hours on end, and she was a very good swimmer. It gave her great pleasure. Tunia listened indifferently, and her occasional comments implied that her thoughts were elsewhere. She mentioned the crops in the fields on either side of the avenue, catching crayfish and Kawecki's plans for a fish farm. Their lines of thought ran in parallel, as if along opposite sides of the canal, without ever converging, but without obstructing each other either.

There was one scene he couldn't tell her about. It was that final summer, a couple of weeks before the outbreak of war. One day towards evening he was on his way back from hunting – for ducks, it must have been – as he loved to wander about with a gun, though he didn't do much shooting. He was due to drop in at Wilko for supper, when suddenly he emerged from a clump of willows into a meadow by the pond. In the middle of the meadow, with her back to him stood Fela, entirely naked, dressing

41

her short plait with a golden comb. Opposite her sat Jola in a red dress, and Fela was telling her something. Wiktor stopped short. The sun was behind him, just on the point of setting, and a golden glow fell on the two girls, clearly illuminating Fela's shapely white body and her sister's red dress. Jola saw Wiktor and looked at him dumbstruck; Fela followed her line of vision, and when she saw him, stared at him in surprise over her shoulder. 'Come on over,' she said calmly, not at all flustered. But suddenly she gave a violent shriek, fell to the ground and hid herself behind Jola. 'I forgot I'd taken off my bathing costume!' she cried, laughing a bit, and at the same time highly embarrassed. Wiktor went back into the clump of willows and waited for Fela to get dressed. He closed his eyes and could still see Fela illuminated before him, combing her hair and calmly turning her profile towards him. Among the willows there was an acrid smell of damp sticks, and now, whenever he caught that scent as he walked along the canal, the same image appeared before his eyes. At the time, Fela had got dressed and run off ahead, afraid to face Wiktor, and he had gone back with Jola. He had felt very manly, with the gun on his back and the lovely Jola at his side, and Fela's comical confusion had filled him with a sense of scornful indulgence. He had thought of Fela as a little girl, just a shade older than Zosia, and had never regarded her as anything but a child. Now he felt he might have been mistaken. It wasn't the first time this scene had come to mind. One of his more typical mental images floated to the surface – the scene at the prison camp, when they hadn't set eyes on a woman for ages. Or during the Kiev campaign, when he had slept in a bed where shortly before a Jew had been stabbed to death. He could smell the sickly odour of blood in the air, but sleep was more important than anything, more important than his aching feet, than the sight of death and wounds, to which in all those years he had become inured – there, too, that scene had arisen in his mind, the image of women bathing, basking in the gentle glow of the setting sun.

Only now, as he thought back, could he see that he hadn't forgotten Wilko as much as he had imagined, and that into every empty chink in his consciousness something from that era had immediately crept, the image of one of these women. He glanced at Tunia, walking gracefully beside him, or rather striding, like the Angel beside Tobias in Giorgione's painting, setting down each long leg in turn. And in this way of walking, leaning very slightly forwards, in her eyes, which glided over distant objects with short-sighted lack of focus, he detected a portent of Jola's walk. 'In fifteen years her walk will be just the same,' he thought.

, They didn't have far to go. Just beyond the mill began the village, and on a hill to the right beyond the first houses lay the cemetery. They went up a slope, then downhill a bit, where there was a spring with a water pump and four silver poplars, and then there was a gate. The graveyard itself was dense with trees and crowded with time-worn mounds, where people lay at rest. Here and there blown-down crosses protruded. They had to pass through this multitude to reach the Wilko family tomb, right under the perimeter wall. But it, too, was already full to bursting. Fela lay nearby in a corner at the convergence of two walls built of stones from the fields. Over the tomb stood a birchwood cross surrounded by railings, but the little grave was neglected. As Wiktor gazed at this mound, with not a single flower upon it, he realised that his question about Fela had been out of place, not because it picked

at a freshly healed wound but because it stirred up something long forgotten. Yes, from what Tunia had told him
today, and from the look of the grave it was plain to see
that no one remembered Fela any more.

'Does your mother come here often?' he asked Tunia.

'Oh, Mama hardly goes out at all now. She doesn't feel
up to it.'

Wiktor stood over the grave, not knowing what to say,
still less what to think. They had forgotten her very existence. Who on earth still remembered her body illuminated by the setting sun? He alone held this secret; who
knows, maybe on the journey here his only thought had
been of meeting Fela again. No, he hadn't been thinking
about her, he was sure of that; he hadn't really thought
about Wilko at all, until he took the first steps along the
road past the station. But he would have found her the
least changed, as then she had been just on the threshold
and today she would have been just at the close of the
finest stage in a woman's life. Almost exactly the same as
she had been in the meadow, she would have been de-
scending towards maturity, and might have calmly turned
around to him and said, 'Come on over!' Now at last he
had come, but too late; everything that might have been
waiting for him had already turned to dust. Ten years –
after ten years there would be nothing left but a few
bones, not a shred of that slender girl's broad white back
as she turned to face the golden sun. He sighed.

Tunia giggled and said, 'You're sighing like someone
in love.'

He looked at her in amazement; this lack of tact in
such a young girl brought him up short. 'How could she?'
he thought, but said nothing. Three ducks flew over the
cemetery and he pointed them out to Tunia. Tunia had

never been duck-shooting, so they agreed that next week they would go to the Ważycki ponds, a few kilometres away, where he knew some good places. There was great duck-shooting to be had, and St Peter's and St Paul's Day fell next week. They left the cemetery without a second glance. What for? They would have seen nothing to remind them of Fela or to cause them to remember her. May she rest in peace.

. But the very next day he went there alone at dawn, just to go somewhere, to go for a walk, and like a sentimental girl he plucked some cornflowers along the way to put on the grave … He laughed at himself, but he wasn't doing it for any sentimental reason, simply because he thought it a shame they had all forgotten the poor girl.

He had wriggled out of lunch at Wilko, whispering in Julcia's ear, 'I'll come back when Jola's gentlemen have gone.' But she had just laughed and said, 'This lot will go, but there will be others, there's always someone here.' Yes, but he would take a couple of days off – he should spend at least some time with his relatives.

He wanted a day or two free to gather his thoughts. The image which had formed in his mind the very first evening had started to blur. In fact he didn't need to gather his thoughts, but rather his emotions. They were all in a whirl; he was ready to turn his back on his entire past and start something new, but he couldn't work out what this new start should be. But yes, of course he could – it was love. It had sprung up inside him despite his former attitude to it; it had started to dominate his actions. Yet the strangest thing about this feeling was that it had no goal or object, it was suspended in a pure void; quite simply, all the joy he had ever felt and that had been crushed into the dust by the onslaught of the exhausting daily grind, had sprouted like weeds beneath the rubble and was rising upwards. He was in an excellent mood, a constant delight to his aunt and uncle. By now he had noticed that his uncle really had aged a lot; he was forgetful and kept asking the same questions, as if wanting to remind Wiktor of everything he had suppressed. But Wiktor took it in a cheerful spirit and told his uncle he didn't want to think about it. And not thinking took no effort at all.

• First thing in the morning he had gone to the cemetery, then he had spent the afternoon in the garden reading some obscure early nineteenth-century memoirs. In the evening he had chatted with his aunt and uncle until late, when they had packed him off to bed. Early next morning he rode over to the Ważycki ponds to find out if anything had changed and who could give permission for a one-off hunting expedition on the waters there. The caretaker and fisherman rolled into one turned out to be the same man as before. As St Peter's and St Paul's fell on Sunday, and the foreman himself was due to go hunting that day, Wiktor arranged to hunt on Tuesday. They were to come around midday, have a swim, and then shoot towards evening, as usual. As for permission, the caretaker would see to it himself. That meant they would have to slip him five zlotys and could shoot for as long as the grapeshot lasted. He got back long after lunch; some food had been kept aside for him, and only his aunt kept him company at table. As usual they talked about Wilko: his aunt said Kawecki was very unkind to his wife's sisters, that they had had furious arguments about expenses, and that he mistreated Kazia, as she had no husband and was obliged to stay at home with her mother and her child. The division of property had already been settled, and the place belonged jointly to the Kaweckis and the Rudnickis (that is, Jola), while the other sisters were to be paid off in instalments. The repayments hadn't started yet, but Kazia had borrowed her capital against her mother's share. In short, she acquainted him with all the financial difficulties of the Wilko girls. Wiktor listened with one ear, letting the other drift as he wondered where to get a shotgun from, and heaped a mountain of lettuce on his plate.

Suddenly someone knocked at the window and Wiktor caught sight of a white parasol, followed by a white hat. They both leaped to the door – it was Jola.

Wilko and Rożki were neighbouring properties, but there was no close or intimate relationship between their inhabitants. The only real link was Wiktor. Naturally, the older generation used to call on each other on saints' days and holidays, but these days the girls rarely looked in at Rożki. So Jola's arrival was a great event. She had come to ask Auntie and Uncle (as the girls always called them) to be sure to come over the day after tomorrow for her mother's name day. The actual name day was on Monday, St Emilia's Day, but they had moved it back to Sunday to celebrate it along with St Peter's and St Paul's. They must come for lunch and then stay till evening; Wiktor too, of course. No, Wiktor can stay at home, can't he?!

Auntie hurried off to the kitchen to make tea – there was sure to be frothy hot chocolate, just as if they were children – so Wiktor and Jola were left alone in the dining room. It was the first time they had been alone since they had met again. Jola looked around the place; it was so long since she had been here, a couple of years now, as she only came to Wilko for a few weeks at a time.

Wiktor's uncle's house stood on its own in a hollow. Out of the fiercest line of fire, it hadn't been as badly damaged during the war as the house at Wilko. The furniture was still the same, even the old crock of a piano, which rattled away beneath Jola's fingers. She looked around the room, rambling on rather self-consciously as she did so, without looking Wiktor in the eyes. Wiktor felt master of the situation and smiled as he watched her moving about nervously, avoiding his gaze. Finally he asked: 'Jola, who exactly were those two fellows at your place the other day? They ruined the entire tea for me and deprived me of the pleasure of your company. You didn't speak to me at all.'

'It wasn't that much of a pleasure. Anyway, they've gone now.'

'There will be others, though, won't there? That's what Julcia said.'

'Julcia's always rattling on. Besides, what's it to you? Just look at him, after fifteen whole years he's jealous!'

'You're right, I am,' said Wiktor, laughing. 'Our conversation has taken a strange turn – you're having to justify yourself and I'm asking pointless questions. It's really none of my business.'

'That's a pity,' said Jola, this time in a different, plainer tone and looked Wiktor in the eyes.

Wiktor had perhaps never encountered such an eloquent look as her eyes stared straight into his. It said far more than words could say; luckily the only thing missing was love. This time it was Wiktor's turn to look away.

'It's a pity it's none of your business, and never was.'

'Were you in love with me?'

'Were you with me?'

'No ... I don't think I was, but I was very fond of you.'

'Nor was I. I was never in love with you and I hope you can tell I'm not now either. But you played a much more important role in my life. Do you realise, I found out everything about you from your aunt and uncle, as if by accident. No, that's not the point. You were a tremendous influence on me then. Just think what a baby I was in those days. I wasn't even seventeen that summer when you stayed with us. And I used to put everything I ever did before the test of your judgement, as I saw it. You never guessed a thing, but I was always asking myself, "What would Wiktor say about that?" I'd read some books and leave them lying about so you'd notice I'd been educating myself, but you never did. Sometimes I'd ask you some quite serious questions, but you almost always used to fob me off with jokes. Of course, I was just a girl, but the strangest thing is that I went on feeling like that for ages. You know, even now I'd be pleased if you were to praise my conduct now and then. Even now I still catch myself thinking, what would Wiktor have said about that … And …'

'Jolka? What?'

'Well, you know – ' and suddenly she looked straight at him again; her lovely eyes were coated in a glassy film of tears. 'Well, and you know, Wiktor, I don't always think you would be satisfied with my behaviour.'

'And are you?'

'What a question. Dammit!' she cursed, and stood up from the sofa. She scrutinised a portrait hanging on the wall. After a while she added, 'Well, that's exactly why I've come today. So you'd know that I know it's no good … what a sentence! Well, in a nutshell, so you won't think badly of me.'

Wiktor smiled. 'Jola, have you ever stopped to think what on earth gives me the right to judge you or anybody else? Do you know what sort of person I am?'

'Yes, I do – you're a noble person.'

'Oh, that's not much at all, but it's a great deal to heap on my humble shoulders. You know what sort of a life I've had. There's not a single thing in it that gives me the right to judge you. Look at it – it's a barren wasteland.'

'What about your work at Stokroć?'

'It's the only work I can get.'

'I know the truth. Your mother told your aunt you devote your life to helping the blind.'

'Jola! Jola!' cried Wiktor, and burst out laughing from the bottom of his heart. 'It's nothing much. What a lot of nonsense about an awful, dreadful life! There's never been anything noble about it.'

'You see, I'm not in love with you and I never was, but what I feel is much more than that – I respect you.'

'Oh, Jola, that's just not good enough.'

They both burst out laughing.

'Oh, but you're so good,' said Jola suddenly, and stopped in the middle of the room. Her eyes had glazed over again. But just then Auntie came in with a tray – hot chocolate and clotted cream really were the order of the day. Jola was fond of sweets, so they all sat down to eat and chat. Tunia, Kazia and the children were coming for her later in the carriage on their way back from the forest. After the chocolate Jola asked Wiktor to take her for a walk, not around the garden but the farmyard. Uncle Robert always had such wonderful things, and it was so long since she had seen it.

So they set off across the huge yard littered with farming tools. Each machine stood beneath a separate bit of roofing, like beehives – such was Uncle Robert's eccentricity. Alongside stood a row of carts, shafts to the fore, pointing towards the cow sheds, stables and henhouses.

Jola found the chickens and pigs especially lovely, despite the powerful stench prevailing in their vicinity. The farmhand had bred a lovely black Italian pedigree sow, and opposite were four of her lovely piglets, already quite big. Jola was delighted, but went on with her interrupted conversation with Wiktor.

'My dear,' she said, 'there has to be some sort of moral influence in life. And the more immoral a life one leads, the more necessary that influence becomes.'

'What do you mean by immoral? Look at the ones with white spots.'

'They're lovely. Immoral, as I understand it, could mean aimless. Drifting along from one thing to the next, with no motive. That's what I call a lack of morality.'

They went over to the hens. Behind a huge chicken-wire fence, which acted as a rampart around special, heated huts, sat a large variety of poultry, including white hens and guinea fowl. In another hut some splendid, tall red cockerels were flapping their huge feet about.

'Look, look,' said Jola, 'they're running along like antediluvian creatures.'

Neither of them had the faintest idea how antediluvian creatures ran, but the comparison sounded apt, and they had a good long laugh about it. They ended up in the middle of the yard, where Jola drew patterns in the sand with her parasol, while talking non-stop. But none of it made much sense. Wiktor grew more and more aloof, detecting a touch of hysteria in her babblings, just a hint of the emotional state of a sick, unhappy, childless woman. It put the fear of God into him, but she was also very beautiful in her classic white hat, which made her look shorter whenever she bowed her head, and taller whenever she raised it. Her speech consisted of a consid-

erable outpouring of confidences, which he hadn't encouraged at all. It was none of his business, and the more
she said the more of a stranger he felt her to be. He drew
himself up straight and leaned away from her.

When she had finished talking she noticed his silence;
bewildered and completely alien to him by now, she set
off towards the house. He went after her, watching her
take awkward, dainty footsteps, while leaning slightly
forwards, her weak eyes fixed on the path. Everything
that ought to bring her closer to him was pushing her
away. He was most upset with her for that, because he
found her immensely attractive, and now as he recalled
the old days, and those outings together, especially the
memorable boat trip to Rożki, the idea that he had been
mildly in love with her kept coming back to him. He
would have to ask Kazia to show him his old letters –
Kazia had been his *confidante*, and there was definitely
something about it in them, though he might have made
some of it up, in an effort to impress a young lady. But
that whole atmosphere of summer, their happy, carefree
times together, full of ideas and jokes, had been very
much like love.

Jola was standing on the porch, looking at him and
smiling. Finally she held out her hand and said: 'I can see
I've spoiled your good mood – you're miles away.'

'Not at all,' replied Wiktor. 'I was just wondering what
sort of pigsty to install at Stokroć – that's what I've got to
do next …'

Kazia and Zosia drove up with the children, but didn't
even get out of the carriage, as they were already very
late, wondering who on earth would have served supper
instead of Kazia and what would come of it. Edward had
been in a filthy mood all day as it was. They just picked

up Jola and left. The entire Rożki household promised to come for lunch the day after next.

Once the carriage had driven off and its rattling echo had died away, his aunt gave him a warning about Jola. He laughed.

'You're forgetting that I'm not twenty any more,' he said. 'And it's not as if in thirty-seven years of life I've never seen a woman before, is it? What harm can she possibly do to me?'

'But I'd like you to marry Tunia,' admitted his aunt, 'and she's sure to spoil it all!'

'She won't spoil anything because there'll be nothing to spoil,' said Wiktor. 'No, Auntie, please abandon all hope. I'm not going to marry anyone at Wilko any more – Kazia, maybe, but she's too old by now.'

It's true, he thought, I'm not going to marry anyone from Wilko, nor would I ever have wanted to; why should that be so?

He only came up with an explanation three days later, at the name-day party, for which a very large crowd of local people had assembled. Apart from the household, there were well over thirty people, and first came an enormous, lengthy lunch. Wiktor sat between two unfamiliar ladies who preferred to talk to their other neighbours; opposite him sat Jola's Captain, who was back again. He spoke most with him, and the Captain learned that Wiktor was a reserve officer with two medals for bravery, and came to like and respect him. His military etiquette was reflected in his unwillingness to drink without Wiktor, and from time to time he asked him a question about his army service. The entire table was very animated, and for once Jola's husband was there. He was stout and very unassuming, although a famous lawyer.

Kawecki was in a good mood, and a toast was drunk to Mama, whose violet dress did nothing to alter her meek expression and docile personage.

Wiktor found the whole thing incredibly boring, and as soon as lunch was over, when the company had dispersed about the rooms and verandas, he went for a long walk around the garden and the woods. He spent at least an hour walking, though rather aimlessly. Somehow now, and over the past few days in general, he couldn't quite pull himself together. He was lost in conflicting trains of thought; Jola and her visit to Rożki were also taking up a lot of space in his mind. Meanwhile his Warsaw and Stokroć worries had waned, as if their importance had been temporarily suspended for a sort of love-life moratorium. On the way back he went around the house and looked in at the pantry.

The house at Wilko was bisected by a vast corridor leading off the hall. At the far end of this corridor there was a small porch, then a covered wooden passage leading to a separate, sizeable building, where the kitchen and its annexes were housed. This was the site of the famous Wilko pantry. The pantry was a large room lined in oakwood shelves, with an enormous table standing in the centre. Wiktor used to joke that this pantry was the substitute for a library, as Wilko didn't have one. Behind the table a staircase led down to the cellar, which was larger than the entire house. On the shelves stood countless pots and jars arranged in chronological order, each appropriately labelled and inscribed; these were jams and juices. A separate shelf was set aside for mushrooms and pickles, another for preserves in kilner jars. A small nook containing glacé fruits, pears in honey, rose-hip jelly and other such delicacies had been Wiktor's and Jola's favourite corner once upon a time. When Wiktor looked in at the pantry, Kazia was standing at the vast table in a white apron, getting the tea ready.

'Come and help me,' she said, without looking up from the enormous strawberries which she was arranging on a dish spread with green leaves.

'What should I do?' asked Wiktor, glad of the opportunity for a chat with Kazia, and of a useful bolthole away from the boring guests.

'Have some strawberries, take some of the smaller ones,' said Kazia, 'and entertain me while I get this dreary job done.'

'You couldn't have made a better suggestion. I can't bear this company. I don't know why.'

'Because they're so vacuous,' said Kazia, setting the largest strawberry in the centre of her fruit mountain.

'That's a bit harsh,' said Wiktor, eating strawberries, 'you're too quick off the mark. You can't expect everyone to be a great philosopher. But they're all perfectly nice and hard-working.'

'Especially my sisters.'

'No, but the rest of them. It's just that I seem to have a different way of looking at things, somehow. Not that I'm anything special – I think what I've been through has cut me off from the rest of the world.'

'You always were different. Right from the start – it's not that you got cut off from other people later on, you were always a bit isolated.'

'You're flattering me, Kazia.'

Kazia set the strawberries aside and drew a large blue bell-jar towards her. She started arranging a pattern of glacé fruits in it, taking them from their tins with a little pair of tongs.

'It's hardly flattery. There's no merit or virtue in it. I haven't any merits or virtues at all, and I'm just as cut off from people, and that's the main feature of my life. These things are decided by some external agency that arranges us on the chessboard, wolves apart on their own, sheep together in herds. There's only one difference – here it's the sheep that devour the wolves, not the other way around.'

'That's a very complex analogy.'

'I spent the whole of yesterday afternoon playing wolves and sheep with Antoś, that's how it got into my head.'

'But I'd like to find a cure for my isolation. You see, that work of mine at Stokroć isn't a career, it doesn't even bring in a decent living, it's just that I want to work with people. But it's not working out at all well for me.'

'Don't you like it?'

'No.'

'So why did you leave the army? Maybe you'd have been better off there.'

'Oh, no. The garrison was awful. You can't begin to imagine the emptiness and desolation of an officer's life. No, I prefer Stokroć, it has got a proper aim and produces instant results. It's only since coming back that I can see how different the future looked from here.'

'And we saw you differently, too, in those days when we were all mad about you.'

'Oh, my dear, who'd have been mad about me?' sighed Wiktor. He put down his teaspoon and began to pick at the glacé fruits.

'Don't ruin my arrangement,' Kazia scolded him. 'You've got whole tins full to choose from.'

'I was just trying one, I won't have any more.'

56

'We were all madly in love with you – looking back, you can see it – Jola maybe not so much, she pretended more than she really felt. That was typical of her – God forbid she should do anything differently from me. She was always imitating me, all through our childhood. And I was madly in love with you.'

'Were you really, seriously?' Wiktor was so surprised that he forgot about the fruits.

'Indeed I was, very seriously,' said Kazia, swapping the tongs for a long, sharp skewer, and skilfully using it to remove gooseberries from a tin. 'It took me ages to get over it. In the first years of the war I thought you'd come back, but then I got married. I had a very good, kind husband, and we divorced amicably. He found someone else, you know.'

'But you're not still in love with me, are you?' asked Wiktor nervously.

Kazia smiled, without taking her eyes off the skewer, working it nimbly. 'Don't worry. I'd forgotten all about you, so I was extremely surprised when you turned up again. You seem so totally different.'

'I've got older.'

'Well, of course you have, but it's not just that. You've lost your spark, somehow.'

Although he was feeling relaxed, once again that unbearable image appeared before his eyes, of the dead soldier wrapped in grey and green rags. He put down his pear stalk and stared at Kazia. He didn't need an explanation, nor could he have found one anyway; it seemed the hardest thing in the world to bridge the gap to fifteen years ago, to the time where he wasn't forgotten, as Kazia said, but was still seen in the heroic light of his twentieth spring.

'Do you know, Kazia,' he said after a while, 'I once saw Fela naked, in the meadow by the pond. What you want to see in me now is the same as if I were to dig up Fela's coffin and be surprised it wasn't the same girl, just as beautiful.'

Kazia looked up at him keenly. 'But I have no desire whatsoever to see you as you were then,' she said in a sincere tone. 'That would be awful. That would ruin my entire life, now that I've managed to get it into some sort of order. No, I just wanted to assure you, for my part, that there's no threat. Once upon a time, as a young girl, not much more than a child, I was madly in love with you; nowadays it makes me laugh. There's nothing left of it now, and I can no longer imagine how anyone could be so much in love. I find it rather funny, but then you must admit, there's something humiliating and funny about every great love.'

'Humiliating, maybe,' said Wiktor slowly, 'but funny?'

'Have you never felt how incongruous, how utterly ridiculous such a strong attachment can be?'

'No, never.'

'Then you've never really been in love.'

'I've never had the time,' he said, standing up abruptly. He went over to the jam shelf and, turning the jars around, checked the dates on them. Some were two, three years old or more.

'Why do you make so much of this stuff?' he asked her.

'So that some of them get served to the chosen few.'

Only now, during his conversation with Kazia, did it occur to him that he had never been madly in love with anyone. He had had the occasional crush on someone, he had had affairs, one of which had forced him to leave the army sooner than planned; and when he was the foreman at Rudki there had been Mrs Żakowa, for sure. But how meagre it was, compared with what could have been. He turned around and glanced at Kazia, who had stopped working; she had put away the crystal sweet jars and, leaning her elbows on the table, was gazing into the distance, no doubt into the very same years on which he was reflecting. She looked almost pretty, her eyes large, black and open; besides which she was slender and her hair fell over her ears in pretty curls. She noticed him looking at her and smiled as she swept the sugar crumbs off the table.

'You're looking at me with regret in your eyes,' she said.

'Oh, no, I never have any regrets,' said Wiktor decisively. He came up and took her by the hand. 'I'm truly sorry,' he said, 'but I really had no idea. And even if I had known, what can one do about such things?'

'Nothing, I'm sure, and I too have no regrets, or any other ill feeling towards you.'

Just then a servant came in and shot a look of amazement at Wiktor – the pantry was no place for guests – and started gathering up the bell-jars and plates Kazia had prepared, to take to the dining room.

'The tea's just brewed,' he told Kazia. 'We're ready to start serving.'

And he was gone. Kazia wanted to go too, but Wiktor held her back. 'Just a moment,' he said, 'it's so nice here in the pantry, it's like being tucked up in a warm coat. And I'm glad we're having another of our "milestones",' he added, recalling old times.

'The last one ever, I should think,' said Kazia, smiling as she untied her apron. 'You see how far they got us, those "milestones" of ours.'

Jarosław Iwaszkiewicz

'All the way to Siberia,' said Wiktor bitterly.

And off they went. The guests had had their rest and were swarming about the rooms again. Kazia went into the dining room. Wiktor crossed the drawing room and went out onto the veranda; this was where he and Kazia had had most of their 'milestone' chats – little had he suspected what seeds he was sowing at the time. He was quite appalled at the vast chasms of past ignorance he had displayed, but even now he could see there were a lot of things he didn't understand as others did. He had become more isolated than ever, a virtual recluse, and in working for society he had somehow grown apart from it, become an outsider.

On the way down the veranda steps into the garden, he suddenly thought of Jurek, his only friend, who was gone for ever. He thought of their conversations and realised how abstract and theoretical they had been, and how impossible it was to test the validity of the conclusions they had reached. 'Jurek's death really put a spanner in the works,' he thought. 'He was gone before he'd had time to discover how meaningless it all is, everything a person resolves to do and manages to achieve, while all the really important things accidentally get left behind, then come back to haunt us, or worse still, we go chasing after them.'

No! no! that wasn't what he wanted to think about; for the first time since arriving he thought of his work at Stokroć. It was a tough job, but it seemed like a haven of purposefully chosen and well defined, though difficult tasks. But everything around him here had suddenly changed from happy potentialities into monstrous crimes he had never even committed.

That evening he went home in the carriage with his aunt and uncle. The night was cold and dark but still summery – teeming with secret life hidden from human sight; only some lingering odours reached one's nostrils, evidence of something going on in the vicinity. Quite spontaneously Wiktor started talking about Kazia, and learned from his aunt what her life was really like. Apparently, Kawecki was unbearable towards her – he had heard that much before. So why did she stay here, working at someone else's home? Couldn't she come and help him in Warsaw? Or at Stokroć?

Back home, alone in his room again, he shook off these thoughts; he didn't get much sleep, but couldn't stop thinking, not so much about Kazia as about himself. These thoughts became much clearer the next day, when tired for lack of sleep he lay down for an afternoon nap. It was quiet now, except for the torrid heat, and as he lay in a sweat beneath the muslin netting, a series of images processed slowly through his mind, vividly bringing home to him the nullity of his experiences to date, compared with the waves he had made by falling like a stone into still water. It was the first time he had likened the atmosphere at Wilko to standing water in a pond, and then it struck him that stones and water could have nothing at all in common.

He awoke from his nap feeling lethargic and feverish. He dragged himself around Rożki, but didn't go to Wilko, in spite of his aunt's suggestions; he had had enough of it. The conversation with Kazia alone was enough to bring him to saturation point for a couple of days at least. In any case, he couldn't go to Wilko because he had to go to bed early and then get up at dawn the next day for the ducks at the Ważycki ponds.

The hunting expedition was memorable, though not for the size of the kill. Quite the reverse – they arrived late, as Tunia didn't come for Wiktor on time, the ducks were hiding, and they never saw a single one. In a tiny canoe borrowed from the fisherman they spent a long time sailing through the rushes; on water covered in duckweed, shallow and silent, they sailed up small creeks lined with sweet flag, stealing their way among the rushes with a rustle and a hiss. They weren't hot, as a fresh breeze blew off the water, both relaxing and invigorating. Wiktor let slip all thought of himself and his problems, and made no mention of past events that could no longer be remedied. He was living for the present, feeling glad to be still young, with a balanced sort of youthfulness. He still had time to start his life afresh, he could still change it all, and his wasted youth could return, in defiance of all the songs and proverbs, in a new, more solid form.

The reason for these thoughts was Tunia, of course, who in the days of his youth had passed him by unnoticed in the guise of a child. She had been too little then to inspire any sort of feeling in him, as Zosia had done, and now the very fact that she was not tarnished with any memory from fifteen years ago, made her into a new person, rejuvenating and worthy of attention.

Without any motive, Wiktor yielded to the pleasure of spending time with this delightful, healthy girl, who said nothing to stir up his melancholy, and had no capacity to evoke memories or regrets. She couldn't remember Fela at all, although she was very like her late sister. And if now and then Wiktor heard an echo of the past which he hadn't fully appreciated at the time, it was in her smile, her laughter, or a nod or turn of her head, which had so much in common with the various poses and gestures of Fela.

Seeing in Tunia all those expressions and mannerisms that he had once seen in Fela, he began to realise the significance of his conversations with the deceased, and of the walks they had taken together. He read it all like a palimpsest, a confession from beyond the grave, a rediscovery of everything he had lost.

But whenever he turned away from Tunia to push the canoe through the rushes and reeds, and, lost in thought, began to realise what Fela had once offered him in the way of flirtation, maybe love even, the moment he looked around at his companion again, it was her smile, her teeth, her lovely eyes and slender waist that he saw, more slender than Fela's had been.

. They didn't set off for home until late in the afternoon, and Wiktor spent hours wandering among the reeds, pretending to look for ducks, while drinking in Tunia's youthful company.

She was enjoying it too; in her eyes, Wiktor was clearly not burdened with any memory. For her alone of all the sisters he was a new friend, unexpected, handsome maybe, and of all the people he had met here she alone did not oppress him with any noticeable changes. In her company he felt free of memories, and it brought his youth flooding back to him.

The persons of Tunia and Fela were so interwoven in his mind that that evening, as he was leaving Wilko, when Tunia was standing in the doorway to see him off after their day together, he suddenly felt as if Fela had come out to bid him farewell. And in this vision he felt no fear of death, but quite the opposite, the joy of life.

He got to Wilko quite early next morning. He went to find Tunia, and together they went to the pine coppice – those few tall pines that stood on higher ground at the bottom of the garden and were so visible from afar. They sat on the grass and began to play the same game that had held Wiktor enthralled throughout the day before; at night he had even dreamed of it. It was a game of jokes and allusions, of sensual intimacy and inaccessibility, the fragrance of the body and of summer, blades of grass tickling them, or ants crawling about their hands and feet, making them shudder and tremble. But it was also a game of age and youth, memories and reality, life and death, Tunia and Fela.

Tunia was twenty-one or twenty-two, but she looked much younger, as she set down each long leg in turn, like Giorgione's Angel. Sitting beside Wiktor on the grass, she vividly reminded him of a trembling bird. Inevitably, what was bound to happen did happen; Wiktor took her by the arms, pressed her to the grass, and kissed her passionately on the lips. Tunia tore herself away and screamed. Then she began showering Wiktor with reproaches, but eventually she burst out laughing and let him kiss her a second time, more passionately and for longer. There was a fragrance of resin about her.

'No,' she said afterwards, wagging her finger. 'Never again, it's out of the question!' She laughed heartily.

This laughter hurt Wiktor's feelings; she should have been more gracious about the kiss, she should have taken it much more seriously. This laughter seemed to be mocking him and his feelings. On the way back to the house he felt disappointed. Tunia walked alongside him, suddenly quiet and more serious than usual. He noticed her sapphire-blue eyes staring blankly from under her shapely brows. It made him feel sorry for her, and his heart ached at the thought of how very much he might have loved such a lively, beautiful creature.

Then there was tea, and what happened afterwards shifted his thoughts onto a different track. They all set off for the forest in two carriages. But as Jola had guests again there wasn't enough room for everyone, so a cart-horse was hitched to a small gig, which naturally was much slower than the team horses. On the way out, Jola and the Captain took the gig. Wiktor sat in the carriage with Julcia, her daughters and Tunia. The children fidgeted, while Julcia chattered in a low, sympathetic tone throughout the journey. Wiktor looked across at Tunia; ignoring the conversation and the children, and wearing the same serious expression he had already noticed that day, she was gazing with rare concentration at the fields along the road. Wiktor also looked at Julcia as she talked, and compared the two sisters. They were completely unalike. Only their eyes were the same colour, but the expression in them was different. Maybe once, when she was thinner, Julcia had been more like Tunia, but now the age difference set them too far apart. Just one feature was strikingly similar – their skin. That warm, sallow satin, forming a rich fabric. Wiktor compared their necks, shoulders and napes, and found them to be almost identically smooth, though Julcia's had a much more substantial layer of fat under them. Once again he was reminded of those nights, when the touch of that skin had stamped itself forever on his memory.

In the forest Jola lost her bracelet. Everyone set about looking for it, which took up a great deal of time. Finally, Kazia's little Antoś found it, and thus became the hero of the evening. Upset, Jola went ahead in the carriage, and Wiktor and Julcia were left alone to take the one-horse gig.

There were masses of flowers in the clearings and Tunia had picked a bunch, from which Wiktor took a large daisy with a pure yellow middle. He slid his fingers across the centre and over the white petals, frayed and slightly wilting. He felt the compactness and resilience of the tiny granules that made up its close-cropped pistils and delicate, silky petals. He thought of these flowers, of Tunia, and of Julcia, as they climbed into the little gig, and Julcia whipped up the idle but weary horse.

Meanwhile darkness had fallen. A slowly advancing cloud had half covered the sky. It wasn't an oncoming storm, it was just that the weather had changed. There was going to be rain, and the sky was changing its dress like a woman. The stars were all out, and the cloud was creeping over, but the air was just as stuffy as it had been all day. Wiktor felt excited.

In the darkness the gig went over a bump and tilted violently. To stop himself from falling out, Wiktor seized the rail with one hand, and grabbed onto Julcia with the other. As soon as they had been left alone Julcia had stopped talking and Wiktor had felt a cloud enveloping them, just like the one that was rising in the sky, uniting them in a heavy silence. Gradually he slid his arm around her, touched the back of her neck, then dropped it onto her shoulders. He could still feel the memory of that skin from fifteen years ago, more beautiful than a flower. But what he was touching so warily now, as the gig rocked and swayed, felt quite different, and shockingly banal. He had felt this sort of skin so often before that it was like touching something as familiar as his own body. There was none of the old, incredible tremor, none of that silent lust that had paralysed his tongue. Julcia was just the same as thousands of other women.

Aware that by speaking he would needlessly break the spell of the summer's night, he said: 'Can you see the road, Julcia? Or we'll tip over again.'

Julcia didn't answer straightaway, though the sound of his voice made her jump. She knew the question had quite another meaning, but she couldn't instantly work out what. To test the ground, after a pause she said: 'No, I can't see a thing, but the mare will find her way home.'

'Maybe she will, but we could still tip over on the way.' Wiktor's hand descended further and grasped Julcia by the waist again. He was surprised how broad it was; once she had been as slender as Tunia. 'You and Tunia are alike, in spite of all.'

Julcia just grunted in reply, and suddenly Wiktor realised he had spoken out of turn, and that Julcia had a very different view of herself. The only remedy for his blunder was to take it to the bitter end, but he couldn't get a grip on himself. No, those fifteen years really had existed.

Finally they got home. They didn't allow silence to descend on them, but the remarks they exchanged were meaningless. Their only purpose was to dispel the summer cloud. Wiktor did so with a certain sense of regret, but at the same time he could feel the memory of those four nights long ago growing, taking on gigantic proportions, making him yearn for the past, even though his present experience was beautiful and fragrant. Julcia chattered on in a matter-of-fact way, and perhaps it was nothing to do with her after all.

Soon they were sitting at supper, and everyone was talking about the lost bracelet, about Antoś, and how many times they had already gone over the very spot where the lost treasure was found. Then Julcia, in her seat of honour, after waiting for everyone to settle down, said in her low voice, laughing: 'I didn't know Wiktor was afraid of driving at night. He kept telling me I'd tip us over.'

'It's lucky our fine charger didn't bolt with us,' said Wiktor, and everyone laughed at the poor old cart-horse.

For the next few days he stayed at Rożki and kept his distance from the avenue down to Wilko. Nor did the ladies from Wilko call in at Rożki, and the days passed drearily. Wiktor emptied his mind of all thought and rested. He had patent proof of how weak he was, maybe because his fortieth year was approaching; at Rożki he had got into the habit of sleeping in the afternoons. This afternoon nap, through the hottest hours of the day, was radically different from his night-time sleep, which didn't always come easily, but as soon as it did, fell over him like a black shroud and brought total oblivion. The hot, heavy afternoon sleep was really just a doze; often it took the form of more intense, more focused thought. His latest emotions would get mixed up with apparitions from the past, radiant with the glory of fulfilment. The dreams and phantoms of these afternoon naps usually had a very erotic flavour. He would close all the shutters and lie down on a small sofa in the drawing room with his legs curled up. This uncomfortable position was one of the charms of the ritual. With a small pillow over his head, he lay listening with equal attention to the muffled buzzing of the flies and his own slackened-off thoughts. A pleasant warmth flowing over his body gradually turned into the sensation of another body clinging tightly to him. It also felt as if all the door hinges and all the wall stays had come loose, as if nothing had contours any more. His body became one with this strange female body, hugging it to him and pulling away from it by turns. Despite this close union he could sense an abyss between himself and the other body, whose owner he couldn't identify or name. Soon the dozing would become a torment as he longed to know who it was, but it never became clear. Once only he recognised it as the body of the slaughtered soldier, but this caused him no distress. On the contrary, the corpse imparted a pleasant warmth, which gave him a sexual thrill. After a while its rags fell away, blending into one with the pillow beneath his head and the pillow on top; meanwhile he felt himself merge with the body lying beside him, then separate from it again across an impenetrable abyss of painful isolation. All together, pain and joy, suffocation and isolation, had blended into one to become a form of erotic excitement, strange shapes in a tormenting dream.

He would awake feeling lethargic and would slowly come to, only vaguely aware of the contours of the objects around him, or of the contents of his head. For the rest of the day he would feel relaxed and never sleepy towards evening. The women from Wilko never appeared in his dreams, yet as soon as he awoke he felt the need to immerse himself in their atmosphere, and had to fight his desire to go there. And so he came to the end of the second week of his holiday. He wasn't bothered by the fact that in just over a week or so he would have to pack up his bits and pieces for the return journey. He was enjoying looking at himself from the outside, as if watching a stranger. He found that he couldn't trace the sequence of his life, and sensed gaps in it that he couldn't fill logically. The break in his lifeline at the moment he had left Wilko in 1914 had radically altered its symmetry. He even amused himself by trying to draw it, but he couldn't, as he didn't know how to continue the curve beyond 1914, even more so beyond 1920; did it go upwards or downwards? In the end he made the following graph: he drew a straight line until 1914, then left fifteen squares blank, then continued the line at the same level, and carried it on upwards. Over the fifteen blank squares he drew a closed ellipse – representing another contained and concluded life.

One fine morning, as he was drawing these lines, admittedly only in the sand, he found himself thinking of Fela. Her life too was in the shape of a closed ellipse, except that there was nothing beyond it. And suddenly, as he was drawing, he felt the urge to see Julcia, Jola or Tunia. Abandoning his diagram he at once set off along the familiar path, taking the shortest route; twenty minutes later he was stepping onto the porch at Wilko.

However, not one of the women he longed for was there. As if on purpose, Zosia was lying in wait for him. He found her in the study, sitting in an armchair, reading. She raised her eyes from a thick, elegant volume to look up at him.

'So you've come at last,' said Zosia, seeming pleased, but at once muddied the impression by saying, 'My sisters have talked of nothing else for days except why you're not here. But not one of them has had the energy to walk or drive to Rożki.'

Wiktor sat down beside her, took the book from her hands and inspected it. Zosia gazed at him, smiling. Finally she said: 'I'm afraid you're becoming our family hero again. They talk of nothing but you.'

'Don't worry,' replied Wiktor, with a seemingly bitter smile. 'Nothing will come of it – I'm leaving in a week and it'll all be over.'

'Me too,' said Zosia, apparently thinking only of herself. 'My husband's being transferred to Avignon, and I must help him with the move.' Then, remembering Wiktor, she added, 'How come? Aren't you ever coming back to Wilko?'

'Right now, I think I will,' said Wiktor after a moment's reflection. 'Of course I'll be back, but I'm afraid that once I get back to my normal life I'll forget you all again.'

'How polite,' said Zosia.

'Politeness doesn't come into it – I'm just being sincere, that's all. I'm ashamed to admit it even to myself, but I reckon my work will engulf me to a point where it's so overwhelming that there won't be any room in my head for Wilko.'

'Do you really manage to get by without any female company?'

'Yes!'

This 'yes' was pronounced with such unflinching certainty, with so little hesitation, that Zosia laughed discreetly.

'You're extraordinary,' she said after a while, and stood up. She adjusted her hair in the mirror and then, turning to Wiktor, added, 'I warn you, not everyone here is so sure of that, and I get the impression that if you're not the object of hope, then at any rate you're the object of desire.' She laughed again and sat down. 'You look horrified,' she said. 'You're still afraid of decisions, just like you always were – you're afraid of everything, even of yourself.'

'So you reckon I've always had these virtues? Were you watching me even then?'

'I was a silly, nasty child,' said Zosia. 'I used to enjoy the fact that you couldn't work out what was going on. It was like blind man's buff – you'd be standing in the middle of the room blindfolded, and now and then everything would change around you. I used to laugh at Jola, although I was only twelve. But I saw more than you did.'

71

'You were a woman.'

'Yes, a twelve-year-old woman notices much more than a twenty-year-old man. Maybe that's why I could never take you seriously – I used to laugh at you and didn't like you.'

'You have nothing but nasty things to tell me,' said Wiktor, smiling.

'Because I know you don't care,' said Zosia smiling bewitchingly. 'That's the truth about you – you don't really care about anything.'

Wiktor gazed out of the window. It was one of those days at the turn of summer when it's very warm but the sky is overcast, and a solid curtain of warm white clouds is gathering. The leaves on the trees were drooping, showing a pale underside. The flowers too looked wilted, the dahlias and fuchsias were hanging their heads. Gazing at the impotence of nature, he could sense its inability to fight off autumn; inside himself he could feel the same lack of resistance that determined the change of season. He went out onto the balcony and stared at the garden, feeling like a different person from when he had arrived a quarter of an hour ago. Zosia came with him; he felt grateful to her for provoking his wilted, but decisive mood with her icy tone.

'Do you know, in a few simple words you've changed me.'

'Maybe I just stirred up something that has long since lain dormant within you.'

'No, no, on the contrary. The season has turned inside me,' he said, and descended the steps. He stopped and waited for Zosia to come down after him, but she stayed on the terrace, leaning on the balustrade and staring at him in keen curiosity.

He turned and wandered off into the depths of the garden.

Locked beneath a tent of clouds, the day was suffused with a sweet and sour fragrance, like the scent of lupins. It was very warm and quiet; the air, despite its purity, bore a smell of carrion. The earth was still, and the sheen of the canal stretching away made it look lifeless. The air was so clear that carts loaded with corn, moving along the hill beyond the garden, looked magnified, as if through binoculars; each ear of corn stood out sharply. The gentle whirr of wheels in motion was the only intermittent music to be heard.

He spent the next hour in a daze, wandering among drooping hazel branches, then sitting on a bank of turf in the little wood. There he sat and marked time, staring into space with no sense of reality. The feeling that summer had turned gave him pain, as if he had cut his finger. From his muddled, ill-defined thoughts one single emotion came through clearly: that it was totally impossible for him to achieve anything.

He knew this feeling from his work – at Stokroć he called it a lack of perfection. But now, on this dead, white, glorious summer afternoon it was like a nightmare. He didn't try to fight it, but let it take him in its grip, driving away all sense of reality: never to complete anything, never to do anything properly, never to master anything fully.

Jola found him wandering alone among a dusty litter of pine needles. She roused him from the sphere of unreality and brought him down to earth with the most ordinary remarks. She chattered away like in the old days, telling him what they had had for lunch, how they had forgotten to call Mama down to table, that they had had

73

ice-cream, how Zosia's husband, who had come to fetch her, had worn a diplomatic expression, although he was only a vice-consul. She kept laughing in a rather forced way, tapping her parasol against the tree trunks. She didn't look at Wiktor once – she had neither the time nor the courage for that. Wiktor avoided looking at her too, his gaze still drawn towards the white clouds in between the black trees.

, On the way back to the house they met Tunia, and the three of them set off on a long walk. Jola talked non-stop, with Tunia occasionally adding a detail, while Wiktor just asked questions or nodded. Towards evening the clouds cleared up; they had turned from bright to dark and then moved away. A few blue streaks remained against the off-white western sky. It was growing chilly.

Wiktor stopped listening to Jola, and thought instead of the hour of silence he had spent in the garden, driven into a trance of loneliness by Zosia's ironical gaze. He could feel the surrounding atmosphere growing heavier, but didn't try to find an explanation. He knew now, once and for all, that nothing that is real is attainable; he must stand alone on the white sea shore, waiting for the sea to creep up and carry him off, and nothing would come after him.

'True mastery of anything is totally impossible,' he said aloud, without considering whether this remark fitted into the flow of the conversation. But although the tone of his voice, more so than his words, surprised even Tunia, it wasn't enough to interrupt the stream of Jola's eloquence. Finally Wiktor realised that Jola was just saying whatever came into her head, as if wanting to drown out an inner voice, or as if she didn't want to let Wiktor get a word in edgeways.

After supper he and Jola went riding together. After the warm day, a cool dew had fallen, and the leaves that slapped Wiktor in the face as they rode by were sopping wet. The moon rose late, tearing its way through the clouds. The patches of moonlight shining through were like patches of snow on the mountains, said Jola, but Wiktor said nothing. Then they both fell silent and rode a long way like that at a walk.

Wiktor felt aware of the impenetrable nature of human solitude, and how impossible it was to show Jola what was going on inside him; how everything attainable, all that he could have achieved, had dissolved into nothing but a sort of pensive mist. He had renounced everything, but he could tell that Jola had no intention of renouncing a thing. Here she was, even warmer and more beautiful than ever, serene and proud, riding beside him, her foot touching his stirrup. 'Do you remember how we used to go riding like this in the old days?' was all she said.

No, he didn't remember that. He even suspected that they had never gone riding together at night before. The summer night had never had such a strong odour of wormwood; never before had he said such a final goodbye to his active life, to his youth. The night was very beautiful indeed, and all of a sudden in its pallor and purity it gave Wiktor the same impression as the day that had passed – pure white. As they rode among the trees, shadowy hollows loomed among them, dark blue spaces where the brilliant moonlight did not penetrate. There was total silence, and without thinking Wiktor leaned over to Jola and kissed her.

By the time they got home everyone else was asleep. Wiktor stood hesitating in the hall, but Jola lured him into the drawing room and on into the little boudoir beyond it which served her as a bedroom. Her daytime loquacity was over and she had become taciturn; Wiktor also had no great desire to carry the weight of conversation, so he put out the light and rolled into an embrace with her, dark as the shadows in the forest. He laughed quietly to himself at the thought of such an end to his day of resignation. But Jola demonstrated so much erotic expertise that she proved herself more than a match for his impulsive, primitive actions. He left the small dark room by the window very soon after, not in the least gratified by what he had done, and walked among the shadows of the garden, then all the way back to Rożki, as if running away from something. Yet he could feel the ground beneath each heavy step he took, he could feel the leaves and branches, he could feel the reality of sensual gratification and real fear of the consequences. He resolved that this evening's events would not be repeated.

Next day he got to Wilko early in the morning; in spite of all he wanted to see Jola and Tunia, and most of all he wanted to talk to Kazia, who was so calm, so determined, and so well-attuned to this atmosphere. Here, in this place which both attracted him and repelled him, where he could monitor his contradictory reactions to his own boorish behaviour, where his inner barometer showed ever changing pressures, that woman with the keys, in the pantry, in the kitchen, on the veranda, had the Olympian calm of a figure from Raphael's paintings. But, as every morning, Kazia was constantly on the move and kept deserting him; he sat on the porch as all the housework, both the provident and the unnecessary tasks, was carried out before his eyes with ant-like diligence.

He felt sorry that he could watch all these comings and goings with a total lack of interest, that he had never entered into the life of this house and never would. In a couple of days he would be off, he would sink back into his own concerns, and he wasn't even convinced that the new memories of Wilko would blot out the old ones. Not even the night before had been able to dazzle him as much as the sight of Fela in the meadow after bathing. He thought how much duller one's senses grow with age, and reckoned nothing would ever compare with that night in Julcia's room. Yesterday's banal episode seemed to have spoiled everything he had experienced here long ago; it had passed into ancient history.

It was a chilly day. The trees stood out sharply against a grey sky, and the yard in front of the house was full of commotion and farmyard noises; he watched all the hustle and bustle, which was in direct contrast to his own contemplative mood.

Just then Jola appeared in a white dressing gown, all scented and lacy. She was lovely, carefree and smiling, and at once began to talk about the day before, as if wanting to explain or justify it. But Wiktor brushed her off with a most decisive 'don't waste your breath', a phrase left over from his army days. He could see that this delicate, pretty woman was startled, as if she really were counting on him, and he was sorry to treat her this way. But what could he do? It really was a waste of his time to talk about something he found so unimportant, and he was afraid lest Jola should blow it up to unwelcome proportions.

She took him into the dining room, where she ate a late breakfast, consisting of bread, butter and cucumber, which she peeled artfully with a little silver knife and cut into pale slices. She ate a good deal quite rapidly, just as she talked. Wiktor was rather irritated that she betrayed not the slightest hint of embarrassment, and that she was even making feeble advances to him, though she was perfectly courteous and relaxed. Now and then the sun appeared among the clouds and spiritedly lit up the dining room, Jola's white clothing and the little silver knife she was wielding. Once again she was saying any old thing, telling him about her husband's letters, which always had an official, businesslike tone. The gleam in her eyes and the tone of her voice seemed false. Finally, as if she couldn't stand his silence any longer, she put down her knife and fork and said: 'I know what you're thinking, but it doesn't matter to me now.'

'That's not what you said the other day ...'

'It really doesn't matter. I'm so confused by yesterday's consummation of things that should have remained for ever in the realm of the unconsummated.'

'So you'd call it a consummation? That never entered my head. It was on such a different plane from our youthful flirtation that they're quite beyond comparison.'

'That's true. But I have such a strong desire for your friendship left over from the past. I'm afraid it's impossible now.'

Wiktor smiled and said, 'Really? No, no, Jolka, calm down. Don't you see that any sort of friendship between us is impossible anyway? We belong ... we move in such different spheres – not in the social sense of the word, but in the astronomical sense.'

'You mean, we can never share a common orbit?'

'Maybe if there were some universal catastrophe ...'

'You're terrible.'

Just then Julcia came in, well-refreshed, well-rested, all pink and white, also decked in frills and laces, but not enough to conceal an old-fashioned corset showing through her light, white dress. Julcia began to laugh at Jola, because however often one entered the dining room, one would always find her at table: Jola's gluttony was legendary. But once she had had her fill of laughter, Julcia drew a plate towards her and also polished off some buttered bread and cucumbers; finally she rang for the maid and ordered some cheese.

Wiktor sat listening to their chatter, then got up and walked about the room, watching both ladies, so sweet and pretty, as they ate their fill, quite greedily at that. He watched Julcia's long white teeth sinking into the white cheese, and Jola leaning forward short-sightedly to spread the butter; she kept her eyes fixed on what she was doing at the table, which made it look as if she were shielding her lily-white brow from Wiktor's scrutiny. The scene made him smile. Here were 'his' two women sitting face to face in perfect harmony, neither of them really serious about him or his feelings.

And he was reminded of a cold night in the trenches, when the touch of Julcia's body had suddenly come back to him. Here was this woman in front of him, and another woman whom he hadn't thought of in the trenches, but whom, as he now realised, he had never forgotten. Were she to look up now, her grey eyes would remind him of so many moments from the past; but she did not. There they sat, face to face, eating quickly and heartily, with relish. Unfortunately he would never be able to discover any more from them or about them. They had husbands, Julcia had children, Jola had lovers (he had guessed it at once, and was all the more certain in the light of the lesson she had given him) – there they sat before him, chat-ting in turn about whatever came into their heads. Jola even seemed happy – sometimes she cast a knowing glance at Wiktor, as if tickled pink that she had become his lover.

Wiktor thought of the days following the first night he had spent in Julcia's room; that mixture of shame and embarrassment, and the sexual charges flying in the air between them, had created a memorable atmosphere. To his mind, what Jola had been saying seemed shameless, even more so now as she gave him a furtive look, hiding her eyes from Julcia. Automatically, Wiktor took Julcia's soft, warm hand in his and raised it to his lips. Both ladies were surprised, but the touch of this hand and his com-plete indifference to it gave Wiktor a sort of incidental pleasure, different from all others. With this kiss he was thanking her for those old, unforgettable nights, and he was glad he had done it in sight of Jola, who had no idea what his action really meant. They stared at him with grey eyes wide open, and once again he felt surrounded by youth.

'Don't be surprised, Jolka,' said Wiktor. 'I've always loved Julcia very much.'

With these words he made his exit, leaving them both amazed at his behaviour. Jola had a look of despair in her eyes as he walked away, but Wiktor reckoned she would soon go back to her cucumber. He went to the pantry, but Kazia wasn't there. He found her in the study; bent over the drawer of an ugly old-fashioned commode, she was taking freshly laundered tablecloths and napkins out of a large basket and putting them away. Wiktor watched this calm industry for a while, and finally he said: 'You know, my dear, I think I'd like to go now.'

'Can't you go on foot?' asked Kazia calmly.

'I could, but it's a long way, it'd be an awful waste of time – I want to get back to Warsaw, to Stokroć.'

'But your holiday isn't over for another four days.'

'I could even extend it if I wanted to.'

'Really?' said Kazia, delighted, then after some thought she added, 'But if you think you'd better go now, you'd best hurry along. Why tie yourself down to anything?'

But he didn't leave at once; nor did he prolong his holiday, because he couldn't see the point. However, he did stay on at Rożki to the very end of it. A couple of days before leaving he had a down-to-earth conversation with his aunt, which tired and annoyed him. He found it very hard to explain to her that he had no intention of getting married, that marriage wasn't really in his nature, and especially that he had no intention of getting involved with one of the Wilko girls, that Wilko and its atmosphere was the direct opposite of the way of life he led and intended to go on leading. At that, his aunt asked, 'Do you really intend to lead that sort of life for ever?'

This question was so full of irony and disgust that it infuriated Wiktor. He got worked up and made a number of very unpleasant remarks to his aunt, which he at once regretted. He apologised, but still couldn't calm down, so he went for a very long walk.

He liked this part of the world; it was rolling countryside, with large, spreading cornfields, and old, rutted roads like little gullies lined in lush grass, at this time of year still thickly speckled with wild flowers. He didn't really know why he felt so annoyed, but the juxtaposition of two such different ways of life infuriated him, and so did his aunt's assumption that he might wish to change

81

his own way of life. He had made his choice, and never had a thought of anything else; he had his blind children, Stokroć and managing the farm, which gave him deep inner satisfaction, and if at times it bored him and didn't seem worth the effort, well, he supposed everyone has such moments of despondency – life's hard for everyone, isn't it? 'The Wilko girls don't have it so easy either,' he thought. 'What a useless husband Jola has, and my God, she's ashamed of it too!' He thought of Julcia's calm way of eating her bread and cheese as she sat in the dining room, and how suddenly the rays of sunlight breaking through the clouds had lit her up with a sort of halo, illuminating her still youthful, golden hair. Her low, pleasant voice rang in his ears, and also Jola's, which had almost been unhappy that day when she had spoken to him of friendship, of respect, of the future, while simply thinking Wiktor would say, 'So just leave your old man and come with me to Warsaw'. Or maybe she was just waiting for him to ask if he could come to see her today, and at what time. He had had enough of it all, and he didn't feel like going to Wilko. Or Kazia, too, who had at once been so pleased that he might extend his holiday, but he had quite deliberately not done so.

But was it for Kazia's sake that he had stayed on? No, certainly not. He had stuck to the original time limit out of fear – if he didn't go now he might never leave. He would get sunk into Wilko and stay on with them, engulfed in all that lily-white warmth, that freshness, that healthy, potent life force flowing through those women's fervent bodies.

On the way home he stopped at the cemetery to visit Fela's grave. It was just as neglected as a fortnight ago. The bunch of flowers he had picked then was still there, dried out and leafless. The little stone wall was the same as before. There were the same sparse acacias, stripped of their leaves, the same forlorn misery of ugly and useless things. No one had been here since his last visit; the beautiful girl's grave lay yawning with neglect. Shedding their leaves all summer, the acacias had littered the dry grass with small tawny ovals, and so it remained, so it was, perhaps with the sole purpose of inscribing itself on his heart in mournful lettering.

>He stood up and looked around him. Over the wall low grey clouds were appearing, intermittently illuminated from below; occasionally triangles of azure unfolded like eyes suddenly opening onto sweet existence.

'No, it doesn't matter to me,' said Wiktor.

He hadn't the slightest doubt now. For instance, it had never occurred to him to get up in the night, walk the short stretch of road from Rożki to Wilko, and knock at the window of the little boudoir beyond the drawing room.

'No, it doesn't matter to me,' he repeated, and leaving the cemetery he crossed the road along the canal that led to Wilko and walked straight on towards Rożki. His only thought now was of his work, which he must get back to. Only as a backdrop, like background music, did certain images keep running through his mind: the slaughtered soldier, Fela standing in the meadow amid the golden rays of a setting sun, or the redness of Jola's dress one fine afternoon long ago.

Once he had got back to his room, quite late in the evening, he was standing at the window, staring out at the sky, clear and blue although it was evening, when he remembered that tomorrow he would have to be off, and he was seized by an unspeakable sense of grief. For a while he felt as if the real events had been then, fifteen years ago, but at the time he had been quite unaware of it. He had put so much effort into the last few years of his life, they had been so exhausting, and only now had he realised they were nothing but dust. There was nothing left of them; even the memory of his past happiness was something he had only managed to grasp today. He could plainly see, to use a bourgeois expression, that he had gone to the dogs. What a great sin it is to be incapable of noticing one's own happiness.

Nor was it true that the war years had ruined him by showering him in a hail of dismal, depressing incidents; no, it was he himself who had stirred up those incidents, wanting them to dominate him. He was quite simply afraid of the thought that he could live any differently, just as for the past fifteen years he had been rejecting the idea of going back to Wilko. He had never been in love with anyone, not because he wasn't capable of it, but because he was too much of a coward.

The grief that engulfed him that evening was heavy, and for a long time it wouldn't let him sleep, as he lay on the hard mattress.

He awoke early; the final day of his stay had come. He spent the whole day chatting with his aunt and uncle, dozing, and walking towards the canal, but he never went down to Wilko. However, instead of taking the evening train he decided to put off his departure until the morning. So next day, as nothing would change and there was no helping it, he neatly packed up his odds and ends and stared at himself in the mirror. He was leaving tanned and looking well; so off he went to Wilko, and with deep self-control bade farewell to the ladies. Julcia accused him of not caring enough. Zosia asked if he would show up again another fifteen years from now.

'Never,' he thought, but said nothing, just smiled, certain that no one could possibly read anything into this smile of his. Kazia brought him a large parcel, carefully tied up with string – some supplies from her pantry, 'a new milestone in our friendship', she said, with rather unfriendly irony; somehow she seemed resentful.

Wiktor saw that Jola had fetched her white linen hat and, leaning forward as ever, she descended from the porch. 'I'll come and see you off,' she said, 'just like in 1914.'

'To the same point?' asked Wiktor.

'Do you remember how far we went?'

'On the way here I stopped at the exact spot. The boundary marker is still there, but the copse has grown a lot.'

As they came out onto the road the day seemed autumnal, though it was high summer; the haziness of the sky and the silence in the air were latent signs of autumn. It was as if summer were already over, although still within reach all around them, ripe and pungent with hay and berries.

Almost in silence, merely exchanging comments on the strange atmosphere of the day, they crossed the road and walked down the highway as far as the copse, now better described as a wood, and found themselves at the very same spot where she had bid him farewell in 1914. Wiktor looked at his watch – there was still over an hour until his train; he had left in a hurry, wanting to get away from there as fast as possible.

They sat down by the old boundary marker. Jola leaned back against the sloping ground and chewed on a blade of grass as she gazed into the sky, across which large ripe clouds were moving. Wiktor, by contrast, leaned forward, hunched, and stared at the ground. He couldn't actually see the blades of grass he was staring at, nor the tiny insects toiling away among them. His mind was occupied with the years between now and the last time he had sat at this very same spot with this very same woman.

Those years seemed monotonous, all the same, and realising how many they were was frightening. Fifteen times he could have come back to this very spot, but not once had he ever done so.

'How do you feel on leaving Wilko?' asked Jola, after a long silence, but Wiktor just shrugged reluctantly and turned languidly to face her. He was sorry it wasn't Kazia sitting beside him; he could have told her more or less what he was thinking, but he couldn't begin to tell Jola. If he were to tell her he regretted the past, whatever he were to tell her, she would try to interpret it as a declaration of love. And he was really so very far from that. All he could feel was a yearning for love, which had trickled through his fingers like water – not now, but then, fifteen years ago. Maybe he did need love – but that didn't mean having to embrace Jola now and kiss her passionately. So he said nothing.

Even turning to face her felt excessive, so he let his head droop again towards the grass and the insects crawling among it. Then he raised his hand to his mouth and held it against his lips, as if to stop himself from crying. Pure sorrow came over him, sorrow for everything that was passing him by and drifting away from him – for everything seen only in the distance, like a boat sailing out of sight around the bend of a river.

'Sad thoughts,' sighed Jola once more.

'Oh, it's just that you don't understand me,' said Wiktor, then added nervously and eagerly, 'You see, I've had such a good time here and I realised … I realised …'

He stopped short and looked at her in dread.

'What did you realise?'

But he waved her aside, as if filled with despair, then stood up. 'Well,' he said, 'the train will be off soon, and if I leave it till tomorrow I'll never get away from here.'

'You're joking,' said Jola solemnly.

'Of course I am. What on earth would I do here among you, like an alien from another planet? Goodbye,' he said, and kissed her hand. 'And then … what else did I want to say? Oh yes, don't neglect Fela's grave so badly.'

Then he walked away, without looking around, taking small, indecisive steps. Jola stood up, unclasped her hands and watched him walk away. She strained her feeble eyes, but the contours of the disappearing figure began to fade from her view. So she shook down her white dress and turned towards home – but no, she did look around again.

The further he went, the stronger and more confident Wiktor's step became. With head held high, by the time he entered the station he was swinging his briefcase cheerfully, wondering what Janek had been doing for the past three weeks at Stokroć.

Syracuse, April 1932

The Birch Grove*

I

Something in the way Stanisław alighted from the chaise before the porch immediately irritated Bolesław. He flew, or rather fluttered out of the carriage. What struck him most was the bright blue colour of Stanisław's socks, which shone garishly from under his short, baggy trousers, laying siege to his skinny ankles. But apart from that he looked perfectly well. Bolesław looked up to his brother's light blue eyes. They were smiling, and there was a smile on his lips as well, sending fine lines radiating outwards. They kissed in greeting; Bolesław's first kindly thought was, 'Thank God, he's in good health.'

It was a very long time since they had last seen each other. Staś, as Stanisław was nicknamed, had spent the past two years at a sanatorium, but it was several years since they had last met. Bolesław had long since buried himself away at this forestry lodge, and Staś had never

---

* *Translator's note*: Where the characters' names appear in more than one form (e.g. Malina/Malwina) the translation follows the original Polish text throughout.

been to visit. Quite possibly he wouldn't have recognised him now.

'How are you?' asked Bolesław after a short, silent embrace.

'I'm fine!'

'So you've remembered me at last.'

'What else could I do? The doctors insisted I go to the forest. So where else but here?'

As he spoke, he kept interrupting himself to do things. He leaped up the steps into the chaise and drew out a light trunk, put it down on the veranda, and cast off his elegant mackintosh, gloves and travelling cap, just like the ones Bolesław had seen advertised in illustrated magazines. At once they sat down to breakfast, laid out on the veranda.

'I'm awfully tired,' said Staś. 'Two days and two nights' journey.'

Little Ola emerged from inside the house. She had startled blue eyes and was carrying a rather threadbare doll. Silently, she curtsied to her uncle.

'Goodness, what a big girl she is!' cried Staś. Bolesław said nothing. 'What an awful doll! I saw such beautiful dolls abroad, but I forgot to bring her one. What a thoughtless uncle I am!'

Ola went down the porch steps and walked quietly into the forest. The forest began just across the road, which ran between it and the lodge. It was a nasty day, drizzling endlessly. The woods on this side were devoid of undergrowth, and as he was animatedly describing his journey, Staś could see Ola's pale little dress glinting between the tree trunks. He broke off his story.

'You let her run loose like that?' he addressed his older brother. Bolesław just shrugged. 'As I was saying, as soon as I got down into the valley,' he continued, 'I felt awfully tired. What a place Poland is! I thought the journey would never end – the forest goes on and on – God knows where it all comes from.'

'Yes, but it's not very pretty. Just woods.'

'Never mind – I adore pine forests. The doctors were always going on about it – off to the pine forest with you, that's what you need!'

'Over there behind the house there's a very fine birch grove,' said Bolesław, pointing, but without looking that way.

The day was overcast, and from the forest echoed a faint rustle of pine needles brushing against each other.

'You know, two hours of listening to the rustle of pine needles and sand beneath the wheels is awfully dull!' Staś went on, without losing his good humour. 'I find the lack of variety in this region rather boring. So how are you?'

Bolesław shrugged again, and made an indeterminate sound.

'You ought to get someone to take care of the little one, you know.'

'I've been thinking about it …'

'Just thinking about it isn't enough.'

Staś pushed back his chair with a wide sweep and took his trunk by the handle.

'Where am I to stay?'

'Left off the hall.'

Bolesław shifted his chair slightly in order to look down the road. The sky between the porch roof and the forest had darkened abruptly and the rain had grown denser. There was an open window right next to the veranda, and he could hear Staś putting his room in order. He plucked at his beard as he listened to his brother rummaging about, unpacking his trunk and washing after his journey, humming all the while. He never stopped humming fashionable European tunes, importing a breath of foreign air. Bolesław frowned and chewed his beard, stuffing it into his mouth.

Staś opened the door from his own room into the next. Bolesław could hear him shuffling about in soft slippers, opening the door into the little hall; he must be peeping into the kitchen. Then he came back down the other side of the house, through Bolesław and Ola's room. Four rooms – that was the entire extent of it.

'I've been right around the house,' said Staś, standing in the doorway. 'I forgot you don't have a piano. I thought you did, and I was looking for it everywhere. It'll be awfully dull here without a piano. Can't we hire one in Sławsk?'

Bolesław didn't answer.

'We'll all be bored to death here.'

Even the word 'death' was not enough to rouse Bolesław from his trance. All he kept thinking was, 'Oh Christ Almighty, what the hell is he doing here?'

Meanwhile Staś had poured himself a glass of hot water from the kettle that stood on the table. He went off to shave, appearing soon after through the window, his face covered in lather. 'Don't you go riding?' he said.

'No, but I've got a saddle.'

'What about a horse?'

'The one on the right,' mumbled Bolesław.

'Does he go?'

'Hm, Janek says he's very good.'

'That's wonderful. I'll do some riding, then,' said Staś and withdrew.

He soon fired another question at Bolesław, asking, 'So how far is it to Sławsk?'

'You came from there, didn't you?'

'But how far is it in miles?'

'About two, two and a half maybe.'

'Do you think it would be possible to bring a piano here?'

'You've seen what the road's like.'

'Of course, but once it dries out?'

'It'll be sandy.'

'But if need be would you let me have the horses?'

'Can't you leave me in peace about your wretched piano?!' said Bolesław impatiently. He stood up and went into the kitchen. Staś went on humming as he shaved. He watched as Ola came slinking up the road, soaked through, but not walking any faster. She stepped carefully across the ruts, shielding her doll with a handkerchief. The sight of her made Stanisław's heart bleed. 'It's going to be tough here,' he said to himself.

Katarzyna, the old servant, was clearing away the breakfast on the veranda. Ola sat down at a little table in a nook and started chatting to her doll.

Staś was inspecting all his knick-knacks, which reminded him of his time abroad. He arranged them on a decrepit, ugly little dressing table standing in the corner. He gazed at the photographs; there he was with Miss Simons and Duparc on the snow at Davos. Smiling faces. The smell of the objects there had been different. Now he was enveloped in the odour of plain pine furniture and freshly washed floors. When he went out onto the porch the sky had brightened.

'Ola, come for a walk. Show me where the birch grove is.'

Ola stood up without a word and took him by the hand. He could feel her cold, skinny little paw in his.

Slowly they made their way down the steps. Heavy drops dripped from the roof.

'When it rains early in the morning the weather's always nice later,' said the little girl solemnly.

They walked around the house. And indeed, on the other side there was a lovely birch grove. The trunks stretched skywards like snow-clad pillars, brittle, as if made of sugar or snow. Delicate leaves were trickling down from on high, but all one could see was the vista of white pillars.

'It's pretty here,' said Staś without smiling.

Ola didn't answer. They walked over damp grass, then a well-trodden path. The white tree trunks grew denser, forming a foggy vista; the humidity among the trees had started to vaporise. It was going to be a sunny afternoon.

'It's just a May shower,' said Ola, ever so slowly unwinding the thread of her thoughts.

They were standing in front of a small mound of yellow sand, going black already, but not overgrown with grass. The mound was enclosed by a white birchwood fence, a very plain structure; sticks had simply been embedded in the ground crosswise. A huge birchwood cross stood over the mound, as white as the trunks of the surrounding trees. Staś was amazed. 'What's this?'

'It's a grave,' replied Ola.

'Whose grave?'

'What do you mean, whose? It's Mummy's.'

'So your mummy's buried here? Why isn't she at the cemetery?'

'It's such a long way,' replied Ola, 'and it's nice and close here.'

'It's nice and close all right, but why wasn't she buried at the cemetery?'

'The flooding after the thaw was terrible. The priest came on horseback.'

'So it was in the spring?'

'On horseback. He heard Mummy's confession and then he just stayed. He was here for two days, he couldn't move – the water had gone everywhere.'

'Did he consecrate this ground?'

'Yes, he did. He said it couldn't be in unconsecrated ground. He kept insisting on taking her to Sławsk.'

'And what did your daddy say?'

'Daddy didn't want to. He said it could be in the birch grove. It's a pretty place.'

'It is pretty!'

'It's very pretty, but I don't like coming here.'

'Don't you?'

'No, I don't. I only come with Daddy. Daddy prays.'

'Your daddy …'

'Daddy comes here every day first thing in the morning or towards evening, and on Sundays he and I come and pray here. He reads from the book Mummy used to have.'

'Do you remember your mummy?'

'Of course I do, it's only a year ago.'

'Right. It's a whole year now. And I only found out in the autumn. Your daddy rarely writes.'

'Daddy doesn't like letters.'

'I wrote more often than he did.'

'But Daddy doesn't like your letters, Uncle.'

'Did he ever read them to you?'

'No … he did read me one, about how you went sledging. I've got a sledge too, but there aren't any mountains here. Are there big mountains in Switzerland?'

'Huge ones. I'll show you my photographs.'

'Then let's go home now. Show me the photographs, Uncle.'

Back at home he began to show them to her, but she soon got bored. Besides, she didn't really understand what 'hotel', 'sanatorium', or 'Switzerland' meant. As he sat on the oilcloth sofa that stood in his room, the photographs slipped off his knees. He gazed aimlessly out of the window, where rays of sunlight had started to shine through from behind the pine trees. The carpet of pine needles beneath the trees was wreathed in clouds of haze; the spaces between the trunks were filled with mist and vapours. But he wasn't watching the doings of nature; he wasn't even thinking about them. He sat still, wanting to be free of all thought. After a while he repeated, 'Oh, it's going to be tough here.'

He had not yet fully divined the atmosphere, but he already knew it wouldn't be good. He was appalled by his brother's state of mind and tried in vain to imagine what it was like; but as he had never experienced any real loss, it wasn't easy. He had been present at his mother's death, but the actual fact of it had seemed unreal. Afterwards he had been unable to understand it or feel it; it was just as if his mother were always in another room, and finally he got used to the idea that she would never come into the one he was in. But the sandy mound in the birch grove was impossible to ignore. He kept on seeing it, and the network of white tree trunks fading into the distance, creating a white, atomised shade, as if painted with the tip of the brush.

Meanwhile Bolesław was sitting across the hall, on his bed, staring at more or less the same landscape of pine trees, at the smoke among the tree trunks and at the first glimmers reviving on the wet leaves of the brushwood, which those same rays of sunlight were just beginning to reveal amid the desiccated tracery of the forest. Bolesław's thoughts were even less focused than his brother's. Nothing had been able to call him out of the fog that had enveloped him ever since his wife's death; he saw everything through a veil, which greatly impeded his vision, but nothing worse. He did visit the grave regularly, that was true, and on Sundays he said prayers there with Ola, which was all the more upsetting as he wasn't a believer. The mound, the body – to his mind none of it existed, but he really could feel the death of that ugly but dear woman who had been his wife for several years. He could feel her absence. He couldn't forget that she was dead. He remembered her dying, and how she had died. And that was the only thing that was real, everything else was not. That was why his brother's socks were such an awful thing; their colour would haunt Bolesław in his rare dreams. The world that the young man had left behind in order to stir up the mist among the pine trees was truly appalling. Stanisław's arrival was like the advent of a Martian. Yet at the same time it evoked an undeniable sense of reality, of which Bolesław had been deprived for the whole year past.

He thought, for the first time, of the fact that it was a year already, that Basia must have undergone a terrifying change in the coffin, that he would never love anyone ever again, that Ola really was terribly neglected – for he gave no thought at all to the need to engage some sort of teacher for her – in short, that somehow life must go on. Where to and what for he couldn't quite think for the moment, just that it must go on. This line of thought was already a very great change for him, and he owed it to Staś's intolerable presence.

Suddenly on the stairs, then the veranda, the firm tread of strong bare feet resounded. A girl, hot from running, abruptly cast her shadow across Staś's view of the pine trees. 'Where's the master?'

He didn't have time to reply before Bolesław's voice responded from the window on the other side of the veranda doors.

Apparently, the girl's brother Janek, the watchman, who lived in the courtyard, had knocked out a pane of glass in the front door with his hand; he had a deep cut and the wound would need bandaging after a good coating of iodine. Both brothers went to see to the matter, which gave Stanisław the opportunity to get to know the courtyard and its inhabitants.

There weren't many of them – just Janek, his sister and mother, and two teenage youths, Edek and Olek, who tended the cows and horses; that was it. The courtyard was small and clean, but cheerless. The horses and cows were stabled in a red brick building at ground level, and upstairs there was a small apartment, where the bandaging operation took place, with two rooms for the rifleman and his family, and another little room for the boys. The windows were very small and didn't admit much light. The pine trees began right against the walls of the building, half of which was occupied by the stable. Separately, there was also a shed, a coach house, a henhouse and a small pigsty.

Stanisław went home feeling even sadder and more disheartened. He still wasn't over his tiredness from the long journey; now and then he broke into a sweat. The air after the rain was sultry and the good weather, which had finally settled in the afternoon, did not promise to last for long. He lay down on the oilcloth sofa and waited patiently for lunch. Bolesław kept pacing up and down his room, although there was very little space between his bed and Ola's. She and her doll were sitting in there too, in a corner behind the bed. The moment his mind went blank, Bolesław could hear her teaching the doll to say its prayers.

II

The next few days were exactly alike, with the single difference perhaps that Bolesław spent less time at home. Not only did he have to drive about the forest, supervising one job or another at a clearing or at the sawmill, which were quite far apart, but he also had to drive to town. He hadn't been there for a year; the road was a bit better now, and he had remembered a lot of business left unsettled for ages, so off he went. He preferred to avoid being on his own with his brother, whose clothes, way of life and manner of talking were enough to tear open his almost healed wound. He couldn't bear the pensive joy at life that Staś was so full of; it was there in his every word and gesture, in his smile. Bolesław wouldn't admit it, but in his own brother he saw so much allure, so much winsome charm that he simply couldn't face, not for anything in the world. He couldn't understand how exactly, but all that charm and allure cut him off from Basia. So he preferred to stay at the sawmill and listen to the Jews arguing. He would be late for lunch, but Staś would be waiting patiently; he had got into the habit of going for very long walks with Ola, which tired him greatly. Bolesław often found him lying on the oilcloth sofa, and in the evenings he went to bed early and didn't want to go out after sunset.

'It's a habit left over from the sanatorium,' he told his brother.

He was very sweet, but still very tactless – he laughed, he joked, he sang and whistled. Ola had cheered up a bit in her uncle's presence and had learned two German songs which he sang to her. She had hardly ever sung before, but now she would hum to her doll in the evenings, after putting it to bed in a birch-bark cradle. This annoyed and upset Bolesław all the more.

It rained again, and cleared up again, and then the moonlit nights set in. Ola went to bed very late; one evening she sat in her uncle's room on the sofa and watched as the red glow of the rising satellite broke through among the pine trees. She was speechless with wonder, for Staś was telling her how the moon rises in the clear mountain air, and how he had seen a total eclipse emerging from behind a red ridge opposite the sanatorium. It was going to be frosty then, and the air, light and pure, gave a hiss as you breathed it in. The little girl was terrified. But the moon changed from red to white, and brilliant patches of light appeared among the pine trees.

Then they went for a walk among the birches. As they walked to and fro, it all seemed unreal to Staś. It took great strength of will to keep on laughing and joking as he held his little niece by the hand. As they were getting closer to the grave, Ola stopped and wouldn't go further, but he told her gently that she shouldn't be afraid, that there was nothing to be scared of. If and when the time came, he too would wish to lie down in the sand among the marbled tree trunks. They went closer to the fence, and then they saw Bolesław. He was just standing there, but his drooping head and broken figure spoke such volumes that Staś drew back.

'Daddy's there,' said Ola.

⟩ They went home in silence. Ola went to bed, and the old cook, Katarzyna, tucked her in, while Stanisław fell to gazing at the pine trees, shining blue in the moonlight.

Suddenly Bolesław burst into his room. He had seen them walking away from him and from the grave, and couldn't resist making some cutting remarks, but Stanisław couldn't understand what was up. Then they went into the dining room and had a cup of tea in silence; finally, Bolesław started telling him the whole story from the very beginning. It was clearly a great relief for him to talk; not only was he casting off a great burden, but at the same time he was breaking the ice between himself and his brother. So, from the very beginning, he told him what Basia had been like, quiet, good and ordinary, but extremely dear; how she had generally been in poor health ever since Ola's birth; what a very snowy winter they had had, and then the awful floodwater, and how the priest had had to come on horseback. It was everything that Ola had summed up in their first conversation, but in far more detail, with references back to themes touched on earlier, with refrains; he spoke very roughly and inarticulately, but Staś listened attentively without once taking his eyes off him. Even if he found his brother's narrative lacking in refinement, through strength of suffering he could feel the full might and tenacity of his whole being, the full strength of his brother's character coming through in his simple words. He realised that Bolesław was a strong person after all, able to suffer terribly and to love deeply. As he listened to this speech, which so perfectly illustrated Bolesław's character, he started comparing himself to his older brother and smiled with compassion. There was nothing deep about him, it was all on the outside, and that was the end of it. And nothing would come of it.

Bolesław wasn't pleased at his own outpouring, and went straight off to bed, but couldn't sleep for ages. To his mind, Staś had taken it all very nonchalantly; he hadn't been at all perturbed – he hadn't shown due concern. He thought this confession of his, by showing Staś what was going on inside him, would bring them closer together. But the next day Staś was even more alien, even more cheerful and unapproachable. Letters had started flooding in for him (the post came twice a week) with foreign stamps, which he carefully cut out and presented to Ola. The days had a fine start now, and they would go for walks. From the veranda or the forest Bolesław would watch Staś's tall, thin figure from afar. Dressed in grey, he almost entirely blended in with the grey glow emanating from the pine forest; he looked almost blue, while Ola's flaxen hair shone like a patch of sunlight trailing after him.

Finally, Stanisław couldn't stand it any longer and decided to have a piano brought from Sławsk.

III

It was a real voyage of the Argonauts. First Staś went to town accompanied by the rifleman who had cut his hand. The journey was long and monotonous in the extreme. It was impossible to sustain one's admiration of the forest and the trees, and for the past few days Staś had been feeling worse: he seemed to have quite a temperature, although since leaving the sanatorium he had promised himself not so much as to look at a thermometer. The sky was grey-blue, like washed-out muslin; pines and birches alternated along the way in a soporific rhythm. Moreover, his attempts at conversation with the rifleman didn't take off, although he was a pleasant enough fellow. Staś wanted to ask him about his sister, but it seemed a bit too forward and intimate. He couldn't think why, but on the way, maybe because of the proximity of her brother, she kept on coming into his mind, common and impetuous, her feet pattering on the veranda floorboards the first time he had seen her. Only now did he remember that in her dark face she had the same limpid grey eyes as her brother. She had watched him closely as he was dressing the rifleman's hand, with the same bandage, apparently, that was now a grey rag, still wound around the palm of his neighbour on the cart. Loose yellow sand shot from the wheels with a faint hum; it was fairly hot and sweat was pouring down Stanisław's neck and body. This gave him a stronger sensation of his own body – the feeling grew more and more ticklish, which was enjoyable but irritating all at once; he gazed aimlessly ahead, as if hearing the humming of the sand inside himself.

The rifleman was simply called Janek, and his sister was Malina. This was the only question which he made up his mind to ask throughout the entire journey. But he was prepared for a lengthy drive, so he didn't notice when the ploughed land began; then on completely flat ground the first rough-cast houses of the town came into sight. They stopped in the market-place; they would have to search about for a piano in working order. Staś started bargaining with the nearest Jew, who consulted another, and soon there were at least a dozen of them crowding around the wagon. They wagged their tongues and waved their arms about, but there was little progress, as first they had to define the problem and weigh up the chances of locating the desired object. Staś listened calmly to all this twittering.

، Finally, an obscure alley was identified where there was an apartment with a grand piano for the taking. It was the home of a redundant railway or bank clerk who wanted to rent out the instrument. His wife, still young, lay sick in the same room as it, and as he tried the keys, Staś began to chat with her. The piano was her property – by no means did she wish to sell it, but she would gladly rent it out for a couple of months; they needed the money, they were terribly poor and their child had just died. In a couple of months she would be well again, and she would need the piano back; in the autumn she would start giving music lessons. Staś stared at her closely, but she averted her gaze. From his days in the sanatorium he had grown all too accustomed to the sight of sick people for this woman's face to make any great impression on him, but he didn't doubt for a moment that by autumn she wouldn't be needing the piano. No, she wouldn't, and neither would he, he thought.

The hardest bit was getting it home. The hired wagon dragged along, getting stuck in the sand time and again. Three horses, harnessed to a single shaft, moved crookedly, and the wheels kept grinding into the sand and slipping out of the ruts. The piano was short and not very heavy. Staś had promised the sick woman that he would look after it like his own flesh and blood, so he didn't want to go ahead of the wagon but ordered Janek to follow it at snail's pace. Sitting up in bed, the woman had wept softly as the piano was carried out, which had irritated Staś.

'The old girl will soon have something to moan about,' he had said to himself as he stood in the narrow street supervising the loading. Now, riding behind the piano, as if following a coffin, he could still see the thin woman's tears, large and lucid, streaming down her cheeks.

Evening was setting in fast, but he hardly noticed. It was a May evening, and among the trees a violet haze was already showing; the sky, too, was half lilac, casting blue shadows among the furrows in the sand. The humming of the wheels was almost a sizzle now; the Jew on the coach box above the piano was braying at the horses. Even Staś had lost his good humour.

Only late in the evening did they reach the forestry lodge. With the help of Janek, the Jew from Sławsk, Edek and Olek, and finally Malina, Staś got the piano unloaded and set up in his room. The Jew led the horses off to the courtyard, and total silence fell. Staś sat down at the piano and, placing his hands on the lid, which shone in the gloom, he gazed out of the open window at the night, at the pine trees and the birches – just there began the birch grove – and his heart ached. He never gave it a thought, but life had become very tough indeed now.

He began to play very softly, to avoid waking little Ola. He began to play irrevocably *passé* tunes, which made no sense here at all, such as the tangos and slow foxtrots he used to dance to at the sanatorium, which against the backdrop of this severe landscape were as incongruous as last year's fashions. Especially the Hawaiian tune he had danced to with Miss Simons. It was very pretty, just like his dancing partner, but like her, it made no sense here. Throughout the unloading of the piano Bolesław had not once showed his face. Evidently he had shut himself in his room and wouldn't even come and look at the offensive instrument. The night was very warm, and Staś was no longer thinking about his brother.

As he was playing the banal tunes he could sense the pain of this black night, and its terror. For the time being he wanted to remain in ignorance of Bolesław's state of mind.

After a while, Bolesław came in with great commotion, and stormed up and down the room; finally he sat down on the bed, tugging at his beard. Only after a time did he say, 'You know, I find that piano of yours and all your playing very hurtful. You just don't seem to appreciate that you're in a house in mourning.'

'A whole year has gone by,' said Staś, without interrupting his playing. His words sounded florid and theatrical, like the opening of a ballad.

Bolesław shuddered. 'I find that music intensely irritating,' he said.

'So do I,' said Staś and stopped playing. 'It conjures up a world I'll never go back to, and which I never really got to know. I used to gaze at it all from my window. I saw some things through the windowpane that would have been beautiful, if only I could have touched them. But I never did, and I never will. It's like glass, like something made of thin ice … Listen, Bolek,' he said, in a serious tone, 'I can tell there's something you haven't realised. You don't know why I've come here.'

'What do you mean?'

'I know my cheerfulness and my music annoy you, but please let me go on just a little longer. You see, I won't be here for very long … In my illness, before the final stage there's usually an improvement. It lasts for a few weeks. The doctors take advantage of it to send the patient off, anywhere at all, back home, or to the country, somewhere private, so that he doesn't die at the sanatorium. My remission is already coming to an end. I'm very sorry, my

105

dear fellow, but I really can't help it. I wish I could ...' –
at this point he smiled – 'but I can't ... So please don't
give me too much of a fight. I came here to die.'

Bolesław stood still in the darkness, but Staś wasn't
looking at him; he was still captivated by the dark night
beyond the open window, and was thinking of Miss Simons, regretting that he hadn't fallen in love with her,
and humming the Hawaiian tune.

'Why don't you have any nightingales?' he asked after
a while.

'There were some ... but they seem to have stopped
singing now.'

Bolesław stood up and paced about the room, but his
step was calmer and quieter now, as if he were trying to
tread carefully. A couple of times he came towards Staś
and stared into his face, pallid in the darkness, his expression fixed, as if on another planet. But Staś took no notice
of him; an inner lament was reverberating in his sickly
lungs. Only later did he say, 'You see, that's what happens
when it passes from the lungs into the intestine ...'

Bolesław left the room without a word and vanished
onto the veranda.

IV

The start of summer was particularly beautiful. The days,
not excessively hot, ended in sultry evenings and the
nights were silent, peaceful and tender. Bolesław was still
getting very little sleep. His brother's confession had
failed to build a bridge of conciliation between them. On
the contrary, they felt even more ill at ease whenever they
sat down to meals together. Bolesław would glance nerv-

ously at Staś, but could perceive no symptoms of advancing illness in his brother's face. He had even started to wonder if what Staś had told him had sprung from his morbid imagination. Staś was still playing the piano a lot and was always writing letters; in the afternoons Bolesław usually caught a glimpse of him and Ola wandering among the white trees in the birch grove. In the evenings, when Staś came home, restless and despondent, Bolesław in his turn would roam about between his wife's burial mound, the blackened buildings of the forestry lodge and the courtyard.

Sometimes he would pass by the servants' quarters, whence he could always hear laughter and merry voices. Although the nearest village was a very long way off, Malina was always being visited by one of her male acquaintances. Sometimes, especially on Saturdays and Sundays, there were several of them, and in fleeing from Staś's piano, Bolesław would fall into the orbit of an accordion, which one of these admirers would be playing. After a time Bolesław started to linger in the vicinity, to listen to the laughter and music. Much as he was annoyed by the Hawaiian songs which Staś kept playing so quietly, the loud droning of the accordion began to give him pleasure. The primitive nature of its tunes touched his soul. He couldn't write this music off as a source of hopeless grief. On the contrary, he thought, how good it would be if Basia were still alive, and they were walking about the forest and the courtyard together, holding hands. Basia would certainly have enjoyed such a fine summer, as well as the fact that lads from distant villages were coming to see Malina. Basia always had a soft spot for anyone in love, and always enjoyed romantic stories. Whenever someone told her about a passionate Polish village trag-

edy she enjoyed it very much, even though there was
plenty of talk around there of murder, manslaughter and
mutilation. For her, love was all. That was what was going through Bolesław's mind. One day he decided to see
which lads came calling at the lodge. He went up to the
doorway, where all the inhabitants of the rooms above the
stable were sitting around. As he approached the conversation fell silent, and the laughter died away. The assembled company greeted him sincerely, but formally. He
noticed that the only outsider was Michał from the
neighbouring settlement. He was a solid, resourceful fellow, and Bolesław was very fond of him.

He didn't know if Michał was courting Malina. But he
didn't even ask; Michał might simply have been there by
chance. He might have dropped in on his way to town to
find out what was new in this backwater.

For a while they chatted about the weather, and their
forecasts for the hay; Bolesław asked Michał what was
new at his settlement, but the conversation didn't
develop. Bolesław realised that he made them feel uncomfortable, but he didn't have the strength to tear
himself away from them. He wanted contact with people,
and the fact that they were simple people was all the
more pleasing.

Finally he had to leave. Maybe something was starting
to age or change inside him, he thought to himself, because he felt so fiercely conscious of a need for company
and conversation. He passed the birch grove and walked
towards his favourite spot, where he could imagine that
the forest had ended. In fact there was a ditch there, beyond which stretched tiny plots of land; past these, in a
clump of cherry trees, stood old Maryjka's tumbledown
cottage, hidden from view, chimney and all, behind the

trees. Further on there were more fields, sown with oats, and only after that did the forest begin again. These fields belonged to the forestry lodge and year after year, unfortunately, they were sown with oats, which grew more and more feebly, providing rather poor sustenance for Bolesław's horses.

He had never come here with Basia. Maybe that was why he liked this spot, and as he roamed about each evening (in spite of being tired from working all day) he often came and stood here at the edge of the forest. He gazed into the distance, imagining that the fields went on for ever, that nothing would ever interrupt them, and that there wasn't really a birch grove on the other side of them. But then he came back to reality with the thought that it was just a clearing, with Maryjka's cottage as a little island in the middle.

Other evenings were warm as well. He couldn't stay stuck indoors, where Staś was so often playing on the old, out-of-tune piano. It wasn't good for the instrument to sit in a house surrounded by dense forest. It was getting hoarser and hoarser, and some of the keys had stopped responding. The waltzes and tangos sounded awful on it, but Staś would never stop playing. Sometimes he did nothing else all day, only rising from the piano for meals or to go to bed. He lay down from time to time now; he especially liked to spend the afternoon lying wrapped in a beautiful chequered shawl, a souvenir of Davos.

Bolesław would retreat into the depths of the black pines, but the hoarse voice of the piano pursued him a long way until, turning a vast circle within the forest, he came out beyond the borders of his district. He sat down beneath a pine tree in silence. His thoughts were empty; the wind was faint and only at the very tops a restless whisper ran through the trees. The black branches of the pines gave a hollow rumble, heralding a change in the weather for tomorrow. He sat there for quite a while. As the wind dropped, he heard the thud of footsteps tramping across the carpet of pine needles; someone was walking about nearby, pacing back and forth among the pines. He turned to face that way and heard a muffled voice, but he couldn't make out who was talking. He found it faintly annoying; even here there's no peace, he muttered, and spat.

He stood up and went home. Staś wasn't playing the piano; he wasn't in the dining room or in his bedroom.

Bolesław carried a lamp from his room into the dining room and slowly drank some stewed tea. Katarzyna was already asleep in the kitchen, and there wasn't a sound from the courtyard. Evidently, Michał and his accordion hadn't come by today; maybe it was him out walking in the woods.

Never before had Bolesław thought so clearly how little his life was worth. Never before had it occurred to him that it really wouldn't matter at all if he were to die. And of course it wasn't the fact that the world wouldn't feel a thing, but that even for Bolesław himself his passage from meaningless existence into meaningless non-existence would have no significance at all – it was just an ordinary, but minor step.

He thought of the rituals surrounding his eventual death, and of the funeral, how the old women would lay him out. Katarzyna, of course, and Maryjka, just as for Basia. And would Malina come? Would she too wash his body, as she had his wife's? Maybe not, she was a young girl, after all. How old could she be?

For the first time he started wondering about Malina's presence at the lodge, what she did here, and what she looked like. He couldn't even imagine her properly. When he closed his eyes and tried to conjure up her image in his mind, her features escaped him. All he could see was the oval shape of her head and her plaits, not covered with a headscarf. He couldn't even remember if she was pretty or ugly. 'I must go there tomorrow morning,' he said to himself.

Stanisław didn't come home for ages. Bolesław was surprised, and walked about the house, looking into Staś's room, but no one was there. The grand piano stood with its lid raised, like a bird's wing. Bolesław went up to the keyboard and with one finger tapped out the tune of a song he used to sing as a youth in the army. At the time they were posted in a small town in the south of Russia, and every day he would slip away from the barracks on the sly to see a lovely girl who came out to meet him; she lived nearby. They used to go up to the loft and sleep together in the hay.

· He was a bit startled by this tune, which didn't sound very loud beneath his clumsy finger, and he was surprised at his own state of mind. I'm afraid it has happened, he thought, Staś's arrival has completely changed me. Only now could he fully understand Staś's confession of a few days ago. It meant there would be another death in his house, another corpse lying on the bed, another grave in the birch grove or in town; that Staś, always such a stranger to him, with his 'European' smile, would be leaving. And once again the old women would come to wash his corpse, just as they had washed Basia's. Only Malina could not. After all, that's no job for a young girl – it's always done by old women. Nor would she even want to – it was out of the question. Who on earth would come running to wash the wretched body of a consumptive? He

111

was going to die. Maybe it was even for the best; he couldn't imagine what else could become of Staś. A consumptive – that was the only career for him.

Then Staś came back with such a smile on his face, with such a blush in his cheeks, so like a happy person, that the gloomy thoughts took wing from Bolesław's mind.

V

The next day there was an unpleasant row between Bolesław and Staś, for absolutely no reason. At breakfast they began arguing about nothing; Staś didn't like the taste of the butter, so Bolesław called him a 'dandy' and reproached him for coming, and even for the cost of it all. Amazed at his brother's cruelty, Staś left the room as soon as possible. It was early morning and cloudy. The sky was white, the pine trees black. Staś took a roundabout route, tearing up straggly, sorry-looking daisies along the way. He came upon the courtyard from the side overgrown with scrub and nettles, which always grow around rubbish heaps. Just beyond the brick stable block, which looked dark as chocolate, stood a washtub on a small table; Malina was there, doing the laundry. She had her profile turned towards Staś, so he took a good look at her. The line of her brow and nose was very beautiful; she had lovely eyelids which hooded her eyes like flower petals, and fine, classic brows. But the lower half of her face was coarse – her mouth was too big and her teeth too white; in her smile, infrequent in any case, there was something feral, though it didn't put Staś off her. As he was wandering among the trees, he had unconsciously started thinking about her, and felt glad of a way to forget the nasty row with Bolesław. He must think that money has been wasted because I'm going to die anyway, he had said to himself, but only for a moment had this thought concealed other, happier thoughts, like a dark pine tree hiding the bright backdrop of the sky: thoughts of Malina's existence.

Yesterday evening, while out walking in the forest with her, he had discovered that on her birth certificate she was really called Malwina, but her parents had preferred the sound of Malina. Staś had assured her that it was much nicer, and that she really did look like a Malina, not a Malwina. She had laughed a good deal at that.

He watched her every movement as she did the washing and saw her arm muscles, arms which were very white; her breasts were crammed into a small, tight-fitting, faded violet jacket, done up with little buttons. Her hands worked briskly and nimbly, with great competence. She was probably washing her own and Janek's shirts. Or maybe Michał's?

Staś did not approach her, or inquire about her work or health, or the weather; after standing there for a couple of minutes he silently turned and walked away towards the birch grove, so splendid at this time of day. The birches, slanting this way and that, in places formed the nave of a church, and today the bleached pillars had an intense atmosphere. That was usual on these warm, sunless days, presaging rain, but still hot, hanging over the earth as if drawn close to the ground by a low, white sky. His mind was a blank; he was conscious only of being still alive. He wasn't even thinking that soon all this would cease to exist for him. He attached no weight at all to his surroundings. What mattered for him was 'the world', 'Europe' – as he called the gleaming corridors of sanatoria

113

and the cupboards under the stairs where sick people's leather trunks were kept during their temporary storage. He had liked the air there, steeped in the smell of ether and the tunes of Hawaiian songs. He gazed at the sloping white birches with a touch of scorn; they weren't like the *melèzes* that filled the high Alpine valleys. He didn't even know that in his own language they were called larches.

Not for a moment did it occur to Bolesław that Staś was so good-humoured because he had already been through the worst. He had bid farewell to that world, as if it were the real world. Slender Miss Simons and the silky muslin of her dress, the sheer tract of the lake, the clouds over the glaciers, the records from Paris, the trunks from London ... that was real life. But here there were birch trees and burial mounds, miserable flowers and an abandoned child – this wasn't proper existence. He had arrived here already broken by his farewell to the world; his final link with life was the piano hired in town from his 'sister in sickness'. That was exactly what Bolesław couldn't sense or comprehend at all. He had hurt his brother with his brutal words – when his brother, strictly speaking, was no longer alive.

Through the trees he saw someone coming towards him. It was Janek, Malina's brother. He felt a great liking for him, he even looked like Malina. Bolesław had once told him that Janek had been suspected of murdering someone in the woods; rumour had it he had shot an old woman who was picking berries or mushrooms. Of course, no one knew for sure, but such things are not unheard of. Janek looked nothing like a criminal – he had a round, rosy face and dark, shaggy hair.

He came up to Staś and greeted him, then sat on the ground opposite, casting his rifle aside. He smiled at

Stanisław, leaned back and asked, 'So it was you, sir, out walking with Malina yesterday?'

'Yes, it was,' said Staś.

'Because Michał was looking for her all evening – he was so angry. Because Michał's courting her now.'

'Who are you courting, Janek?'

'Michał's very angry. Watch out he doesn't do something to you, sir.'

Stanisław laughed. What on earth could he do to him? Besides, Michał could relax – he wouldn't go out with Malina any more.

'Don't you like her, sir?' said Janek.

'Don't worry. Quite the opposite. I like her too much, and I wouldn't want to get in Michał's way.'

'You can go out with her, sir,' said Janek confidentially, 'as long as Michał doesn't know. Malina likes you, sir, but she's afraid of Michał.'

'So why does she care what he thinks?' said Staś indignantly.

'What do you mean? Michał's going to marry her.'

Then Janek left, as he had to walk his beat. Staś was left alone in the glade and started gazing at the birches again, but something in the landscape had changed. It was no longer so neutral; it had grown sadder, and at the same time happier. Staś smiled at his own delusions. But he was glad – the feeling suddenly swept over him – he was glad that he still had a few days left to live. These days had now grown in his mind to infinite proportions; the hours that were left to him until evening had taken on immense length, and every moment felt like a priceless object, a special gift.

That day for the first time in ages he had taken his temperature. It was 37.9, not so very high yet. His

115

morning weakness passed off towards evening, when a desire for life uplifted him. He asked Bolesław for horses, as he fancied going for a drive. He fetched Ola, and off they went, with Janek driving. As before, sand came pouring from the wheel spokes, but this time the melody didn't sound so sad. Towards evening the sky showed its face for a while, pale and wan, high above their heads and above the tops of the pine trees. The drive was great fun, and stayed in Ola's mind for a long while after, in memory of a particular era in her life. It was the first of the outings which Uncle Staś arranged, and this first had been without Malina. They went to the lake; flat and black, with low shores all round, it was more like a great big puddle, but they liked it very much. Near the shore there was a battered canoe, but in spite of Janek's encouragement, Staś wasn't eager to risk a ride in it. On the way home the sky clouded over again and it began to spit with rain, nothing torrential, just a few warm drops, heralding a long stretch of bad weather. Staś wrapped his little niece in his cloak and gazed at the murky backdrop of trees, warm and green behind a blue veil of rain. The horses were shining wet, and the evening was turning blue and hazy as they drove into the lodge. There was a fragrance of pine needles, and raindrops falling from the leaves and branches onto the decaying veranda roof kept up a gentle tapping, as if holding a conversation. The tapping grew denser and denser, now and then changing into a solid hum, which broke off and then came back again, like a refrain in a soulless piece of music.

Staś sat alone in his room, thinking that he wouldn't see Malina again today. The samovar standing by his window steamed gently in the rain. Michał must be playing his accordion inside the little room, for as soon as the raindrop conversation fell silent, his ear caught faint noises coming from the courtyard.

⸱ He was reminded again of all his lost opportunities for love, in Warsaw before his illness, and then in Davos, and it made him feel so sorry that he had never been able to fall in love with anyone.

By the time Miss Simons left, the snow had all gone. On the afternoon of her departure she had worn a black satin dress with sleeves embroidered in silver stars. Leaning over the railing of the wooden staircase she had cast her amorous blue gaze on him, but he was unable to respond. He could feel so much sadness and disappointment in her look that pity welled up inside him. He was so very sorry. He had wanted to tell her something of the kind but he didn't know how to put it. Outside, splendid violet clouds were gathering below the Schiahorn and the Seehorn, and the sky was cold and lilac; Miss Simons's eyes were sad. He really didn't know, nor could he have known, why the feelings that had made her heart sigh had no equivalent in his, neither before nor after. He thought he was a sort of sexless, stupid creature, incapable of summoning up the nerve for even the feeblest of emotions. He may not even have rationalised it like that at the time, but he ascribed these thoughts to himself after the event, sitting here in the dark, listening to the murmur of the rain. He was still forcing them on himself now, when he thought he should do some summing up, to refine and extract the meaning from those days, which had absolutely no meaning at all. Of course, the result of this exercise was futile; he couldn't put it right or interpret it any other way. In the final reckoning, he ascribed this void purely to the fact that he had never been in love.

Jarosław Iwaszkiewicz

But not even this idea could keep his attention for long; in mental images his thoughts went racing across the forest and the birch grove to the spot beyond the lodge, behind the blackthorn bushes, where there was a sort of rubbish heap, from where you could see the yellow doors of a brick building and the gateway into the stables, where a short while ago he had seen a young girl washing her brother's and her lover's clothes. Her lover's? He spent a while trying to explain to himself the colloquial expression that Michał was 'courting' Malwina, but he was quite unable to define the range of this word. It could have so many meanings, but it certainly didn't have to mean that Michał was her lover. Perhaps, in passing, he could ...

The rain kept resuming its roof-top scale-playing more and more often. Finally it began to fall in earnest; fully clothed, Staś lay down on his bed and stared out of the window at the motionless shadows of the trees. After a while it seemed as if the shadows had broadened, and as if someone were shaking the leaves and slender branches of the lime tree that grew under the window.

But no, it was just that the leaves had bowed beneath the weight of accumulated water, then sprung up abruptly as they shook it off. From Bolesław's room light fell on the rain-drenched forest – in its beam the fine threads of raindrops flashed by, but the world beyond remained deep, dark and impenetrable, murmuring mysteriously.

To Staś, life amid this murmur of rain and rustle of wet leaves was pure bliss. Just as outside, there was a gentle pulse in his temples, and his heart was beating stronger. Isolating himself at the forestry lodge, closing the doors to the rest of the world behind him was a unique experience, and he reckoned he had composed an

118

unusual finale for himself. But then it wasn't a finale at all
– it was an overture. His life was only just beginning, and
it was beautiful, full of harmony.

VI

The next three days, as it poured with rain without the
slightest let-up, were the happiest days of Staś's life.
The harmony of the world which had revealed itself to
him that evening brought him a rare sense of repletion,
above which rose the whisper of warm, incessant rain.
Everything was beautiful, as if composed like a piece
of music or a painting. Leaning its soaking leaves against
the roof and almost against the window of his room, the
lime tree was as well-constructed as the perfect novel,
artfully dividing into branches and topped with a crown
of greenery.

As he began to wake up in the morning, the sound of
raindrops dripping rhythmically from the roof and the
rumbling of water trickling down the gutter into a barrel
set below permeated his still sleeping consciousness.
Blending with his dreams, this music was like the sounds
of an orchestra, the sort that plays at night. He imagined
he was in a vast hall, with a great crowd of people, all listening to the murmuring of instruments. Then gradually,
without opening his eyes, he became aware of a greenish
glow coming from the windows, and then a shudder of
deep delight ran through him at the thought of existence.
And so the day began, to be completely uneventful
throughout, but filled with an inner light. In the radiance
of this light even the gloomy Bolesław seemed a being full
of joy. Towards evening was best; Staś could feel the heat

of his fever, then the weakness would pass and the pulse would start to beat more keenly in his temples. He would wrap a rug around his legs and stretch out on the veranda, where moisture was hanging in the air, and where he only had to reach out an arm to grasp a handful of wet lime leaves, broad and very pleasant to the touch. All the 'European' images, as Staś called them, would recede; it was as if he had never left Poland, as if he had been here since childhood, gazing at the pine trees, the limes and the birches.

Evening would come over the cloudy sky abruptly. The night would deepen along with the rain. No longer able to see, he could hear the rustling sounds even better, which went on vibrating in a range of tones all around him, moving ever closer, until they had taken him entirely into their possession, and he would fall asleep. He would come in to supper frozen through and drink a glass of vodka.

Bolesław would be sitting by the oil lamp, stiff, sad, silent and unapproachable. Taking no notice, after not speaking all day Staś would start talking about everything under the sun; about Davos, the cafés, the sanatoria, the ladies, of whom there had been so many there, about the music, and the strummings of the symphony orchestras which were like the whisper of the rain here at the lodge. Over these three days he only saw Malina twice, when she came to see Katarzyna on some errand or other and ran past the veranda, pulling her skirt up high, showing her very white bare calves. In a shrill voice she greeted Staś and vanished around the corner of the house without looking up. These moments sent a thrill through his emaciated body like an electric charge. He didn't look round at her either, or stare after her, but he could feel her temporary presence with every nerve in his body. He was shivering more, yet above all, over and above the shivers of cold and the humming of raindrops, one feeling predominated – the feeling of discovery. All his travels and all his acquaintances seemed merely a preparation for these three drizzly nights, when he slept with the feeling in his heart that the greatest possible secret lay hidden there. It all combined into a joy so great as to be too heavy to carry, so it was hard for him to raise himself, to stand up and walk with such a feeling in his heart.

He stood at his bedroom window and gazed at the cloak of grey threads behind which the world lay hidden; he gazed at the uniform ranks of pine trees, as if seeing them for the first time, and suddenly he thought of that girl. 'So this is life,' he kept repeating under his breath, and this phrase, which didn't really mean anything, but was simply a way of offloading all the feelings that had welled up in his heart, became the leitmotif of those memorable days. 'So this is life,' he kept saying at every opportunity.

He felt that at the moment when he had said goodbye to a part of his life, when he had walked away from everything that he imagined to be 'real life', as soon as he had slammed the door shut on it, to die here in peace, only then had life shown him its true face. He didn't stop to wonder why he thought of this life as having been captured or revealed at that particular moment, he was just glad that before leaving this world he had managed to experience all these feelings in one, all-absorbing sensation.

At midday the rain became denser, heavier and more penetrating; one would never have suspected that behind the clouds, sunk so low onto the pine trees, there was a summer sun and a blue sky. But Staś wasn't looking for a blue sky. It might never appear again as far as he was concerned; the rain gladdened him and the cold delighted him, pervading him as he stood gazing out at the grey veils of mist draped over the black branches of the pine trees, washed clean of dust. So I have found it, he kept repeating to himself; he didn't need to ask what exactly he had found. It was a sort of hidden, inexpressible inner meaning, a sort of flip side, the inside lining of everything he could see – trees, houses, buildings and people – it was the background and at the same time the essence of everything, and it filled him with a steady, constant joy. He was afraid it would all change at the first ray of sunlight, and he nervously kept watch in case the sky was clearing over. But the rain kept beating steadily on the roof shingles, simply changing its rhythm from time to time, while the stream flowing down from the gutter into the barrel kept up its hum, loud and strong as ever. So he went about amid this humming sound, as if in a cloud of bliss.

He listened to his own breathing and kept watch on his body, the throbbing in his temples and the pulse in his wrists. Now and then he combed his hair, which fell over his eyes; he looked at himself in the mirror, as if seeking confirmation of his own existence. Then he went into the kitchen and stood by the fire, watching as the water boiled. The blisters forcing their way to the surface, and the steam pushing up the lid gave him a childlike pleasure. He watched the flames leaping from the short dry sticks that Katarzyna had laid beneath the hot plate. The smell of potatoes steamed for the pork tickled his nostrils. After all this warmth and crackling his own room, damp, quiet, grey and murmuring, was an even nicer refuge for his unadulterated bliss.

On the third day, just before evening, blue and green patches of sky appeared in the west and it stopped raining. Staś turned his attention to little Ola, who for all this time had not changed her routine and came in from the rain each day with a dripping wet head and plastered-down hair. Yet the little girl had lost her trust in her uncle and reacted very coldly to his interest in her rag doll, and in the general state of affairs in the nook behind the bed, where she spent all her time when not out walking. For some reason she had developed an aversion towards Staś; it was impossible to tell why. But this aversion soon passed before the patches of sky had changed from green and blue to deep azure, before that azure had coated the entire ceiling of the sky, before a fine, cold evening had set in. Coughing, Staś took Ola by the hand and they went out onto the wet leaves and grass. At first they were in total darkness; only once their eyes had grown fully accustomed to the closing-in of night above the trees did the washed-out expanse of the sky become apparent. All Staś knew was that above the stable there was a little window that should be lit up by now, a very small window, almost square, with four large panes of glass. Through the bushes and leaves, which shook raindrops onto their hair, that was where they went; the window was lit by a small lamp and they could see faint shadows flickering on the walls. There was no one in sight, but from inside the little room came the sounds of an accordion. Ola squeezed Staś's hand more tightly.

'Uncle,' she said, 'can you hear? They're playing music in there.'

Staś had caught the nasal sounds long ago, the chords constantly striking against the seconds, all stamping their mark on his dead heart like a seal on wax. He could clearly hear the tune of a popular song he used to sing in Switzerland, which only now, rearranged in Polish style, had finally got through to this obscure forestry lodge. It sounded completely different now, just as different as his life had become among the birches and pines, his redis-covered life, rediscovered at a moment of utter ruin. So he and little Ola stopped and looked up at the four little squares shining out of the pitch-black wall. He listened keenly to the nasal sevenths and seconds called out of the damp, black nothingness by Michał.

From now on to the very end, he thought, that tune will accompany me, in that same arrangement, trans-formed from a slow foxtrot into a sort of Cracovienne or fast march, more suited to the performer's Polish tem-perament. It was quite another tune from the one crooned a couple of years ago by all the street urchins in Zurich, where he had had his first operation. As much as there are any street urchins in Zurich, he thought, and started in a rather rambling way to tell Ola all about the regattas on the beautiful, colonised lake. But his mind wasn't on what he was saying, nor was Ola listening. She tugged at her uncle's hand again. 'Come on,' she said, 'let's go in and listen to Michał.'

For a moment Staś hesitated; Ola's suggestion was the exact expression of his own desires but he was afraid it would be too awkward for the company gathered above the stables. Finally, however, he made up his mind to go in; but no sooner had he entered the cottage than he re-gretted his step. They were all very embarrassed – the old mother, Janek and Michał. There was a bottle of vodka on the table. Malina alone was not at all confused. She dusted off a little stool with her apron and drew it up for Staś; without so much as looking at her he took Ola on his knee and started up a polite conversation with Michał about the difficulties of playing the accordion. Janek was sitting in the chimney corner before the semi-circular maw of a Russian stove, where wood chips were burning. On the floorboards stood kneaded loaves of bread covered in sackcloth; the fire crackled.

Without looking at the girl Staś could see her every movement, her every glance; she alone existed for him in this company. She poured him a glass of vodka and carried the lamp away to the back of the room, as she had to check that the dough had risen enough. For a while they were left in silence and in shadow; flashes of fire flickered red and gold across the walls. Suddenly Michał leaned back against the wall, stared into the fire and began to play, so languorously and so mournfully that Ola hugged Staś tighter, without taking her eyes from the coarse but expressive face of the performer. They listened to the music in silence.

Stanisław could feel the vodka radiating warmth along his veins, as he ceased to feel the dampness of their walk on his hair, shoes and clothing. He bowed his head and listened to the awful wheezing music, a truly unpleasant sound, stirring up his raw feelings, which until now he had so hastily rushed through the dimly lit recesses of his consciousness. His entire experience seemed a downward slide, and he had so little time left now before the ascent. He had noticed that he was measuring out this time calmly, not thinking about himself or his own death – it was just the world that was going to die.

He noticed that Ola's eyes were wide open, staring at Michał in speechless wonder. He could feel the little girl's heart beating beneath his fingers, and he was afraid his own was beating just as fast. He turned his head and saw

Malina standing at the back of the room, in a corner behind the shadow of the stove, leaning against the wall,
listening to Michał's music with her head thrown back.
Her exquisite, flawless eyelids hooded her eyes; a faint
glimmer of light fell on them, on her plaits, and on the
wisps of hair protruding from under her headscarf.

Michał played on for some time, until at last he
stopped. Staś thanked him, gave him his hand and left,
without looking at anyone. Ola wanted to stay longer, so
she dragged along after him reluctantly. He scolded her
sharply, then at once regretted it.

Out in the night, amid the damp smell of the forest, he
picked her up in his arms; light as a bird, he hugged her
to him and rained kisses on her brow and hair. She wound
her skinny little arms around his neck and pressed her
cheek to his, hugging him tightly. He sensed that she was
crying, the tears dropping silently from her eyes.

'What's the matter?' he asked.

Choked with sobs, her voice was like the breath of the
night in his ear. 'I love Michał so much … And Mummy
… And Mummy …'

Staś felt these words send a cold shiver through him.
He pressed the fragile figure even tighter to him and covered her mouth with his hand. He was afraid he would
start crying too, that beneath the burden of unknown and
unadmitted things he would die before his time. He cra-
dled Ola in his arms and walking at a gentle pace towards
the house he rocked her to and fro. Now her feet, now
her head kept nudging the leaves and bushes and a murmur of raindrops fell on the brushwood. After a while he
started talking in a happy, steady voice.

'You're prattling nonsense, Ola, awful nonsense,' he
said. 'Just for that I'm going to give you a bath in the

raindrops, I'm going to give you a proper bath, a proper bath, I am, I'm going to throw you in the air!'

Ola was laughing now. 'Uncle, Uncle, you'll bash my head against a tree!' she cried. 'No, I'm a cat, I can see in the dark,' said Staś solemnly. And laughing out loud they reached the veranda.

He handed Ola over to Katarzyna, but Bolesław wasn't in. Staś's sense of regret and fear had changed by now into good humour, and at the thought of his brother's loneliness he was overcome with pity. He wanted to go and find him, he wanted to tell him that he wasn't at all upset with him for making a scene, or for the things he had said. He thought he must have gone off into the night again, and would be out among the birches, standing over his wife's little grave. He thought how awful his vigil was, and that it wouldn't do him any good; also that it was wet and that the moisture and rainwater were seeping through the sand covering the coffin where Basia lay, which must be a terrible thought for Bolesław.

Slowly he walked over there, thinking as he went how little focus their life had, how much time they spent escaping from the lichen-blackened lodge, how they were always out and about, how even meal-times were becoming mobile and unfixed, rarely gathering the family of three around the same table.

The damp air had warmed up a bit before nightfall and the ground was steaming. He walked on slowly; as he stretched his legs his heart grew calmer and his shallow breathing deeper. He stopped near the grave and rested his hand on a slanting trunk, feeling its rough and smooth grains beneath his fingers. But Bolesław wasn't there. For a while Staś went on standing there forlornly, trying to feel his way into his brother's thoughts. What went through his head as he stood like this at the spot where a couple of metres away the woman he had loved lay buried beneath the sand? Staś had never loved anyone, so he had never been able to understand fully how Bolesław felt. Only now did he wonder, in this place of decay and new life. And he wasn't even counting how many weeks were left before they would be burying him here. Bolesław was very strong and healthy and would certainly have to go on wandering from the birch grove to the clearing where Maryjka's cottage stood for a long time to come ...

Michał's music had evaporated from his head; now he was listening to the gentle rustling of the trees, and he was thinking that if one could hear while lying three metres underground, would he be able to hear music played at his graveside? Maybe not. Earth, solid and heavy, did not let voices in, and deep down a desert-like silence reigns.

He heard a footstep, then a sigh close by. He took his hand from the birch tree and touched the person standing beside him; he felt the same roughnesses and smooth-nesses as on the birch bark, the same drops of dew, the same coolness – except that beneath the fabric he was touching a hidden warmth lay slumbering, announcing its presence with a sigh.

Without a word to each other, they moved a few paces away from the grave. To one side a few small bushes grew and the moss on the ground was drier than elsewhere. With gratitude Staś thought how she had come all this way after him. They sat down. Silently he embraced her, his thin arm feeling her broad back, and the ridge of her spine girdled in fleshy muscles. He thought of that other woman, lying in the grave, and then tenderly, gratefully, with a languor he hadn't suspected in himself, he nestled his head against her breast. Just as silently she embraced him, warm and moist with dew, she leaned him back and they lay down together. There they lay for ages, without moving, listening spellbound to the nightlife of the forest, to the murmur of frail birch twigs. Then Staś silently moved his hand to her heart; beneath his palm, beneath the swell of her breast, beneath her ribs he could feel it beating steadily, evenly and earnestly, as if it would never stop.

Then he got up, while she remained lying down, sleepy and serene. He stood up and felt how damp his clothing was; he took out a handkerchief, flicked the earth from his knees, mopped the water from his hair, and dried the scent of love from his face. Then he knelt down and leaned forward, tenderly wiping Malina's face; as he did so, he could feel the perfection of her eyelids, like spring leaves beneath his touch. She lay without moving, saying nothing, just as from the very outset. He thrust his handkerchief into her hand and whispered in her ear: 'Take it as a keepsake.'

Then he got down again and lay on his back; she put her hand beneath his head. He gazed upwards; the sky was pale and distant, and way up high among the branches a star was twinkling.

VII

On days when it drizzled but brightened up later Bolesław was continually on the move about the forest, never taking a break from his work, and it was the same at home where he fretted like a caged animal; he wasn't especially sad, he just felt weighed down. He was physically aware of himself standing up, walking about and eating, as if he were carrying a burden. All these activities and functions seemed drained of colour, and all the more laborious for that. His feeling of desolation had grown so much deeper that he had even stopped going to Basia's grave. On the last few evenings when he had gone there as usual his thoughts had contained such a mixture of elements that for the first time since her death he felt inclined to suspend his visits for the time being.

He grew numb at the thought that there might be another death on the way. Sometimes it felt as if the life they were leading was nothing but a dream, just their imagination, easily dismissed. He thought Staś had told him about his illness for a silly joke or to give him a fright, and he wasn't in any real danger. But the rainy days when his brother had lain at home on the veranda, numb and silent, had filled him with fear that this was the end. So on the evening when the weather cleared and Staś, in a good mood, had gone for a walk with Ola, he was very pleased and even smiled at his own fears. He walked slowly after them; slightly surprised at the direction Staś had chosen, he followed to see where they had gone. When they stopped to look up at the lighted windows above the stables, so did he, and when they went inside he was left alone in the shadow of the rainy night. The accordion music grated on him as he stood and stared up at the lighted window. He saw the lamplight slip away into the depths of the room, and reflections of firelight began to flicker across the walls and window panes. Michał's music struck him as wild and even more piercing than before.

There could be no doubt now that Staś had 'fallen in love' with the rifleman's sister. That was the last straw!

130

What on earth did he see in that simple girl? There were trollops like her by the thousand in these woods, but he had to fall for her, didn't he? All those fine young foreign ladies whose photographs he had set up on the plain wooden table in his room were not enough for him. To put it bluntly, Malina was ugly, though her eyes were pretty and nicely set, with even brows, lids and lashes.

He closed his eyes, though it was almost entirely dark, and tried to imagine the girl's face again. But raindrops were dripping noisily from the roof, bits of debris were rattling in the gutter, and these sounds at close hand prevented him from concentrating. He kept seeing some other pair of eyes, other faces and other eyelids. It felt as if he had only been there for a moment, and hadn't yet managed to do all his thinking, as if Michał's music, muffled from here, though audible, had not yet told him the whole story. The pine forest came almost right up to the building; there were four mature pine trees opposite the small square window, and he was tempted to climb up one to see what was going on inside. But the lowest branches started quite high up, and then he felt ashamed of the idea. 'What's it all coming to?' he said, almost out loud, and drew back against the wall to hear better.

The music stopped, Stanisław and Ola's footsteps rang out, and then came the little girl's smothered whisper, 'I love Michał so much ... And Mummy ... And Mummy ...' He didn't know if Ola had failed to complete her sentence or if the rest of it had blown away on the night breeze. He heard them walk away quietly at first, then making louder and louder rustling noises in the bushes, while he stood still, rooted to the spot, unable to comprehend the words he had just heard, or his own feelings.

At a calm and steady pace he walked a long way into the forest and got home late. There he kept pacing his room again, stopping occasionally at the foot of Ola's bed, where she lay fast asleep. He didn't consider trying to find some hidden meaning in Ola's words; such a very little girl could not possibly know of some awful, vulgar secret, and anyway, it was well over a year now since Basia had died. Michał hadn't gone there at all in those days, he hadn't been courting Malina then; the thought never even crossed his mind. He just wanted to know what the little girl had been saying, but he couldn't ask her that directly. The real meaning of her words would have to remain a mystery, the secret of a dewy night, never to be disturbed. Let silence reign supreme, like the silence in the birch grove, the silence of the grave.

What upset him most was that his dismay at the words he had overheard was almost equal to his rage at Staś's visit to Malina's home. All right, he had only been there for a short time, and only to listen to the music, there were several people in the house, and Ola had gone with him, but all the same it was improper. He decided to have a word with Staś first thing in the morning to point out the inappropriacy of his behaviour. But as soon as he got up, he had to leave at once for a far-off district, where from early morning he had to supervise the job of marking trees for felling.

The weather had not settled; it was rather chilly with a sky full of clouds. He stayed in the forest till evening, overseeing the work, marking the trees with numbers and trying not to think about yesterday evening. In fact, it was like a vision in a dream. And of course he was thinking about Basia a lot and missing her terribly. He remembered her buying berries from an old woman and pouring a mound of wild strawberries from a jug into a dish, he remembered her walking through the forest with Ola in a white dress, and accepting a hare from Michał, which he had brought her as a gift. Yes, so Michał did come by in those days too – but he was a rifleman, wasn't he, a peasant, someone one took no notice of, just as he took no notice of Michał's fiancée, for instance.

He wasn't the hysterical type, and he had too much respect for Basia to think anything bad of her, but the mere mental association of his late wife and carnal thoughts, or the body in general, caused him acute distress. For the first time it occurred to him that Basia could have found someone else attractive. That Michał's perfect build, for instance, could have made an impression on her, could have evoked thoughts he had never suspected her of in the course of their short-lived marriage. That she had realms of sensual existence that had never been any of his business.

He didn't go home for lunch and spent his break at the edge of a clearing, watching the wind dispel the clouds. It was getting ever warmer and finer, and the earth was drying out before one's very eyes. He lay down in a ditch, half-closed his eyes and felt a lassitude come over him which hadn't been able to touch him while he had been blindly occupied with the matter in hand. This lassitude was so very unfamiliar to him that it felt as if some completely alien element were flowing into his veins, like an injection of some magical liquid, changing the very essence of his being.

The afternoon was hot now, crickets were chirruping and there was a scent of June catchfly, blooming pink in the ditch. He scratched at the grass and flowers and felt crumbs of dampish earth beneath his fingernails, and a verse of the Bible came to mind: 'Dust thou art, and unto dust shalt thou return'. Basia had already returned to dust. It was painful for him to think of it; his misfortune was stronger than he was. Moreover he felt his own strength to be a misfortune, his health, the muscularity of his arms, his step, so very confident and resilient, even when he was loping from corner to corner, not knowing what to do with himself, with his life and his distress.

Finally, as he lay there amid the warmth and scent of the flowers, he fell into a fitful sleep, the sort slept on the ground and in grass by people who have slept their whole lives in a bed. When he awoke the workmen had got down to their task without him. They were moving in line along the young forest, scratching marks on the bark of some of the trees; the junior forester from the neighbouring district was walking along marking numbers with a red pencil and a brush soaked in tar.

The birds were singing like mad. The leaves were rich and green. The sense of composure in nature brought him a kind of solace. He sat in the ditch for a while longer, not even wondering if the work were going to plan. Nor was he thinking of his worries; he only had one thing in mind – that if he had still been married, he would never have slept through his lunch hour in a ditch, and that it was better like this, because he could stay here and keep a proper eye on things.

Although the days were long now, it was almost dark by the time he went home. He dismissed the workmen, then stopped to chat for a while with the junior forester, a very genial fellow; then the rifleman came and told him of the damage caused recently by people from the nearest village, about twenty-five kilometres away. Apparently they had sawn into a magnificent old larch but had not managed to bring it down. For a day the tree had stayed standing – the rifleman had seen it – but before he got back the next day with the men, the wind had blown it over, destroying a lot of young trees. Krępski, the junior forester, was annoyed. Bolesław drove him to his lodge, for it was quite a distance and he wasn't in a hurry to get home.

When he got back, he found only Katarzyna at home. She told him that Staś had gone for a walk, and Ola had run off somewhere. In silence he ate his reheated lunch and went out onto the porch. Just as Staś's piano-playing had upset him earlier, now he was maddened by the silence. He would have liked to hear the stupid, hoarse tunes tearing his nerves to shreds. He remembered Michał's accordion and went out into the courtyard. Janek was feeding the horses; upstairs a light was burning. He hesitated for a while, then went up the stairs and opened the door without knocking. He stood in the doorway unnoticed. His daughter was sitting on a bed in the gloom, leaning against Malwina's high pillows. By the bed sat Michał, telling her a complicated fairy tale about some silly people. There was no one else in the room. Ola saw her father, sprang to her feet and ran up to him. 'Daddy, Daddy, Michał's been telling me such wonderful stories.'

Bolesław kissed his daughter. Michał stood up straight and Bolesław took his first careful look at him. He was tall and magnificently well built, with coarse but pleasant features. He had very fair hair and a blond moustache, his eyes were small and very blue. Bolesław smiled at him. Michał gave him a deferential look. He was clearly a good man.

'Don't get up,' said Bolesław, unusually softly, 'let Michał finish the story, then quickly home. It's time for bed!'

Jarosław Iwaszkiewicz

He turned and went out, trailed down the stairs and wandered off to one side; he wanted to go into the forest so they couldn't see him, and so he couldn't see anything either. He didn't know how to tell fairy tales, he didn't even know how to talk to Ola, he never knew what he should say to her. But she was all he had left in the world. Staś was right, the little girl was very neglected. But what could he do about it? He was so busy with his work.

Today had been a day of new elements: within surroundings so familiar and so ordinary he had noticed new things. And he didn't regret it; it was as if life had been reawakened in him – it interested him. His midday lassitude had coloured his entire afternoon and evening in an unfamiliar way. He felt as if he were fighting off a dangerous narcotic. For the first time today he had had a good look at Michał, and he could tell he was a fine lad, a likeable sort. For the first time he had felt a pang in his heart at Ola's neglect, a lonely little girl, off to the watchman's room for fairy tales.

Emerging beyond the stable and the pine trees, again as if for the first time, he saw the birch grove where his wife lay buried. The white trunks stood out against the late evening sky, illuminated by the remains of light like pearls set in velvet. Those tree trunks, smooth, white and sculptured, reminded him of women's arms, lots of entangled arms, rising upwards imploringly or exultantly, sometimes bent back downwards in a gesture of submission and resignation. High up, the clusters of arms joined hands, entwining fingers, though some of the trees stood forlorn and single. Moist, steamy air filled the gaps between the birches with condensation, and all together it gave the impression of a sort of temple of the senses. The arms created a glittering colonnade. Never had the forest looked like this before, this forest of anxious whispers, of chill breezes, of wintry nights when the stars were so immense; of autumn days when petals fell like golden rain onto the burial mound, when they hung in the air in a rippling, golden stream. On this June evening there was neither death nor anxiety in the birch grove, but there was life, the forest was breathing it; it had become so powerful and unsettling that Bolesław's own regular breathing suddenly grew troubled. The air caught in his throat and his heart ached. There he stood and gazed; now and then a gentle shudder ran through the forest, the arms slanted and changed formation, then fell back in line; each time the darkness, into which these white limbs were plunging, gave a sweet murmur. Suddenly, like a single point of gold riven into the shadows, the first note of a belated nightingale rang out. It made him choke, still standing there, like a lump of ice. And the lump was melting in his throat, becoming sweet and salty, filling his eyes to overflowing with warmth.

VIII

Neither that evening nor for the next few days did the brothers meet at table. Only over a rapid lunch did they exchange a few banalities. Bolesław had taken to spending the afternoon wherever his work found him, whether at fellings, plantings or land clearances. Staś was free to do as he liked. In the early evening he often took the horses out, driving them himself and taking Ola with him; Malwina would be waiting for them at an agreed spot and they would all go out together. During the drive they hardly exchanged a word. They would travel a stretch of the sandy road, or wander about the forest, and then go home, all in total silence. If Ola was with them she did most of the talking. Staś did not stop to think about what he was doing; Malina just came along for the ride and that was it.

However, he found the girl's silence extremely worrying, as if it must be concealing some sort of ambush or secret that he wouldn't be able to cope with. While driving at her side in the trap, or standing next to her in the forest, he would often take a sidelong look at her calm, pensive profile. There was so much cheerful serenity in it that it had a soothing: effect on his nerves. And his heart needed soothing; his nerves were in tatters, at night he was having hallucinations and he could hardly digest a thing. But whenever he looked at Malwina's low brow, whenever he kissed it, his heart beat steadily.

He had decided not to ask her any questions or to tell her anything. He wouldn't answer any questions about his life, or ask any about her past. He didn't even want to know about Michał. But once he got home, for a long time he would be unable to fall asleep; he kept seeing her face before him and couldn't stop thinking that now it was Michał's turn. Yet Michał seemed to have stopped coming, for in all these days Staś never saw him once.

The whole day was filled with anticipation. In the morning he lay for a long time listening to the sounds of the house – the tapping of Katarzyna's knife as she chopped onions for lunch, or the monotonous crowing of a cockerel shut up in the creaking henhouse. Slowly his body would come to life, drenched in cold sweat from a night full of bad dreams. A shiver, then a shudder would pass through his numb hands and feet, and only then would he have the strength to open his eyes. At once he would notice the windows curtained in green leaves and the light, either sunny or dull as the weather varied. When it was raining he liked to listen to its whisper before looking at the world. But he preferred bright sunlight and fine weather. Then he felt more alive and got up a bit sooner. He would have his breakfast, then sit at the piano, but all the time he would be waiting to hear Malina's firm footsteps and rough voice. During the day she often had something to do in the kitchen and would come running in to see Katarzyna. At one point it did cross his mind that while leading such an idle, inactive life he shouldn't really be listening out for Malina's voice or footsteps. But those other, furtive footsteps seemed to have gone away. He too was starting to think the doctors had made a mistake, and although he didn't feel too strong, he hadn't noticed any changes for the worse. The progress of his illness wasn't making itself apparent. He was hardly eating a thing, but nor was he aware of any particular symptoms. He only felt unwell until midday, but he didn't know whether it was the burden of love or of illness. He knew nothing of either kind of feeling – he was experiencing both love and death for the very first time.

Only by about five did he feel his strength gathering. He was extremely happy with life, although he had a feeling of being obstructed at every turn, as if there were a barrier between himself and reality. At dusk Malwina finished work, smelling of earth and soapsuds. They would meet at a pre-arranged spot and be gripped by a meaningful silence. Sometimes the mere fact that their hands touched as they swayed along gave them pleasure and coloured Staś's entire view of life. Indeed, he was brimful of emotion, he was overflowing with a pure joy he couldn't even talk about, for Malwina wouldn't have understood him.

Gradually he realised that the woman who went walking along the sombre forest paths with him was pure deceit from head to foot. Neither the cause nor the effect were apparent; suffice it to say that the few words Malwina spoke to him were all patent lies, so much so that Staś believed nothing she said, not even things which must have been true by force of nature. At first she denied whatever he asked her. He had soon given up his policy of not asking any questions. On the contrary, the more he could tell that they got him nowhere, the more it annoyed him, and the more inclined he felt to shower the girl with questions. To every single one she answered in the negative – no, she had never loved anyone; no, she had never had a lover; no, Michał wasn't courting her; no, she didn't know any lad intimately. She went so far as to claim that she had never known any man before Staś, which was patently untrue. He didn't believe it, but eventually such a blur of 'no, no, nos' went running through his head that he stopped believing his own eyes and ears. Miss Simons had confided everything in him; she had been noble and sincere, telling him he wasn't the first man she had loved, that she had had three lovers before him, even that she had stolen money from her father and was a bad daughter. It didn't bother him at the time; he hadn't let any of these confessions upset him. As he looked back at himself during that period of his life, what annoyed and infuriated him most was his own vacuousness. A single day in this wilderness seemed to him fuller than that entire life. He had stopped answering letters with foreign stamps. They had become rarer too; Bolesław no longer had the irritation of finding them in every post.

Malwina's lies were like a cloud of butterflies swarming around her. They were all part of that special aura that both excited and intoxicated Staś. Every day before seeing the girl he promised himself he would keep his mouth shut, but every day he asked her the same questions, which soon became a stereotyped litany, as regular as a ritual. It always ended the same way, with 'I'm boring you, aren't I?', which was met with the final, unfailing and adamant 'No!'

There was only one question that she answered with a wholehearted, sincere 'Yes'. Staś had risked it a couple of days after their first meeting – the question was 'Do you love me?' He realised that this 'yes' was just as false as all the 'nos', but even so it gave him such pleasure that he kept asking the same question, not just daily, but several times a day. What should he say, while she said nothing, as they lay in the bushes together on the damp fabric of the forest, feeling the grass and last year's fallen leaves beneath their toes? As he tightly embraced her warm, ample body in his skinny arms, as he touched her skin, feeling its whiteness at the mere touch? So he kept on mindlessly repeating the same questions in various tones of voice, and she always gave the same answers, without changing her intonation in the slightest. Her answers were like dilatory raindrops falling from leaf to leaf. Only once did she give a different answer.

It was a hot evening. Staś had been feeling reluctant to go out and had put off their meeting until late, at the edge of the forest in view of Maryjka's cottage. That day he was exceptionally weak and could even feel how tired his fingers were from tinkling away at the piano. It was a postal delivery day and he had just received a letter from Miss Simons, who was off to Davos again. With a wry smile he thought of the landscape and houses, and the air smelling of medications, as if made up to a prescription. He rattled out a tune, slowly warbling each note as he hit it – the same old tango that he used to dance to in his former life. The heat was tiring him, but maybe it wasn't tiredness that made him delay his departure for the edge of the forest. The chance of a meeting with Malina was his greatest joy – it was everything, it was his only privilege in life – and he thought of the forest where they met with immense, new-born love. The earth they lay down on was like a loving pet, a tame animal that he could cuddle up to. Malina, the earth, and the forest – it was all as if the good health he would never recover was still cosseting him. Very slowly he descended the veranda steps, looked around at the forestry lodge, dark and sloping, and took in the silence that slumbered in the forest. 'There's sure to be a moon tonight,' he thought.

But there was no moon; as he went by the trees he passed between warmer and cooler streams of air, like a swimmer between currents of water. He found Malina lying stretched out, half asleep beneath a low leaning pine, which had often cloaked their caresses within the canopy of its lower branches. He woke her and passionately repeated his daily questions, and heard the daily answers. The only thing he didn't feel like asking was if she loved him. He hesitated, kissing and embracing her. Only towards the end, when it was time to go home, did he fail to keep his promise to himself. 'Do you love me?' he said; to which came the stifled whisper, 'Do you love me, sir?'

The memory of this unusual inquiry rocked him to sleep faster than usual that night, and woke him earlier, giving him greater strength for the following day. But this strength proved illusory. Towards evening he could hardly lift his feet, but in the light of her gentle question of the night before Malina seemed quite another girl, and all the blatant lies she had told him before took on a ring of truth. He had found her to be capable of feelings he hadn't expected. Strange hopes began to take possession of him. He thought that if all this were to develop into a passionate and impulsive love, his life would end in the clouds, in wonderland. It would be a fabulous finale. But even as he said it he no longer believed such an ending to be possible; he was just pretending to compose a finale for himself, but what he really felt was that he was only just beginning, with a great deal of effort, to construct some meaning for his life – he was only just beginning to live. All his thoughts revolved around the strong, white body which he held in his arms each day; he decided that from this body he was drinking in the juices he needed to conquer his infirmity.

He thought that from then on Malwina would change her replies to his constant questions, that she would answer with something akin to emotion and that maybe she would start to do the asking. But no, she was just as before – meek, quiet, shy and deceitful. She went on saying she had known no men before him and that Michał wasn't courting her. And to the question whether she loved him she answered 'yes' again.

He wanted to change it all, stir it up and get to the heart of this frigid body, but his efforts were all in vain. Only once, a couple of days after that evening, when tired of her passivity, wanting to find out more, he shook her by the shoulders and demanded an answer, she again said something that revealed a darker side.

'What about Michał?' he had asked. 'Do you love him?'

'Yes, I love him too,' she had answered very softly.

143

IX

That day they had met earlier than usual because it was a Sunday and Malwina didn't have to work that afternoon. It had been unusually hot since early morning and Staś was very tired. He had walked all the way to the lake, a lifeless, black-and-white eye of water, as he had arranged to meet his lover there. At least it was far from home where no one could see them. It was there among the waterside reeds and grasses that Malina had told him she loved Michał too. At first he had taken no notice of this remark, and once he had left the girl, who wanted to stay and bathe, he trailed homewards. The trees stood rigid, perspiring in the hot, static air. All day the sky had been a pure and cloudless sapphire blue. Slender shadows cast a sparse net among the trees. The azure depths of the forest had become strangely crisp and sharply patterned. Bathed in sweat from heat and weakness, Staś could only drag his feet along, stopping now and then for a breath of air. But nothing could refresh him. Breathing was becoming torment. By the time he reached the lodge, it was already fairly late. His brother had gone off somewhere. Inside, the house was cool and pleasant. Ola was lying asleep on her father's bed; flies were buzzing and crawling about her face. In Staś's room the windows were curtained in the green coolness of the lime trees; he sat down at the piano and gazed out of the window at the leaves and trees beyond. Then he began to go over Malina's words in his head.

Altogether it had been a bad day. He and his brother had quarrelled again at table. Bolesław had slammed the door and left his lunch unfinished before rushing out. And now there was Malina's remark. There was something infinitely stupid in those words, as well as the deceit, the simplicity, the utter lack of ability to articulate emotions. For the first time he felt abased by the emotions that had taken such a firm hold on him.

He placed his hands on the keyboard and stared at them mindlessly. Then he noticed that his fingers had grown terribly thin and were extremely bony. From this alone he could tell that the end was getting nearer, but he didn't want to summon up the thought of it. On the contrary, he started imagining a long life.

Later he started to play his favourite Hawaiian song, the one that had played as he danced with Miss Simons. He could remember that occasion perfectly. Now something was starting to happen – a rare event that only occurred when he heard an exotic song. With a deep, cold shudder he was beginning to sense the enormity of all the things he would never, ever see. The great expanse of cold, green oceans, blue seas full of palm trees and islands, ice-cold and blazing hot lands. Women in ports and villages, people, people, people. All the people he might have known, or loved, or simply come across. They weren't here, and he would never get a glimpse of them now. Whenever this feeling had come over him in Switzerland he had immediately obliterated the scenes conjured up by his imagination. 'I shall have far more in life,' he had told himself. But now he knew he would have nothing more in life than the body of a very simple woman, and the flood of unknown, inexpressible worlds engulfed him to the point of choking and gasping for air. How much of it there was in one simple Hawaiian tune, which he had drawn out of the old piano with an easy bit of fingering. The fact that not only would he never know those worlds, but wouldn't even be able to express

145

the thrill they sent running through him was even worse torment. He could feel the omnipotence of nature, the menace of its inexorable rights, its vastness and its indifference. He was staggered by its indifference to his little death – it made his blood run cold, in spite of the heat; it made his hair stand on end to think that death was gradually consuming him, while nature would do nothing, nothing at all to alter the fact – it would just stand by and watch his demise impassively. Billions of people died just as young. He stood up and slammed the piano lid shut with a crash. He was overcome with terror. In the doorway stood Ola, awoken by his music, pale and as if hypnotised.

He took her by the hand, drew her onto the bed and in a tired voice began to tell her once again about the lunar eclipse he had seen in the mountains, how the lifeless red disk hung suspended above the frosty peaks; about the sense of space created by the shadow of the earth as it falls on the moon; how the stars appear larger, more deeply set in the frosty black sky; how the dogs howl with fear in the mountains; and about the eternal murmur of torrents and waterfalls which slowly and relentlessly erode great rocks and sweep them away into the valleys. In the face of this great game of the elements, human life is nothing.

Ola didn't understand any of this, and it frightened her. Staś kept nervously repeating, 'I know you don't understand, but it doesn't matter.'

Then he left her on the bed and walked about the room, bumping into the piano. The little girl sat startled, holding her threadbare doll dangling from her hand.

'It doesn't matter if you don't understand, there's no harm done,' he repeated, 'but I've got no one to tell, and once I'm in the ground you'll remember, when you grow up you'll remember. Just don't remember in the middle of the night or you won't be able to sleep ... Or maybe you will. People do sleep, in spite of being surrounded by such terrible things – trees, clouds, animals. But none of it means a thing, people do sleep ...'

He prattled on in this vein, until all of a sudden it grew dark. It took them a moment to realise that it wasn't just nightfall but a storm as well. Now and then Stanisław had a strange but pleasant taste in his mouth, and wiping his tongue on his handkerchief he saw that his spittle was pink. A few drops of blood had trickled from his nose as well. 'That's brought on by the storm,' he thought.

Finally he felt weak from all this chatter. He glanced at Ola, who was sitting on the bed weeping quietly and clutching the doll to her chest in fright. He stopped talking abruptly; moved to emotion, he seized the child in his embrace. And it all ended in tears. They both cried, and along with the tears their fears melted away. They were back on solid ground again, they could no longer see any terrors, just the walls that shielded them from the approaching storm.

They heard the first sough of the wind, and at the same time Bolesław's footsteps on the dark veranda, then in the house, now dark as pitch. 'Shut the windows,' he shouted in a harsh, down-to-earth voice that made them both shudder. They rushed to the windows and shut them quickly. By now it was pouring.

Bolesław lit a lamp, put it in the dining room and stood quietly in the middle. Suddenly a stream of rain dashed against the windowpanes and drops of water lay flattened against the glass. Thunder and lightning came one after another at regular intervals. The sky kept opening, pale blue, revealing the incredible shapes of twisted trees.

147

'Go to your room,' said Bolesław abruptly to Ola in a menacing tone, his face flashing sternly, doubly illuminated by the lamp and the lightning.

Staś was puzzled by his tone of voice, but before he had worked out the reason for it, Bolesław had explained it.

'Fine things you're up to here,' he said.

Staś was unspeakably alarmed by the start of this scene, not because he feared what Bolesław had to say to him, but because it would be nothing but futile, idle nonsense, which would not only make no difference to his inner state but which could not change his feelings for Malina in the slightest – his final refuge before plunging into the vortex. He just made a wry face in reply. 'Well, what?' he said after a short wait, since Bolesław was still standing there without moving.

Slowly Bolesław turned his own twisted face towards his brother. Staś noticed that the right corner of his mouth kept dropping abruptly of its own accord. In the end he had to hold a hand to his face to get control of it. His teeth flashed between his lips.

'So what am I up to here?' Staś asked again waywardly, though he could feel the blood draining to his legs and had to sit down for a while. He was feeling weaker and weaker, and wanted the conversation over as soon as possible.

'That trollop,' uttered Bolesław throatily.

'Don't be so moralistic, you know perfectly well I haven't taken an oath of chastity.'

'Yes, but in my house.'

Stanisław laughed heartily. 'What an extraordinary thing to say. What on earth do you think? Do you really think a young chap like me can stay celibate? What a daft idea!'

'Well, what about me?'

'What do I care how you manage? Do as you wish – I've had quite enough abstinence in the sanatoria, thank you.'

Bolesław seemed to relent, removed his hand from his face and took a few paces about the room. He stopped at Staś's side. 'It might do you harm.'

'Oh, don't worry. Don't be so concerned – nothing can ever hurt me again.'

The scene appeared to be ending calmly. Staś was smiling almost amicably, but he didn't yet feel strong enough to get up from his chair. He cast his brother an ironical glance. 'You've been spying on us,' he said.

This ironical glance was a mistake. Bolesław scowled again and suddenly started stamping his feet in the middle of the room in a fit of helpless rage. This stamping was answered by a powerful bolt of lightning that struck in the forest somewhere very close by; then an intensive onslaught of sheets of rain laid siege to the windows. Staś stared in helpless amazement at the madman, who was glaring again and had started spouting incoherently.

'You go gadding about, you're always gadding about with her ... you're everywhere ... at every turn ... today ... always ... everywhere ... today ... by the pond ...'

Staś was slowly getting a grip on himself, feeling ever greater disgust. He would long since have left the room and fled to his own if it weren't for the strange heaviness he could feel so sharply in his legs, and which was still rising up his body. He looked at his brother with pity almost, quite unable to understand his state of mind. 'There was no need to spy on us. Why should it bother you?' he said.

'Why should it bother me?' exploded Bolesław, more coherently this time. 'How could your behaviour not bother me? One day you tell me you're dying, and next thing you're running after trollops night and day, every single day ...'

'Once and for all I'm telling you it's none of your business!'

'Yes, but I know more than you do, I know things you don't. I know things you wouldn't even guess.'

Staś felt colder; he was gradually going numb and the thoughts that were flashing through his head were not comforting. Finally, by making a superhuman effort, he stood up and took a few steps towards the door of his own room. But his legs refused to obey him. He stopped and leaned against a small table by the door.

'Wait, wait, I have to tell you what I saw this evening just before the storm. I saw her kissing Michał – more than kissing.'

Staś's view of the world had gone hazy and he could no longer hear the intermittent thunderclaps; it had all fused together into one great crashing in his ears. With the greatest effort of willpower he spoke very calmly, separating each word with long pauses. Even to himself his voice sounded alien. 'What – do – I – care – what – the – girl – gets – up to? She's – not – my – wife – so let – her – kiss – Michał – if – she – wants.'

Bolesław clenched his fists in front of his face and staggered. That was the last thing Staś saw, as the lamp, jolted by his brother's hand, fell suddenly to the floor and went out with a clatter.

'Thank God it didn't catch fire,' said Staś normally. But at that moment a flash of lightning illuminated Bolesław's face as he stood leaning against the wall. In the blaze of light he looked very pale. Staś noticed that he was holding a black object. Suddenly the strength came flooding back to him, and at a single bound he was beside his brother, had seized him by the hands and spread-eagled him against the wall. With all the fingers of his left hand he squeezed Bolesław's wrist. 'Let go,' he hissed, 'let go of it. You'll be the one who's sorry.'

The revolver fell noisily to the floor. Another flash of lightning illuminated both brothers, but by now they had let their muscles slacken and were slumped. Bolesław gripped Staś's arm and whispered in his ear: 'I saw them, you know – there was no one else at home, Janek's in the forest, the old woman's gone to the church fair, and Michał's been waiting all day for her to get back from you, then she came, and it was already dark, so he lit a lamp, I saw them, I did!'

'It's not true,' said Staś, suddenly falling into his brother's tone of voice. 'It's not true, you can't see anything from down below.'

Bolesław's whisper was barely audible. 'I climbed up,' he said, 'I climbed up a pine tree, you know, there are pines there, opposite the windows. I saw everything, clear as day, they didn't put the light out …'

Staś pushed his brother away. 'You spy. It really does bother you.'

He set off for his own door, but his legs turned to lead again. Once he had found the chair he sat down in the darkness, but the heaviness had passed higher up his body, to his heart and lungs, obstructing his breathing. He coughed and suddenly felt relieved, too much so, for his head felt light as a vacuum. He pressed his handkerchief to his lips, but it proved a poor defence as the blood poured through his fingers.

X

For the next few days Staś lay semi-conscious in his room with the windows shaded. Katarzyna and Ola looked after him, taking regular turns at feeding him ice-cream and taking his temperature. Meanwhile, in Bolesław something had snapped; he couldn't even turn to face his brother's room. Worse than that, he found it very hard to speak, and in reply to his daughter's questions he emitted noises resembling animal grunts through tightly clenched teeth. On the first day he didn't go to work at all, but sat without moving at a little table in his room. The daylight was reflected in his clear pupils, which had contracted like a cat's eyes; he saw nothing and was aware of nothing. Twice he was sent for to come to the forest, but he didn't go. Only in the afternoon did he drag himself from the hard stool; he didn't touch the lunch left out for him, but went straight to the forest clearance. To the young forester who had been waiting so long for him he simply whispered, 'My brother's very ill,' without further explanation. Nor would he have been able to say more, or maybe it really was the truth for him at that moment. He instinctively felt the seriousness of the illness as an excuse for the rage and impotence which, tangled up inside him, had so completely drained him of strength that he could hardly take a step. He sat on an excavated tree stump, told the forester to do as he wished, and with head hanging waited for evening to set in. He was greatly astonished at the humiliating acts he had so recently performed; he had always regarded himself as a noble sort and it was hard for him to take in the fact that he had actually sat in a pine tree opposite the lighted window of the servants' quarters and with eyes wide open watched Malina and Michał making love.

He had wanted to climb that tree before, but it had seemed a bit inaccessible. However, that evening before the storm he had spotted some knots, which had got him up to the level of the window in a trice. He had been convulsed with fury ever since he had discovered Staś and Malwina's love-making by the lake; in the blazing heat he had crept after them, keeping at a close distance because, confident and carefree as they were, they never looked round once. By squinting a bit, through the network of trees he could clearly see their slowly moving shapes – the tall, thin stooping figure of Staś, and Malwina's yellow headscarf. There they went, hiding among the grey tree trunks, sneaking about among the bushes and low forest under-growth, while he went after them with a feeling in his heart which he had never felt before. He had gripped the re-volver in his pocket, and that was when it first occurred to him that he might make use of it. Anyway, he thought now, it turns out one wouldn't need a revolver to kill Staś.

His feelings when perched in the pine tree had not been so simple. He was watching not only his brother's lover, but also Michał, towards whom he had lately devel-oped some ill-defined feelings and strange suspicions. Of course he couldn't, nor did he want to substantiate these suspicions, but he regarded him with a certain curiosity. In any case he couldn't identify these feelings. They were like the storm, which had suddenly taken hold of the tree he was in and had bent it violently towards the ground.

Now he squeezed his eyes tight shut and kept repeat-ing, 'It's terrible, terrible!' These words, however, referred chiefly to the unlikely capacities that he had discovered in himself.

Three more days of relentless dread lay ahead of him. He couldn't get enough of a grip on himself to issue a single word in a normal voice. The simple instructions he gave Katarzyna were squeezed out through his teeth with the greatest difficulty, and it was just as impossible to speak to the forester or the workmen. He kept his mouth clamped shut all the time, and as much as possible, his eyelids too.

˴ On the third day he ran across Malwina in the forest. She was picking mushrooms, which had sprung up after the storm and were lurking under the bushes in great abundance. He was walking across a spinney, entirely divorced from his surroundings, when suddenly Malwina's purple-and-white striped apron came into view. He stopped and stepped back abruptly, but she smiled placidly and invitingly. Without a word, she drew herself up among the hazel branches and was soon standing tall and slender. Then she showed him her basket full of milk-white mushrooms and said, 'Look how many there are this year, sir.'

Bolesław had never seen her so close up, or on her own before. He kept staring at her straight nose, the perfect arch of her brows and her low forehead. She really was very beautiful. He went on staring at her in silence until finally she blushed and looked down at her basket of mushrooms.

'They'll be for supper tonight,' she said. 'Ola loves them.'

He saw the blush spread to her forehead, covering her entire face; he went on staring, until with an effort she turned her head away, not even looking at the mushrooms now. The simple country girl was embarrassed. She couldn't bear that cold, relentless, cat-like stare.

Suddenly Bolesław spoke, but still with great difficulty, in a strangled voice. 'Master Stanisław is very ill.'

'Yes, I know,' she replied, 'Katarzyna told me. I don't know, should I come and look after him?' she added uncertainly.

At first Bolesław said nothing, then he spluttered out: 'You cannot go on meeting.'

The blush turned a deep purple, she looked away and swung her basket feverishly.

'There's only Michał left now,' Bolesław pitched in.

She bridled and gave him a hard look. 'And what's it to you, sir?'

She leaped up and started to make a run for it, but Bolesław didn't want to let her go. He rushed after her, suddenly feeling the suppleness of his legs. He kept shouting, 'Stop! Stop!', but she was off, and ran headlong into a clearing, in the middle of which stood a single old pine. She leaned against it, breathing heavily and laughing open-mouthed, as far as the heavy breathing would let her.

'Oh, I'm so silly,' she said.

Bolesław, no less exhausted, stopped right beside her. He felt as if he should throw himself on top of her, throttle her and shut that trap of hers. But gradually his fury passed, and his breathing became regular; he stretched out his hand and touched her body. It was warm and silent in the forest. Then he leaned over and kissed her, and turning around suddenly walked off towards the work site at a calm, steady pace.

All his malice was gone; he spoke with ease, imparting some valuable instructions to the young forester, then sat on a stump, lit a cigarette and whistled softly. His eyes didn't close tight, they just blinked a bit.

That same evening he called in at Staś's room. It was the third day since the haemorrhage and Staś had recovered a little strength now, but he could hardly move and his pale white face remained impassive at the sight of his brother. It was already dark and the candles were burning. Bolesław walked about a bit by the piano. Staś took no notice of him. Bolesław wanted to keep moving, but he was arrested by the indifferent, aloof expression on the face lying on the pillows. The only thing apparent in Staś's compressed lips was pain; that alone gave his face a semblance of life. The fact that his brother was suffering and wasn't indifferent drew Bolesław to him with a sudden sense of communion. Neither of them spoke, and it seemed just as difficult for either of them to do so.

At last Staś raised his eyelids and gave his brother a dull stare, in which there was so much perspicacity that Bolesław looked away. It was a terrifying stare, lacklustre and final. Merely raising his deathly heavy eyelids was enough to make speech impossible. But Bolesław did feel capable of speaking; he thought it was the last time he would ever be able to talk to his brother on equal terms, his last chance to ask him some vital questions.

Resolutely he stepped up to the bed and put his hand on Stanisław's prominent collarbone. Meanwhile Staś had looked away, closed his eyes and turned his stare inward; he was back to being lifeless and indifferent.

'Do you know something about Basia? Something I don't know?' asked Bolesław quickly, keeping his hand where it was.

Staś raised his eyes again in pure amazement. 'About Basia?' he just managed to whisper.

'Yes, because you said ... you don't have a wife, that a wife ...'

'How could I know anything about Basia?' said Staś more confidently. 'I just said that, because ... that's what one says, ... because I don't have a wife.'

For a while Bolesław went on standing over his brother, waiting for him to say more, but nothing happened. He leaned a touch further forward, but Staś was silent; finally he opened his eyes and said quietly: 'Off you go now.'

Confused and distressed, Bolesław retreated to the door. Only from there did he see that under the piano, squeezed in against the wall and hidden behind the lyre-shaped pedal, sat Ola. Her blonde hair was sticking out like ears of corn around her little head, gleaming in the shadow of the instrument. Bolesław called to her, then felt shocked that she had been there all the time. But she calmly scrambled out from under the piano, clutching her inseparable doll. Bolesław took her by the hand and left the room, crossed the hall and went out onto the veranda. The evening was warm, damp and fragrant. Only now did he sense how very stuffy it was in Staś's room, and how pervasive the sickly smell of illness.

They stepped down from the lighted veranda and into the night, into the darkness, which suddenly enveloped them. In the darkness they could sense the trees they were passing, and it also felt as if a gentle, joyful breath of earth were fanning them, cloaked in black but watching over them. They crossed the familiar road and for the first time in many days stood at Basia's grave. Ola noticed that everything had changed greatly since they were last here. She no longer felt afraid, or bored – on the contrary, she enjoyed repeating the words after her father. Ever since Uncle Stanisław had arrived and told her so many important things the world had grown larger, and ever since Michał had been coming to play his accordion the world had grown beautiful.

Indeed, as they stood there among the birches they could hear the sound of his music nearby. Ola felt her father's hand tremble, then he fell to his knees and she heard him weeping with all his heart.

XI

Staś found Bolesław's question about Basia disturbing, though he had no wish, nor was he even able, to let it show. Having fallen into a weakened state of consciousness he just lay still, calm and silent. All he could hear was a loud buzzing, as if a swarm of bees had built their honeycombs in the bedstead. For lack of shutters or curtains the windows were draped in large headscarves, and there he lay in the dark, conscious of nothing but his own pain. His entire intake of life had suddenly been arrested, and everything external had ceased to exist; suddenly left to himself Staś had realised he was nothing but a wretched scrap of humanity, not even fit for death. Everything he had ever done was a pointless hullabaloo, and now only one thing really mattered: how to conceal the pain and reach oblivion. It all reminded him of the piano which he used to play so loud.

On the fourth day of his illness the piano had in fact been taken away; its owner had died, her heirs wanted to realise their property as soon as possible, and without a word of warning, one fine morning they drove up in front of the lodge. Bolesław tried in vain to explain about his brother's illness, but they didn't want to know. He had to agree to give up the instrument. The porters brought the daylight into the sick man's room; the scarves on the windows were lifted and Staś was surprised to see how fine and beautiful it was outside. Then Janek came in too, and all together they encircled the piano, mustered their strength and with a concerted effort lifted it into the air. Slowly they shifted the black box towards the door, tilted it upright and carried it out of Staś's sight, like a large black coffin … 'Mine won't be that big,' he thought. He was sorry to lose the piano. He had been feeling the urge to drag himself out of bed one of these days to strike up the Hawaiian song again, which might allow him to feel once again the staggering mass of all the things he would never see. It was easier to evoke that sea of things and to look down into the sweet abyss of the unknown to music. It made him feel a bit drunk, it made his head spin. But now, as he stared at the open door through which the piano had disappeared, he felt a flood of other things – the conclusive ending of everything that was not fear or pain.

So far he had not experienced any particularly onerous physical symptoms, but now sheer torment had set in. His emaciated body ached from lying down, but he couldn't move, for every movement cost him a huge effort and ended in pain, spreading from his back into his limbs. He couldn't eat at all. Katarzyna brought him clear soup or milk, and every other day she mixed ice-cream for him and from early morning he was disturbed by the noise of the machine grating at the ice with a great clatter. Although it disturbed him, this sound from the hall outside was also a source of joy. The clattering of the ice-box was the only sound that could reach him, bearing witness to a great big life still going on beyond his reach. He lay like a tree stump flung onto the riverbank by the current. He was like one of the withered branches he was always noticing on spruces and pines. Now he was just waiting for the final break with life.

He did get up again for a couple of days, with a very great effort indeed, though he managed to move about normally. He went down from the porch, crossed the road and went for a short walk into the forest. The next day he whistled and hummed as he shaved, just as on the day of his arrival at the lodge, and Bolesław even smiled as he listened to him whistling. 'Maybe he'll get better again?' he thought.

› But once he had been up for a couple of days, Staś had that stupid sensation of having lost something, which he couldn't shake off. He felt like someone who has worn a ring for years and years and leaves it on the wash-stand; he was dogged by the feeling of having lost some very ordinary, everyday object, and he couldn't think about anything else. It wasn't the lack of the piano, because he had managed to deal with its absence. It was some other, more serious loss, the loss of the element that until now had combined everything he saw and felt into one organic whole.

Now everything around him seemed to have scattered, like the beads of a rosary, like the glass pearls Miss Simons used to wear around her neck. He was still aware of the green light in the windows of his room each morning, but it no longer shone from the inside, it wasn't coming from within him, and on waking he would push it away resentfully; it did nothing to enlighten him, nor did it embody the essence of what he had so joyfully recognised earlier as a new discovery. The pines and lime trees, the rain and fine weather had all disintegrated, they were somewhere else, somewhere separate, tucked away rather nonsensically on another wavelength of his thoughts and senses.

It caused him intense suffering. Neither his illness, nor his lack of strength, nor his incapacity to consume any sort of food at all caused him quite so much pain as losing the entire world, which was turning into chaos and inertia before his very eyes.

He was still whistling and crooning, just as on the first days after his arrival, but even then the whistling had been a way of clouding over reality, from which some new shape for the world was supposed to emerge. But now, as everything went spinning to the rhythm of the song he was humming, he knew that nothing of the kind would ever surface, that it had all collapsed and this was the end – and that made him burn with a worse pain than in his sickly lungs and bowels.

Whenever he stopped humming there was a fearful hush. All of a sudden the house, the forest and the veranda were filled with an emphatic silence. The rustle of pine needles was the only backdrop to his fear and suffering. He got into bed, and each thing that wounded his heart, each thought of loneliness, of the end, of fear, came separately, wildly stabbing him at random – in the head, in the heart, and then at once moved off to make way for another.

This was so terrible that he summoned all his strength just to keep moving, to hum, or to sit on the veranda with the others. Once when he entered the kitchen, the smell of boiled potatoes made him feel violently sick, nor could the murmuring flames catch his attention. He retreated to his bedroom, but he was starting to overcome the fears and weaknesses. Time and again Bolesław noticed a smile on his lips (it really was a smile, not a grimace), but suddenly the smile would vanish, and the expression left on Staś's face was a dreadful mess. Bolesław followed these changes with dismay.

Staś was sitting at lunch with them, but Bolesław could see from his face that he wouldn't get better now. He was horrified by the deadness of his drooping eyes, which didn't even liven up when laughing. They were eating lunch on the porch. Staś was sitting with his back to the light, and Bolesław kept casting short, searching glances at his shaded face. It had slipped away into a vague shadow, it had ceased to represent a person; his brother was dying. Clearly they all sensed it, for even little Ola sat very quietly, making large round eyes at her uncle. But Staś didn't notice their stares; he kept looking around at the forest behind him, and then a gleam would shine in his blue eyes, like a smoky reflection in two dust-caked mirrors. He laughed and, God knows why, started telling them about Miss Simons again. He had had a letter from her that day; she was in Davos again and described everything that was going on at the sanatorium. He remembered a dress she used to wear, and described it in detail to Ola, who listened, staring intently at her uncle and finding it hard to swallow her stale bread; Staś ate nothing and drank only milk. The dress was green, edged in green fur, with a short green velvet jacket to match, with golden stripes. Just like the lake in the forest.

'Just like the lake in the forest,' said Staś, and suddenly glanced at Bolesław, who turned away. This simple comparison reminded them of bitter scenes, and at the same time proved how utterly meaningless they were in view of the change of situation.

When Ola had left the table, Staś asked Bolesław to bury him in the birch grove beside Basia. It might not happen immediately – today he felt fine. He didn't want to mention it to his brother again as there was something rather affected and pompous about it, all very unpleasant; pure showing off. But surely he didn't fancy a twenty-something kilometre trek after all that, for what? Better to bury him right here. 'Won't it be painful for you to have me so near?'

Bolesław said nothing throughout, but after the final question he felt that indeed it would be very painful for him. A new grave beside Basia's would be a great burden for him. He would prefer to take Staś somewhere far away, and then not to have to think about it; he would rather not have those graves constantly in sight. But it occurred to him that he could easily transfer to another job, somewhere round Suchedniów, for example, or to Szydłów. Then he would leave the graves here, and it would be hard for him to come and visit them. He would come once a year, or once every two years, perhaps. Yes, Staś could be buried in the birch grove.

, Meanwhile Staś was sitting at table opposite him smoking a cigarette; a grey thread of smoke was escaping like breath and dissolving on the heated air, against the backdrop of the trees across the road. For a short while they were silent, then Staś smiled and said, 'And after my death do help yourself to Malina.'

At that Bolesław slammed his fist on the table, but then restrained himself, frowned fiercely, turned away and started stuffing his beard into his mouth, which, recently trimmed by Janek, was too short and he couldn't chew it. This made Staś laugh heartily but he said nothing more. He could feel the afternoon sun warming his back, and the sensation of warmth filling him with bliss.

That day he saw Malina again, and the next day too. A couple of days later he lay down for good and all.

Malwina never came into the room where he lay; it wasn't appropriate. As soon as he took to his bed all contact between them ceased. This did not cause Staś excessive pain; he didn't need Malwina's actual presence – he could imagine her perfectly, and spent days on end thinking about her. Not even thinking, just comparing everything he remembered with everything he had learned from this strong, quiet, loving girl. He knew she was telling lies and that Michał was really her man, that she would marry him and live to a great age, untroubled and robust. He imagined her in old age, common and ordinary, with none of her beauty left. 'Now that's what a life should be,' he said to himself.

. Each day now he just lay there getting weaker and weaker, amid the humming of the imaginary hive, in the light of the veiled windows, and he could see it was beautiful sunny July weather. He felt rather abandoned now, as Bolesław was out all day, Katarzyna rarely looked in on him, and Ola preferred to play outside; she was bored with her sickly uncle's smile. One day towards the end of July, when he was already very weak and only felt like looking out of the window as sunset approached, he sat up a bit and propped the pillows higher, which took him a great deal of effort. Sitting up at last, he gazed at the sunlit window frame. The leaves of the nearest trees dangled down the glass and beyond stretched the same never-ending scene: tree trunks, greyness, forest. There wasn't a soul in the entire house or courtyard – everyone had gone off somewhere, and it was very quiet. Yet Staś didn't find the summer silence oppressive; it was full of warmth and benevolence. He was lost in thought, about what he didn't know himself; his bones no longer ached, which brought him a sense of well-being, as amid the dormant silence he melted into the summer afternoon.

Then he heard footsteps crossing the road and coming up to the porch. The steps kept coming nearer and then moving away again; he recognised the tread, which he had so often waited for over this summer: it was Malina. His heart thumped like a hammer, there was a roaring in his temples and cold sweat coated his brow, his back and shoulders. But she didn't come into the house; instead, she withdrew and he could hear her departing footsteps running down the side of the house and off into the forest.

Then a high-pitched voice rang out – Malwina was singing. It was the first time he had ever heard her sing, but knew at once that it was her. She drew out the long, droning notes with trills. She sang better and finer than is typical of our country folk, but lost none of the pure simplicity of sound. The top five notes came downwards, then rose five tones again and soared on a high note at the top, persistently repeated with the full force of her lungs. From the very first phrase an echo went ringing around the forest, blending in with the singing and acting like an accompaniment with choral undertones, creating a harmony.

The primitive passion of this song sent a shudder through the invalid. His strength gathered as he strained to listen. He knew Malwina was singing for him, and that her song was an alternative for everything she had to say to him. This was what she really wanted to say, not those monotone answers to his meaningless questions.

'The first close of day
Is my look that's to say
I don't want to know you no longer ...'

Among the high-pitched, drawn-out notes he recognised these words. His mouth fell open, all at once he could hear and see so many things. His childhood came to mind, and his mother; they were sailing along on a broad silver river, then everything went into a dream. He was kissing his mother, though he knew she was long since dead, and then he was caressing her fingers, soft and plump. The silver of the river mingled with the light coming from the windows opposite his bed, and with the song of his unseen lover.

She repeated the first verse twice, then broke off abruptly, and for a long time there was silence. Staś thought she wouldn't sing any more. He leaned back against the pillows, turning slightly on his side, so he could see the entire world float past his eyes slantwise, a tangle of greyness, coolness and greenery. In vain he sought his mother's eye, just as on his first day at school, but he could see eyes everywhere, half-veiled beneath leaflike lids. No, his mother's eyes were different – these were the dejected pupils of Malwina.

Suddenly the stream of illusions was torn apart as the simple song began again; Malwina had come up closer, she was very near by, and the notes and words of her song were almost tangible, physically entering Staś's room, though he didn't have the strength to get a grip on them.

> 'The second close of day
> Is the vault far away
> About which I ever must wander ...'

She repeated each verse twice without stopping, shifting into a slightly higher key, but returning towards the end to that persistent, high-pitched note.

The setting sun permeated the woods, flashing among the pine trees and the forest aisles, lining them in rosy vapours. Staś saw his own figure in the forest, tall as in a fairy tale, and knew that his judgement had come. It was a bit like the uprising in which his grandfather took part, and a bit like a dream. The rosy clouds were filling the forest and changing into birds, singing in Malina's voice, '... the vault far away, the vault far away', and Staś saw the forest transform itself into a sky-high wooden structure, over which he went leaping, nimble as a squirrel, while Malina was a tiny little figure, as if far off in the mountains, moving along the very bottom of the wooden tower, and it was impossible for them to come together.

Suddenly, from beyond the woods the silver river appeared, and he felt extraordinary relief as he gently slid across its steely expanse, glassy tracts of water unyielding to his touch.

Malina fell silent. He became aware of the room again; the empty corner where the piano had stood now weighed on him like a bereavement. On his lips a salty-sweet taste, a sickening odour struck his palate. Another haemorrhage on its way, he thought.

He heard steps right by the front door and someone leaning against the lime tree that grew beneath his window. He was afraid he wouldn't be able to bear the singing so keen and raw, right under his window. Pressing both hands to his pounding heart he cried out, 'Malina, Malina ...'

But it wasn't a proper shout, just a plaintive, dried-up whisper. Malwina couldn't hear him, and she might have thought Master Stanisław couldn't hear her singing at all. But it was clear she did think he was listening, for she checked her voice and didn't sing as loud. Yet this made her singing even more intense, like a plaintive lullaby.

At the first note Staś went floating out onto the river again, as it ran around a bend. As she went on singing the banks of the river contracted, folding on top of each other, trying to smother him. He struggled to draw breath.

> 'The third close of day
> Is the stone slab so grey
> Beneath which I ever must slumber …'

Before she had finished singing the same verse twice, her breathing ever softer and deeper, all the illusions had gone. The longest to linger was the sensation of his mother's presence, but even that passed. He woke up leaning against the pillows with the taste of blood on his lips, his eyes fixed on the carmine spaces between the trees. He was deeply struck by the words, 'the stone slab so grey, beneath which I ever must slumber'. And for the first time with heart and soul he could feel death within him. It was as if his entire essence had clouded around him in the form of a damp, reddish mist and was slowly dissipating, leaving a terrible void.

> '… and the stone slab so grey
> Beneath which I ever must slumber …'

With the last of his strength he called back his departing life, and this time it did return. But he knew it wasn't for long; he calmed down a bit as he heard the footsteps retreating. He didn't see Malina. Then, as he repeated the words about the stone slab, he felt childish resentment as he imagined really having to sleep for long, long years in a dark vault beneath a grey stone slab. And he began to weep like a child, until his pillow was wet with tears.

When Bolesław came home that evening, he told him for the first time that he didn't want to die so young. Bolesław was alarmed, but soon got used to it, as Staś kept repeating these words until the very end.

XII

After Staś's death Bolesław realised that finally his own life had sorted itself out. With his brother's absence came peace and quiet, a feeling of harmony with everything around him, which he hadn't had before. All the stopping and starting had finally come to an end, and above all he felt great relief – it was easy to work, and with very little trouble he wrote a letter to the administration asking to be transferred to another forest; he knew he was well regarded and that they wouldn't move him to a worse post. The autumn days were fine, the sun shone relentlessly, the leaves were yellow and the colour itself had a warm and calming effect. The lake, so black in summer, had now changed colour, becoming much more pleasant and alluring ever since it had started to reflect the pale trees, now dying, but destined to regenerate. Now Bolesław was meeting regularly with Malwina by the lake; there was nothing passionate about their meetings, but with every passing day they brought Bolesław greater fondness for life. Not that he was distressed to hear the news she had just given him, namely that Michał wanted to marry her in October. 'That's good,' he said, and bit at his beard, which had grown again. 'That's good. In any case I'm leaving for a new post. I'm to have it from the first of November or from Christmas, and you'll have your wedding before then, so I'll see you married before I go. Are you going to live in Michał's village, or will you both live here?'

She didn't know where she would live; either way, somewhere in the forest, for sure – whether here or there, it was all the same to her. Then she added, 'It's a pity you're leaving, sir, it'll be sad without you and Ola. Only Master Stanisław will be left.'

Staś had in fact been buried in the birch grove, as he had requested, though there had been more than a little difficulty with it. This time there was no excuse of floods – he had died on a fine summer's day after rain, when the road to town was at its most passable. But Bolesław had stuck to his guns. There were no outsiders at the funeral apart from the priest, and the whole thing had passed off with remarkable speed and simplicity. Janek and Michał had carried the coffin on a stretcher, the priest had sprinkled holy water and consecrated the ground alongside Basia's burial mound, then they had buried him, vigorously heaping up the earth; next day, with the help of Olek and Edek, they had made a birchwood fence and a short, stout birchwood cross. No one had wept at the funeral, not even Ola, and everyone had gone straight back to their occupations, because it was high summer and they all had work to do. The priest had harvests on his patch, and Bolesław was busy with autumn fellings. Malina was doing the laundry for her mother, Janek and Michał. Only Ola had nothing to do, and sat all alone in the empty room her uncle had been carried out of, which hadn't yet been cleaned. The little room seemed quite large now that neither the piano nor her uncle's body were in it, and Ola found it rather unnerving. To build up her courage she started talking to her doll. That was how Bolesław found her when he got home; she insisted that from now on she would live in her uncle's room, so the next day Bolesław ordered the floor to be cleaned with lye, the walls to be freshly whitewashed and his daughter's bed to be placed where the piano had been. A new, rather intense but quiet life began to flourish in the dead man's room.

Bolesław didn't go straight home from the lakeside after hearing Malina's news that her wedding to Michał would happen in October. He wanted to make the best of the beautiful evening, to wander about the forest, looking in here and there; or rather what he really wanted to do was to listen to the thoughts and images stirring inside him, leaving a gentle hint of intoxication. It really did feel like intoxication. Love had come out of the blue, and for a short while had changed what was going on inside him, making him quietly cheerful. But it had all started in a dreadful way.

Staś had died in the afternoon, and at once the old women, Janek's mother, Katarzyna and Maryjka, had come and bustled about over washing and dressing the body. Although it was light outside, candles were lit, then the windows were draped in headscarves again. Staś was dressed in two rather tight pairs of pyjamas, one blue and one green, one on top of the other, and it was hard to undress him. Yet the old women managed to unwrap the corpse and laid it out naked on the counterpane. Bolesław was in the room throughout, standing in a corner, mournfully watching the preparations. He was ruminating over what he wanted to say to someone, but there was no one to say it to; nor was he really sure what he should say or what exactly he wanted to say; there probably weren't any words for the things he was thinking. In any case, everything going through his mind was bad – hard, bitter and unruly. He had had enough of it – though he wasn't entirely sure what 'it' was.

Staś lay on the bed, his extreme emaciation pitiful to see: his skin, white and pitted with rough tubercular lesions, was a tight, perfect fit for his narrow chest; his arms lay inert and at ease, the hands much darker than the body. His nipples had gone almost completely black, shrunk by the chill of evening and the chill of death. His

171

face was covered with a handkerchief, while another red peasant kerchief bound up his drooping jaw. But no facial expression was needed: the abandoned body, thin, limp and dry as sticks, was all too expressive. The old women fetched a bowl of warm water and slowly, ceremonially dipped a sponge in it, murmuring prayers as they rubbed down Staś's wretched chest.

At that point Malina came in. Bolesław tensed and took a step forward. Malina stood at the foot of the bed, wanting to stand and gaze at the shameless nakedness of the corpse stretched out before her, but the old women wouldn't let her.

'Fetch some more water and vinegar,' said her mother. But she refused to budge. She looked avidly at Staś, then stepped forward and took the handkerchief from his face; she gave a gentle shriek, or rather sigh, but very quietly. Then she stepped back a pace and started trying to sponge him with the others.

Bolesław took another pace forward and said firmly, 'What's Malina doing here?'

Malina turned around and stared at him. Her eyes were dull, almost white, with narrowed pupils; she stared as if blind, and her large, chiselled features looked almost as dead as Staś's pinched face. She stared around her and turned away, her breasts quivering in her tightly fitting bodice. She was strong and sturdy, expressionless and indifferent.

'Malina, please leave.'

She didn't answer. She picked up the bucket of water and set it down nearer Staś's head, then plunged a long white towel in it.

'Malina, please leave at once,' repeated Bolesław in a hushed, almost desperate tone.

172

But she went on nonchalantly drawing out the towel, then wrung it out, unwound it and covered Staś's chest with it. The black nipples were hidden beneath the white expanse of the towel.

'Get out!' screamed Bolesław suddenly, and grabbing her by the arm he pushed her forcefully towards the door. She stopped and stared at him again, then she opened the door, went out, and closed it behind her. Throughout it felt as if the terrible words 'Get out!' were still shuddering and swaggering in the room. At once Bolesław came to his senses and bounded after her. Outside he was amazed to find it was already dark. He didn't know which way she had gone, so he softly called out her name a couple of times. He ran down the porch steps and walked briskly over to the courtyard, where he almost tripped over the girl. She was standing impassively beneath a tree, leaning against its white trunk.

Quickly Bolesław said, 'I'm sorry, I don't know what I'm doing, you see, I didn't mean it, Staś is dead, Master Stanisław is dead, he was my only brother, we're going to bury him beside my wife …'

There stood Malwina, large as life, impassive, saying nothing. He could sense that she wasn't even looking at him. He touched her: she was warm, her body was hot. He thought of Staś's cold body, of his thin ribcage, lying torpid on the counterpane. He grasped Malwina's arms and suddenly burying his face in her proud, hot bosom, he burst into a fit of weeping. He felt her hands on his head as she pressed him to her. But he didn't weep for long; suddenly he tore away from her and hurried home, where the old women had finished washing Staś and were dressing him in his foreign Sunday-best.

Now, as he walked along the edge of the forest, Bolesław no longer thought of that scene, although for some time he had gone on seeing it vividly. It had often come back to haunt him, thrusting itself into view; meanwhile, his only conscious thoughts were of his new job, the autumn fellings, the impending move and the fact that something needed to be done to care for Ola. The pines had not changed into autumn dress, except that flimsy flakes of reddish bark were floating down from the treetops. He ran into Edek and Olek; Maryjka's cows had strayed into the forest and got into the courtyard, so they would have to drive them home. The brown cows were stealing their way through the yellow hazel thickets, with the boys after them, calling out now and then and cracking a short string whip. For a while he followed in their tracks, then stopped at his favourite spot. Maryjka's cottage was drowning in mists and shades of yellow, and it was impossible to see that it was just a clearing. He felt as if he had come out onto broad, open fields. He watched as the large cows, then the boys went down the sandy path. Their silhouettes were blurring as the early autumn evening set in. Peace, peace – almost happiness.

Zakopane, Atma, 1932

The Mill on the River Utrata*

Blue, blue heaven,
Dark, dark shadow …
Negro spiritual

Not long ago I had to help arrange the funeral of one of our country neighbours, and in doing so I wandered deep into the deserted cemetery at Sulistrzyce, a village beyond the suburbs of Warsaw. The cemetery is unremarkable, with only a few fine trees whose branches overhang some time-worn burial mounds covered in lush grass. Here and there broken crosses protrude, with the remains of inscriptions on them. In this wretched rural backwater my eye was caught by a monument standing in a corner of the cemetery. It was a large black stone, with two names engraved on it. One was that of a once noted, even fashionable writer and poet whom no one remembers nowadays. The other was at one time very prominent among Warsaw's property-owning classes, and would also have been forgotten by now, had it not lived on as a relic of generations past in

---

* *Translator's note*: Where the characters' names appear in more than one form (e.g. Jadwiga/Jadwisia/Łowiecka/Mrs Łowiecka) the translation follows the original Polish text throughout.

the name of one of the capital's largest construction firms. The young age of both the deceased and the proximity of the dates of their deaths – only a couple of weeks apart – the isolation of this splendid monument, on which the rain, wind and frost of the Mazovian plain had already begun to wreak their destructive art, and finally the addendum to the inscription, stating that it was 'erected in memory of his friends by Desmond King, poet', greatly stirred my imagination.

Soon I had struck up several friendships in the district, which is not far from the place where I now reside, and I found out everything there was to be known from the locals about both of the deceased. It is a great deal, and at the same time very little, because people form their opinions imprecisely, seeing only what they want to see. There were certain statements and accounts of the events that I had to temper, and others that I had to fill in on the strength of my own intuition. And so, as I broadened the range of my conversations, the lives of these two people surfaced before me – three even, for I found out a lot about Desmond King as well. Any person's life, even if it had no particularly unusual features, can be interesting and informative if described in detail. The lives of Juliusz Zdanowski and Karol Hopfer were indeed remarkable, even though they were lived against the sparse backdrop of a village on the outskirts of Warsaw. That, at least, was my view, so I decided to devote some time to writing about them. I may not have done it in as much detail as they merited, but I lacked more precise information which, even where I had it, I often had to supplement rather liberally, for which I beg the reader's pardon.

*

This then is their story.

It was an established custom for Julek Zdanowski to spend the holidays at Krzywizna. Krzywizna was not far from Warsaw, but like many such places it was right off the beaten track. To get there one travelled to an out-of-town station, then came a drive of some three or four kilometres across a sandy vale, next there was a small birch wood, and then on a green carpet of clover loomed a small red-brick manor house. As soon as one passed through the walls – like the drawbridge of a medieval fortress – Warsaw was immediately forgotten, a million miles away. A permanent inhabitant of Warsaw would never guess how many such places there are just outside the capital, how many manor houses there are within a radius of a few miles from Szymanów or Radziwiłłów, where nature preserves the most primitive elements of rusticity, the primal state, the elemental, or whatever one wishes to call it, as if saving it up for the right moment to replenish the degenerating capital.

Inside the walls was a large courtyard overgrown with chickweed, a vast stable and barn made of rough stone, and areas overgrown with bushy elm and elder, with an unexpected pastoral idyll beyond: a rectangular white house with bright windows, an apple orchard and a pond half-covered in duckweed, on which there floated an old tub of a boat. Surrounded by a jungle of lilac, the banks of the pond were covered in reeds, and there were times of year when it was very pretty: in the summer twilight, for instance, as the sky was going pink, or even in winter around Christmas, when the water, not yet frozen over, looked black as agate next to its snow-covered banks. But most often the pond looked run-of-the-mill, with white and saddlebacked ducks swimming about on it; sometimes fair-sized roaches would toss their white bellies out of the water in trying to escape a pike. Running off the pond was a small stream, hidden at first among the dark green foliage of nettles, lilacs and burdocks – then emptying into the greenish subsoil of a levee; peeping out here and there it created little pools in the fields, each one full of reeds and brambles, and around St Peter's Day, wild ducks as well. In spite of its modest appearance, this stream was one of the main tributaries of the nearby river Utrata.

Altogether it was not without charm, especially towards evening when the workers were back from the fields, and the spacious courtyard, carpeted in chickweed, was filling with life at the end of the day's labour. The fields became deserted, veiled in blue twilight, the chill intensified, and with it the scent of clover; birds could be seen diving for cover in the undergrowth and shrubbery. That was Julek's favourite time for a walk on the modest fields, not at all flattened by excessive cultivation. If Karol was at home he would accompany Julek, and they would go for a long walk along the boundary strip between bird's-foot and beets, discussing matters far removed from this secluded village. So much so that on returning to the manor house sometimes it seemed odd to them that ordinary life was still going on there; water would be gushing into bright buckets and it would take ages for the horses to draw it, gently snorting the while. They would sit on the porch or the balcony overlooking the garden and drink buttermilk, which the kindly Mrs Sikorska brought them. On Sundays there was invariably chicken, and Karol was served a little vodka. But he was so often away that Julek's strongest image was of sitting alone on the balcony gazing at the spreading apple trees, with black-and-white bean flowers blossoming beneath them.

The scent of bean flowers and clover came to be the very essence of the fine summer days spent at the manor. Krzywizna was the remains of a once wealthy estate, which over three generations had been built up, reached its peak and then collapsed, leaving Karol, the last offshoot of the property-owning line, with this small scrap of land and some lordly habits. The fortune had at one time been so vast that Karol was still living on its remnants, and was always discovering some forgotten house in Radom that had finally been sold or some mortgage that had happily been repaid at a time of need. In any case, Karol's needs were not great: he didn't have a car, he didn't travel abroad, and what he and his friends squandered on vodka did not come to much. He was fond of horses, but there were never more than four in his stables. He did have one rather strange whim: a very good cook, whom he paid as much each month as all the other servants put together – only to have buttermilk for supper and meat and potato soup for lunch. So the cook, Mr Kletkie, spent all day wandering by the pond, and once he had taken up position, would gaze at the clouds reflected in the water. Sometimes he took Karol's fishing rod with him and cast a line among the reeds, but he rarely caught anything but frogs.

No city on earth leads such a chaotic life as Warsaw, and Karol Hopfer was a true son of Warsaw. His method of time-keeping was truly exasperating. He had reached the point of not wearing a watch, and his doing so while living out of town led to constant confusion. He never arrived on the promised train, and the cabriolet, harnessed with a pair of sturdy greys, with old Łukasz on the coach box, would stand at the station for days on end in the shadow of a great poplar tree. It wasn't a complete waste of time, for through boredom old Łukasz had redis-covered the art of reading, into which Karol's grand-mother had initiated him many moons ago, and would read the *Morning Express* from cover to cover, borrowed from the local kiosk, whose owner he had befriended.

The strangest thing of all was that Karol didn't really do anything – he had no proper occupation. He had a great many friends of the most varied age and calibre, whose business he took care of like his own; he had a great many women, among whom he had to steer his way carefully (for this reason he kept his Warsaw flat a strict secret), and once in a while he had to 'chase money', as he put it, which took up a lot of his time in these difficult days. Sometimes he 'chased money' all the way to Lublin or Lwów, Częstochowa or Katowice – and Krzywizna got nothing but telegrams: 'Am in such and such a place, arriving such and such a day'. Whenever Julek received a telegram from Katowice, Karol would already be in Kraków, and never arrived at the appointed hour, of course.

Once he finally got there, though, life at Krzywizna was merry: he told stories, chatted and joked, more per-haps than was appropriate for the 'squire', as he was still called. And almost every time he arrived after a long ab-sence he brought some new fad, some curious idea or new friend with him. So it was that he had once brought Mr Kletkie back from a journey to Kraków, and so in the last holidays, somewhere in Warsaw, he had come across Desmond King, who for a time was a key figure at Krzy-wizna, although he was just a humble black man who taught English and elocution and had strayed along paths known only to himself as far as Warsaw. There he had been starving to death, reciting poetry – Longfellow's and his own – on the radio and giving lessons wherever he could, for he really did speak English beautifully, but without being too proud to give an occasional demonstration of Negro dances in some second-rate cinema or small cabaret. Now he was supposed to be teaching Karol English, or rather reminding him of his studies of long ago, by reading the English classics with him. And so one day Desmond King had arrived at Krzywizna holding a briefcase containing a pair of pyjamas, two shirts and a faded beret. He gave Karol three or four lessons; at first people treated him as an oddity, and then they got used to him, especially when it turned out he was a Catholic and a regular churchgoer. Out of boredom he picked up a smattering of Polish and finally ended up spending whole days on end by the pond, with a rod in his hand. However, he always chose the opposite bank to Mr Kletkie, and somehow was never able to befriend the cook, though their common lack of purpose and fondness for roach-fishing should have brought them together.

That summer was especially intense for Julek. He had passed his final exams in philosophy and was preparing for his doctorate. As the subject of his thesis he had chosen the works of Sts Thomas Aquinas and Francis of Assisi, and had decided to contrast the full richness of St Thomas's teaching with St Francis's meagre offering. Julek's religious belief had lately found a quiet, deep and already very confident conduit in his soul. He was no longer visited, as a few years ago, by any paroxysms of fear or tragic doubts. Whenever he had to make yet another decision about himself and the path he should

181

take, he could easily raise his thoughts from the dust in which he lived to the Lord on high. He called it 'putting oneself straight inside', and he would say, 'we only have to put ourselves straight enough and our heads will be plunged into the enlivening and salutary current of eternity'. Karol, with whom he sometimes talked about such matters, used to say Julek had the Lord God at his beck and call. And even though it was a joke, it was apt for the happy certainty that thrived in Julek's soul.

Julek and Karol were such good friends, and had been for so long that they took up even the most intimate topics, such as religious feelings. On this subject Karol was troubled by certain worries and problems, whenever between excursions to Warsaw he sat for a while on the balcony at Krzywizna, and in the rare moments when he was surrounded by the silence of a country evening. Forgetting his own fits and starts, Julek treated these problems of Karol's with a certain contempt, typical of those who possess total conviction and have found a safe harbour once and for all. Julek couldn't restrain himself – regarding it as proof of his faith – from displaying to Karol the superiority of his own religious stance, and would dismiss all his friend's doubts with a wave of his hand. For there were doubts too – alongside the purely religious issues, alongside mystical experiences Karol ranked some plainly sexual emotions. He compared his act of charity towards Desmond with the exploits of St Francis of Assisi, and supplemented his vague understanding of St Thomas with images of Platonic idealism and the fire-bearing angels of the neo-Platonists.

'It's a muddle, a complete muddle!' Julek would assert in conclusion of such conversations, most conspicuously pursing his narrow lips.

'Oh, my dear fellow, does it really matter?' Karol would say dismissively. 'All the same, I'm not going to make something up like everyone else out there! But where is the truth? Either we shall find out on the other side, or else no one will ever know.'

'We shall find out,' Julek would mumble, pointing his chin upwards, 'we shall, but I pray it's not too late.'

"The parish church of Krzywizna, where Julek conducted his rites of worship throughout the summer, was not far away. It was a very small parish, covering one other manor house besides Krzywizna, a hamlet located next to the church, and the mills along the nearby river Utrata. The church was old, but plain, surrounded by acacias which only looked fine in their brief flowering period. Behind the church stood the presbytery, a wooden cottage rather like a Russian villa, completely overgrown with wild vines. Beyond that lay the cemetery, which all but blended into the gardens of the tiny hamlet of Sulistrzyce. To this minute parish old, ailing priests were sent for a rest, or as a prelude to their final retirement. So now there was a white-haired, ugly old fellow in residence, with huge glasses and a raucous voice; his name was Father Górski. His hands shook as he raised the chalice, he used to take his handkerchief out of his pocket during mass to wipe his brow and blow his nose on, and he was barely able to turn around to face the congregation in order to say his quavering *Dominus vobiscum*. Julek had got used to this church and this priest by this time, although he could have placed much greater demands on his confessor. Julek valued his own sophisticated brand of Catholicism very highly and rightly regarded the view of the world which he had achieved as a great treasure, so it

183

was hard for him to bare his soul before a simple little priest. Yet he regarded it as an act of humility which he should make himself perform. He made his confession to Father Górski as mortification for his proud spirit, as a special exercise to refresh his reclusive godliness.

Karol used to make mild fun of all these rituals. For two days before such penitence Julek would be moody and out of sorts all day, and would shut himself in his room in the evening with a look on his face, as Karol put it, as if he had drunk castor oil. But on his return from church his face would have changed, his mane would be sticking up again, in token of his confident superiority over his surroundings. In short, Julek would be back to normal, and would respond to Karol's varied and complex questions and Desmond's helplessness with the slight smile of someone who has been let into a secret.

The summer was exceptionally fine that year. The trees and flowers at Krzywizna had sprouted all the more exuberantly as there was no one eager to cut them back or train them in any manner. They grew as the good Lord intended, filling the hollow by the pond with a green-and-pink sheen. First the apple trees blossomed, then the daisies, then the peonies, and lastly the roses, which grew in abundance. Over the little bridge on the far side of the pond a small hazel thicket was growing into a copse, and one could spend whole hours there, with the water, the roses, and the plain white house in view. Inside the house was bright, clean and quiet. There was cretonne-covered furniture and a great many books scattered about here and there. In the attic was Desmond's little room with the famous sofa on which more than one 'great man' had slept in the past, and next to the anteroom were Julek's and Karol's rooms. Aware of Julek's devout faith, Mrs

Sikorska had hung a huge, gilt-framed portrait of Pius IX
above his bed. A small black cross, Julek's personal property, stood out against the whitewashed wall at the head
of his bed. In a simple earthenware jug there were always
roses or wild flowers. Everything in here exuded the
tranquillity for which Desmond so envied Julek. He, by
contrast, with only the help of his pyjamas, three shirts
and a beret, and books brought up from downstairs, had
managed to create the epitome of chaos in his little room
upstairs. Mrs Sikorska and her helper, Genowefa the kitchen maid, couldn't help wondering how he managed it.

Part of Desmond's appeal for Karol may perhaps have
lain in the fact that he possessed an equally limited understanding of the concepts of time and space. He was
capable of coming in late for lunch from just in front of
the house, and whenever his question, 'Am I late?' was
answered in the affirmative, he was greatly amazed. He
regarded the Poles as very ill-mannered people. His lack
of punctuality provoked the cook into burning all his
soups.

One day in June Karol had come back from a particularly long and tedious journey to Wilno, where he was
involved in litigation over a bequest; it had been pouring
with rain for a week and both permanent inhabitants of
Krzywizna were bored to tears. They rejoiced at Karol's
arrival, and all of a sudden that afternoon there was an
excited, unusually jolly atmosphere. Karol summoned Mr
Kletkie, who set aside his rod reluctantly, as the fish were
biting well just then, and spent some time conferring with
him on what to have for supper.

'Well, your Lordship,' said Kletkie, emphasising 'your
Lordship' with specially fulsome intonation, 'I would rec-
ommend some of our good old-fashioned vol-au-vents.'

Kletkie's manner of speaking was as ornate as the get-up he wore on Sundays. Now, too, he was at pains to display stocking-clad legs and chequered plus-fours, while stroking his neatly trimmed moustache. On his neck he had a goitre which had appeared, if one could take his word for it, as the result of a 'high C sharp', sung at full voice on a frosty morning somewhere 'in the depths of Russia', and in his right eye there was a leucoma, which made it hard to tell which direction he was looking in.

Of course, the idea of some good old-fashioned vol-au-vents was not at all well received, but to Karol's sharp rebuke Mr Kletkie simply replied that a horse may have four legs, yet it stumbles. So they resorted to buttermilk, with which Karol knocked back one cognac after another, while Desmond kept him company.

The conversation came round to Father Górski. Karol told a couple of stories about the funny old man. Apparently the old fellow had a single obsession: in the course of the year he dispatched as many novenas as possible to St Anthony, Sts Peter and Paul, to the Transfiguration, and to the Sacred Heart – all asking to be granted the chance on this earth to see a real saint. Not to have the ghost of a dead, canonised saint appear to him, but a living saint of flesh and blood, who through his real, earthly existence bore witness to the might of the Catholic Church.

They spoke in French. Desmond was not in the least surprised by Father Górski's plan; on the contrary he regarded it as entirely natural. The church has its saints in every era, even if no one is aware of their existence, apart from their confessor, perhaps. If a saint were to come to Father Górski for confession, he would surely be able to recognise him, all the more since he himself, apparently, led a very saintly way of life.

'Yes,' said Julek in reply, 'but in everyday life a saint is a perfectly ordinary person. If one were sitting among us right now, his heroic virtues would not proclaim themselves to us so clearly that we would throw ourselves on our knees before him. In my view saintliness really depends on not creating the appearances of saintliness – it's rather a matter of commonplace virtues. It isn't hard to blow your horn at Easter, but to keep on placing your head beneath the yoke day after day – now that's a real virtue!'

Desmond protested, saying, 'Saintliness is something so unusual, something so exceptional, so out of the ordinary, that it must be immediately self-evident. Father Górski is right – I too would like to see a saint.'

Then Karol threw in his twopenny worth. 'Well, I think a saint must be distinct from other mortals for his tranquillity. Just think what human life is like – take mine, for example. I travel all over Poland on business, but maybe I only do it to try and forget that the night is always very black, and one's soul is even blacker. To avoid looking at the sky, to avoid what is happening inside oneself – that takes a great effort. It's like the Arab who was told that for his whole life he would be happy and successful and would enjoy all kinds of prosperity, so long as he never thought about a camel – of course he thought of nothing but camels! So, too, a man dreams up thousands of things in order not to think of the eternal night, or to put it bluntly, he thinks of nothing but the night.'

Julek smiled. 'He who thinks of nothing but the night has not seen the day,' he said. 'But you started on something completely different. You said a saint could be recognised by his tranquillity.'

'Yes, indeed. Only by his tranquillity, like yours. I think you're rather saintlike on the whole. Ha ha ha, we must let Father Górski know there's a little saint at Krzywizna. Don't you like it?'

'I think you've had too many cognacs,' said Julek with a touch of irritation.

'Yes, yes,' cried Karol eagerly. 'Just look at him, Mr King! He's a little saint, *un petit saint*, small, but saintly!' And Karol began to laugh uncontrollably, pointing at the pursed lips of his friend, for whom Desmond had to take up the defence. 'But,' said Karol, calming down, 'I get the feeling there's a basic misunderstanding creeping into our conversation. Here we are talking about saintliness, without stopping to wonder, quite simply, if it really does exist.'

Desmond leaped up on the sofa and cocked his skinny neck. 'My dear sir, my dear sir,' he went on in his comical English accent, 'how on earth can you say such a thing? Saintliness … saintliness … what about St Francis of Assisi? Or St Teresa of Lisieux? Or that Belgian priest who lived with the lepers for ten years in the Pacific?'

'Anyway, I reckon,' said Julek calmly, though in his dark blue eyes a silent passion was at play, 'if we assume that saintliness doesn't exist we don't really have anything to talk about. Saintliness is simply a form of sacrifice, laying everything on the altar and being resigned to everything that can happen to one's individuality …'

'Is it a sacrifice of the individual?' asked Karol.

'No, no …' contested Desmond, 'it's the dedication of one's life in the interest of individuality.'

For a while Karol said nothing, and the others were silent too, lost in thought.

'But I do think,' said Karol gently and seriously, 'it's a renunciation of fear … of our greatest riches, which are terror and longing …'

'We're crossing into the realms of poetry now,' said Julek.

'You as a poet should know that these things do not have any strictly defined borders.'

Desmond smiled. 'For me too,' he said, 'a poet is something saintly. And not because, as you put it, he renounces fear. Quite the opposite – it's because he has the courage to look terror in the eyes. Because he doesn't walk away from the open window, beyond which lies the night.'

ι Then, without any connection with the conversation, but quite naturally, like a refrain which comes back in moments of silence, its inner music corresponding to the mood, he began to recite some English poetry. He did not move away from the window. Beyond the low windowsill stood the June night, clearing over, aromatic and tangible. On the pond, the frogs were playing their music, mocking Mr Kletkie; the Negro leaned out towards the dark blue yonder and the roses growing under the window, as he repeated in his faultless Oxford accent:

'*All night have the roses heard*
The flute, violin, bassoon …'

Julek had bridled a bit at the word 'poet'. He didn't like being called a poet, although of course he was one. He found the theatricality of comparing poetry and priesthood somewhat tasteless. Oh, what a pity he wasn't a priest!

As Desmond was reciting these verses, facing the window and the deep blue night, Julek suddenly caught a glimpse of his own frailties, failings and sins, and the hint of conceit he could see in himself. He was overcome with regret to be wasting the great gift of grace that he had

189

been granted, and he resolved not to postpone his confession any longer, but to regain his sense of the pure simplicity of a choice made for ever. He had chosen Christ, since when it was easy for him to qualify his every deed; if his action brought him close to Him it was good, and if it distanced him it was bad.

Julek looked across at Karol, sitting on a small silk sofa in the lamplight. In the apricot-coloured glow his greenish complexion and ash-grey hair were clearly reflected. His broad, black eyebrows were knitted with tiredness and anxiety. He was staring at a small silver object, toying with it nervously, staring so hard that his grey eyes were glazed in tears. He was thinking about something acutely and intensely, while at the same time listening to Desmond's resonant words. Julek suddenly felt terribly sorry for his friend. Meanwhile, when silence fell, Karol sighed and, turning to the Negro, repeated,

'*All night have the roses heard*
The flute, violin, bassoon …'

And at once he translated it into Polish. Julek smiled. 'In your case saintliness has taken on the guise of poetry,' he quipped, 'but not necessarily the best.'

A couple of days later Karol went off to Warsaw again. These conversations at Krzywizna that June were the happiest and most peaceful time in their entire friendship, and who knows, maybe their entire lives as well. In spite of his frail constitution Desmond had the relaxed good humour of youth, and knew reams of English, French and Danish poetry by heart. After the rain the days were fine and not too hot. They wandered rather aimlessly about the fields, as if they couldn't bear to stay indoors. The skylarks poured forth an endless stream of joyful song, which flowed over the green rye fields, regretfully full of cornflowers. The lupins were in bloom, and at sunset their fruit-flavoured scent settled on the fields and came drifting up to the porch. It was all very beautiful.

But as soon as Karol left, everything fell apart. Desmond went back to his rod and stopped reciting poetry. His small, slight figure could be seen by the pond, wearing his ancient sweater. Almost buried in the reeds at the water's edge, now and then he could be heard exclaiming in his English accent, 'Ooooh! Ooooh!', giving these cries a tone of astonishment, admiration or impatience, whatever the circumstances.

One evening Julek finally made up his mind to go for the long delayed confession. He made sure Father Górski would be expecting him, and before sunset walked about the garden, copse and fields, to focus his mind properly before partaking of the sacraments. On his way back to the house he stopped at the dam above the pond. Pink streaks of cloud threading their way across the sky were reflected in the patches of black water that were free of duckweed. On the right stood Desmond, and on the left Kletkie. Both had cast their rods into the water and were wearing a look of concentration, as if expecting a revelation. They didn't look up at Julek, or at the lowering sky. Kletkie just drove off the mosquitoes with an occasional faint curse. It crossed Julek's mind that it wasn't fish they were after, standing there opposite each other in such religious concentration; it was as if beneath the cupola of the darkening evening they were hoping to catch something more essential.

The next day was one of fine weather and hard work, as the mowing of the meadows had begun and the farm steward had driven out every living soul to come and help,

equipped with scythes and rakes. There was no one to take
Julek to church, so they decided to take advantage of the
unproductive energies of the cook. A small carriage was
harnessed, Mr Kletkie readily clambered up onto the box,
and off they went. The cook did not shut his mouth once
throughout the entire journey – he never stopped describing all the finery he had spied out over the years from his
kitchen. This didn't amuse Julek at all, but for the sake of
politeness he had to pretend to be listening, bending an ear
to Kletkie's confidences about the wretched duchesses or
countesses for whom he had once fried fowl or boiled
broth. Anyway, it wasn't a long journey. The little church
had an air of utter desolation. The whitewashed walls, rug-
ged and uneven, sloped and sagged with age. Against them,
in black frames and black with age, the Stations of the
Cross opened out like windows onto another world. The
actual windows were caked in dust and festooned in cob-
webs, with the meagre leaves of the ugly acacias brushing
against them. There was a smell of lime, dust, congealed
incense and wilting herbs. On the side altars dusty branches
and bundles of reeds left over from Whitsuntide gave off
a rather offensive odour of dried-out vegetation. Total
silence reigned, with only occasional bird noises audible in
the distance – a hen cackling in the village, a cock crowing
on the cemetery fence, or larks twittering in the sky.

Father Górski came out to the confessional box seeming rather confused. He sat down in the black chair, shut
the grille in front of his face and closed his eyes for a
moment while he prayed. Julek boldly genuflected on the
step, and bowing down, quickly recited the Confiteor in
Latin. Then he raised his head and Father Górski leaned
towards the small barred window. Covering his lips with
the end of his stole, he said, 'I hear you, my son.'

Very calmly and slowly Julek began to speak. He was trying to make sure that what he said was as banal and as humble as possible. In recounting his sins he was trying to appear a quite ordinary penitent with no ambitions towards great faith, and that he wasn't going through any major upheavals. And so his admission of his sins was extremely brief. When Julek had finished and was hesitating, Father Górski raised his ugly, swollen lidded eyes to him for the first time and, apparently accustomed to a totally empty church, spoke far too loud.

'Don't you remember any more sins, my child?'

'No, I don't,' said Julek, just as loud.

Father Górski cleared his throat, waited a while and then said, more quietly, 'And tell me, my child, is your faith deep? Is it pure? Do you never have any doubts? Do you not enjoy questioning it? Do you not like to philosophise? Or do you simply believe?'

Julek replied without surprise, 'Ever since I have known the grace of God, my faith has been constant.'

Father Górski cleared his throat again and after a longer silence he said, 'Examine your conscience and beware lest your confidence be not born of conceit. Beware lest your faith be born of pride. Doubts are better than confidence that arises from a sense of superiority.'

Julek did not understand this instruction, which to cap it all was uttered in a wavering, fractured voice. The priest was having trouble finding his words, and it felt as if they didn't match his thoughts. At last he hesitated and broke off, clearly wanting to say more, but he let it drop. For a while he was silent, and then, casting a sidelong glance from behind his glasses, he added: 'And now repent your sins …'

Julek bowed, beating his chest as the priest recited the words of absolution. When he rose, the priest said, 'In

Jarosław Iwaszkiewicz

repentance you will recite for three days, three times morning and evening, the Confiteor, and you will repeat the words of the Communion of Saints three times for the benefit of the Holy Church.' Then he knocked on the grille three times.

Julek left the confessional box with a feeling of pure relief. The sense of lightness did not leave him as he fell to his knees in one of the pews. Before opening his prayer book, he sank for a while into a state of bliss, brought on by the resolution and remission of all his offences, both those he had confessed to, and those he couldn't remember.

The priest came out to say mass. In these days of haymaking the church was so deserted that the altar boy had not even come to serve at mass. Instead of playing old Cracoviennes and new foxtrots on the broken-down harmonium in the organ loft as usual, the old organist, dressed in a shabby surplice, genuflected and rattled a small silver bell.

The mass proceeded at its usual calm pace from the moving *Introibo ad altare Dei, ad Deum qui laetificat iuventutem meam*. The murmur of the priest's voice, now rising, now falling into a whisper, and the rapid, rather mumbled Latin responses of the organist were at odds with the chirping of the swallows outside. The sound of the bell reverberated around the empty walls, and the withered reeds gave off an ever stronger odour. The silence, the whispering, the chirping and the odour all eased the way for prayer and remorse. Julek felt his soul cleansing itself layer by layer, burning with a calm flame of certainty, filled to the brim with purity. He could feel the grace of God envelop him.

When the Gospel was over, the wooden entrance door creaked open and swift but erratic steps rang out. A woman had come into the church and knelt down beside Julek's pew. Julek took no notice. He moved up a bit to make room for her, but the woman didn't enter the pew. She went on kneeling, hiding her face in her hands.

When Julek returned to his pew after communion, his soul brimming with the presence of God, he noticed that the woman, still hiding her face, was weeping bitterly. He sat down, then leaned towards her and said, 'Won't you sit down, Madam?'

The woman did as he bid, without ceasing to cry. Julek opened his prayer book, took a pencil from his pocket, marked a passage and offered it to his companion. She shot him a glance. She was not in her first youth – dark-eyed, tearful and unattractive. Then she looked up at the book and read through the marked passage:

> I regret, O Lord, my dark desires, the yearning of my soul for all that is beautiful, my struggle with the hindrances that keep me from Thee, my distress, misfortunes and earthly sorrows.
>
> I regret, O Lord, the mystery that surrounds me, the despair that torments me, the anxiety that never lets me rest, the impatience that tears me from what I have grasped towards that which I cannot.
>
> A flower does not desire, it does not weep – it grows and blooms without hope, and dies without despair. No thought occurs to it, for it is a constant part of Thy reason! Thou created it, but Thou art not enamoured of it.
>
> Thou hast granted me to live in Thy image – Thou hast loved me with Thy heart – Thou didst not want me to live in ignorance of being alive.
>
> Wondrously hast Thou ennobled me through my suffering, O Lord! And therefore I strive towards Thee without rest, conscious that I am myself and a part of Thee in one.

Having read it through she closed the book and passed it along the bookrest towards Julek. The mass was coming to its end. Julek was deep in prayer, while at the same time looking forward to the happy summer's day that lay before him. He took no notice of his neighbour as she stood up before the end of the service and went out, just as she had entered, at a fast, erratic pace.

Father Górski bowed over the altar and embraced it, fanning the scent of incense and reeds from it as he did so. Leaning on the altar, he turned to face the congregation, at this moment represented by the solitary, morose young man with messy fair hair flopping over his brow, his lips pursed with the confidence born of unwavering faith.

The priest gazed at the young man, standing alone in the empty church, hung with faded banners. As if fighting his way through the slanting rays of sunlight that fell from the skylights and criss-crossed inside the church, he reached out his hand in benediction and traced a cross in the air surrounding Julek's head like a golden halo.

Still the priest went on standing before the altar, for he could only move with difficulty, and watched the young man bowed in ardent prayer. It occurred to him that this was how a saint might look, if ever he were granted to see one on this earth. He felt panic at this thought, the realisation of his dreams, and turning to the Gospel he began to recite, 'In the beginning was the Word, and the Word was with God, and the Word was God …' As he stepped away from the altar he decided to pay a visit to Krzywizna.

Meanwhile Julek had left the church and found that the woman who had been sitting beside him earlier was now in lively conversation with the cook. As he came up to the carriage, Mr Kletkie said, 'Madam was just asking if we're going towards the mills. I replied that as befits gentlemen we can go in any direction she would wish to go …'

She turned to face him, and without a word gave him her hand. She had a black lace scarf on her head, the kind peasant women in Russia used to wear. Mr Kletkie went on elaborating, 'What's an extra three or four kilometres if one can be of service to a lady?'

The 'lady' gave an enigmatic laugh. The traces of her tears, along with the traces of any emotion at all, had faded from her plebeian face. She jumped into the chaise and Julek sat down beside her. Mr Kletkie whipped up the horses and they set off in the opposite direction to Krzywizna.

'Do you live at the mills?'

The woman laughed and said, 'At one of them, of course, one of the mills. It's called Tarnice.'

Juliusz didn't know this road or the place they were heading for. It was very pretty there. The dry, sandy fields suddenly came to an end above a green hollow; a green meadow stretched away far into the distance on either side, while a small, winding brook shone through, overgrown but moving quite rapidly. Here and there white lilies bloomed on the water, which looked clean and bright as the sky.

They drove along a sandy, bumpy road on the border between an arid field, where sparse rye was growing, and a freshly mown meadow, where grass was already shooting up again, showing a limpid green. When they came out onto a slight rise, or rather a turn in the road, a further expanse of meadow came into view ahead of them. Here the river made a couple of arcs and, its motion checked by a series of pools, poured out into a fair-sized pond. Now it was broad, edged in alders and willows, lying still and sleepy. The sun burned more and more fiercely.

'Don't you know these parts? This is Tarnice,' she said, pointing towards the pond.

Above the pond stood a mill. It was a strange edifice, clearly very old. There was a wooden ground floor, almost completely black with age and rather badly affected by rot, above which, connected by a large staircase, rose an upper living storey, rendered and topped with a hip roof. It was extremely simple, and yet there was great charm in its four identical, three-windowed façades, each facing in a different direction. On each of these façades there were small balconies, with the largest one overlooking the pond. By the weir in front of the mill the limpid river Utrata came streaming out from under a raised sluice gate and flowed away across the meadows, to link up some way off with the grey silhouette of another mill, and gleam forth again in the form of a pond. Julek gazed in that direction.

'There are mills over there too,' said his female companion, without alighting from the chaise, just pointing with a broad sweep of her hand, 'but they're almost all idle. Ours is still running, though. Mama makes such an effort,' she added with some pride, and sniggered again.

Julek leaped from the chaise and tried to take his leave, but the lady wouldn't hear of it, and invited him to breakfast. 'You're out on an empty stomach, aren't you? I saw you going to take communion,' she said, in a rather flirtatious tone, cocking her head to one side with a faint smile. This made him feel all the more impatient to be off, but he had to give way.

Afterwards he admitted that he really had enjoyed this meal in the large central room of the mill's upper storey. The balcony overlooked the pond, which lay glittering in the sunlight. On the table, spread with a colourful cloth, Mrs Rygielowa, mother of his companion and owner of the mill, laid dark blue plates of bread, butter, cheese, cucumbers and honey; she poured fragrant coffee into large campanula-shaped mugs which bore the legend, 'A Souvenir of Częstochowa'. Mrs Rygielowa, a brisk and slender elderly woman, did not hesitate to acquaint Julek with the state of her financial and family affairs, as if she had been just waiting for him. She always referred to her daughter as 'Łowiecka', which confused Julek at first. It was fearfully hot in the mill, because the large baker's oven in the neighbouring kitchen adjoined the room, keeping it warm even in summer. Mrs Łowiecka disappeared for a while, but Mrs Rygielowa never stopped chattering as she treated Julek to coffee, bread, salami, and finally a special sloe gin made of blackthorn, which grew there in great abundance. In the end, the whole mixture made him feel drowsy.

He began to look closely at Mrs Łowiecka, who at that moment was standing on the balcony, gazing out at the summery pond, which lay steeped in the silence of a blazing hot morning. The mill wasn't running, and whenever Mrs Rygielowa stopped talking silence reigned. Mrs Łowiecka leaned out over the balcony and called, 'Boys, please don't touch the boat, it's an old wreck.'

'Those are her sons,' said old Mrs Rygielowa, leaning towards him knowingly. 'She's run away from her husband with them.'

Julek did not make further inquiries. It was of no concern to him. Mrs Łowiecka wasn't pretty and had undoubtedly long since passed thirty. Her sons must have been about ten or twelve years old. She wasn't pretty, and yet Julek kept asking himself, 'why not?' If here in her place there had been someone beautiful and unusual, then the entire mill would have taken on a different character; it would have been a beautiful majestic mill that had strayed onto this lush green meadow by the Utrata. He had a vague sensation, after a couple of glasses of the sloe gin, of becoming more and more befuddled, and the June day seemed incredibly, unreally beautiful. More beautiful than such a day could possibly be, with a blue sky half-filled with clouds.

It was time to get back to Krzywizna. He found Klet-kie standing by the horses, in the midst of a very animated conversation, of course, with the handsome young mill hand. He was holding forth tenaciously, casting his sickly eye up towards the clouds, floating by in a flock like birds. Apparently he had not done all the chattering, but had also been avidly listening to the inhabitants of Tarnice, for all the way home he entertained Julek with news of the mill and its lady owners. During their short stay he had discovered a good many details and now, adding his own colour to it all, he was handing it down to posterity, that is, to Julek. Meanwhile, distractedly following the clouds above the green meadows and the twists of the Utrata, Julek was listening equally distractedly to Mr Kletkie's tales. The only thing he found out, that is, actually took in, was that Mrs Łowiecka's husband, a forester in the state woods at Huculszczyźna, had beaten her badly a number of times; fed up with such behaviour, as a last resort she had run away to her mother, taking her sons with her, confident of her husband's pursuit and a reconciliation. However, the husband had shown no intention of chasing after her or of coming to fetch his sons, and the whole matter had reached an *impasse*.

They drove up to the house in the midday swelter. All the shutters were closed and the summer's day lay lurking in their golden chinks, and in the buzzing of flies spinning around the ceiling. In the drawing room, amid the red and white cretonne covers and the green mirrors in their heavily gilded frames, stood Desmond King, reciting out loud while watching the movement of his own lips in the glass. Julek stood in the doorway undetected as Desmond, peering at the looking-glass, slowly recited the opening verses of Longfellow's poem:

> *'It was the schooner Hesperus*
> *That sailed the wintry sea …'*

Julek turned, went upstairs and washed, still repeating the words in English,

> *'It was the schooner Hesperus*
> *That sailed the wintry sea,*
> *And the skipper had taken his little daughter*
> *To bear him company.'*

The air was so still that he could hear the sound of the midday Angelus bells ringing at Sulistrzyce. Julek felt a great sense of tranquillity, as if his ultimate moment of peace had come. Repeating the words of the English poem, he went outside, despite the heat. He walked past the pond and sat down on a knoll that rose behind it, facing a pine copse. From this spot he could see the pond shining like a green eye with duckweed for lashes, the spreading apple trees, old and bowed beneath their abundant green fruit, the plain white house and its red roof. As he sat down, he could feel that the torrid heat had turned sultry. From behind the copse, out onto the sky a great, round rain cloud was slowly creeping, slightly washed out by the heat, but with a violet tinge that heralded a storm.

And suddenly in the burning stillness there came to him an unexpected sensation, an experience which he hadn't had for a long time now. All at once this entire silent landscape seemed nothing but a veil before his eyes, behind which he could sense the presence of another world, so real and acute that the strength of the experience made him feel physically weak. The leaves and water, the trees and objects seemed like something imagined, the reflection of another world, while at its most intense moment, the sense of revelation literally threw him sprawling on the ground. He leaned his head back, and as he felt the blades of grass tickling the nape of his neck, he could feel the immensity of everything above him and the immensity of what was going on inside him. He closed his eyes and repeated the words from a few hours ago: 'O Lord, I am not worthy to receive Thee under my roof …'

Yet despite that he felt that the Lord was gathering him up and engulfing him like an infinite ocean, seizing him up and drawing him into an infinite vortex of reality, more real than anything he could see and feel. He surrendered himself to the vortex and, penetrated to the core by its coolness and its pain, he surrendered himself entirely to his Lord God, who fell upon him like an eagle, greater than the violet cloud that came bearing the storm.

It only lasted an instant. As he half-opened his eyes he saw Desmond bending down to choose his bait, and once they were open he saw the Negro stand up straight, swing around in a circle and cast his line into the water. In the past few moments he had been through more than other people are ever given the chance to experience in their whole lives. He sat up on the grass again, and the immense happiness of faith and certainty settled comfortably inside him, filling his entire being. Calmly he followed the progress of the approaching rain cloud.

The storm passed over short and mild, just enough to freshen the air and wash the leaves of the apple trees. All nature breathed a deep sigh and, once the cloud had gone, resumed its activities with redoubled energy. High up the birds were singing and the silence was gone.

Julek was standing in the drawing room with the English words on his lips again:

'It was the schooner Hesperus
That sailed the wintry sea …'

He looked out at the garden, cleansed of dust, and at the battered roses and campanulas, gradually raising their heads as they dried out. Fragrance flooded in through the open window. At the same time, in his tranquil, happy mind, in his soul, occupied by God, a certain vague yet negative sense of anxiety was starting to grow. There was nothing serious or bad about it, just a slightly uncomfortable feeling, nothing worse. It intensified after an excellent dinner which Mr Kletkie had 'knocked together' on his return. It even seemed superficial enough for him to ascribe it to nothing more than a surfeit of pancakes and custard, which Mr Kletkie prepared so superbly. So to aid his digestion he went out to the meadows to join the haymakers. He wanted to help the workers, but he didn't 'have a way with' the scythe, so he took a rake and went over to the women, who were scattering haystacks that had been dampened by the downpour. Only now did he realise that the brook flowing through these meadows was

the Utrata, and that the Tarnice meadows were the con-
tinuation of Krzywizna's, which, bypassing Sulistrzyce,
stretched in a distant arc all the way down to the mills.

Karol spent that day in Warsaw, rather unusually. He
loved these hot days in the grey, ugly city. The atmosphere of open-air restaurant verandas, of ice-cold vodka,
crayfish and cucumber soup, with which he always ordered a good Burgundy, too heavy in such a heatwave,
had a lot of charm about it.

   Karol's flat, or rather his poky little bachelor's room,
was kept a strict secret, in spite of which a whole crowd of
friends and acquaintances were always assailing him in his
hide-out. Each one ostensibly came in search of some sort
of advice or help, but in fact all they wanted was to pour
out their hearts, borrow some money or go out for a free
dinner. Karol was so constantly disturbed that he had no
chance of settling his affairs, which usually involved a visit
to a lawyer who handled complicated commercial matters.
He and his friends ate lunch at Wilanów, then took shel-
ter from the approaching storm at Rydz in Ujazdowskie
Avenue, and although the storm blew over, by the time he
got out of the restaurant the lawyer's receiving hours
were long since past. So they went for coffee to the home
of one of the company, who lived in Saska Kępa. The
man was a sub-commissioner of police, still young and
very handsome. He lived alone, he was a widower, and
had a very nice flat. He had transferred to the police from
the army, and they had a lot of friends in common. So a
genial atmosphere was soon built up, and to drink a toast
to *Bruderschaft* they had to set off *en masse* – about twelve
of them in all – to a restaurant, where once again a large
amount was drunk, and of the most varied mixture. In

short, long after midnight Karol ended up on a bridge over the Vistula in the company of the police commissioner, and was very drunk indeed. They couldn't bear to part, and had long since been on first-name terms, constantly repeating with drunken insistence, 'Felicjan', 'Karol', when suddenly the commissioner stopped on the bridge at one of those pretty, rounded bays where there are benches and, becoming serious, said, 'Karol, you know, my wife, here, from this spot ...' And with a telling gesture he indicated the pitch-black current surging below, inky in the first green glimmers of daylight.

Karol sobered up on the instant and caught hold of the commissioner by the arm. For a while they walked along in silence, but Karol's heart was pierced by a sudden, violent pity. 'Poor man, O God, O God ... this is man's lot,' he kept repeating. A vast and substantial wave of pity had overwhelmed him, pity for the whole human race, not just for this stranger, from whom he would soon part, never to meet again. No, he felt pity for all mankind, for every single human being who, like a drowning beetle, cannot be saved. This shocking sensation went running through Karol so strongly at this moment that he was incapable of uttering a single word. The vodka had so completely blunted all his inner resistance that he felt tears coming on. He walked meekly after his companion. Dawn was coming over the sky with large splashes of light above the towers of St Florian's.

Suddenly the drunken commissioner turned on the spot, buried his face in Karol's arm and started to weep. The shoulders of his navy blue uniform shook as his loud weeping broke the silence of the night. Karol didn't know what to do. He was crying too, but in spite of himself and from drunkenness, and embracing his new friend he

205

stared out at the broad rush of water and the riverbanks lined in tall poplars. 'Hush now, Felicjan, hush,' he kept repeating.

'Don't think it's just because I'm drunk,' said the commissioner, sobbing – then all of a sudden he seemed to feel ashamed of his own weakness, got a grip on himself, straightened his jacket and said in a steady voice, 'Well, goodbye then, goodbye. Go home, it's late, and you live a long way off. Goodbye. Call me some time,' he uttered the familiar formula, but without giving his telephone number.

Before Karol knew it, the commissioner's military steps were echoing on the concrete paving, growing more and more distant. He stood for a while, gazing after the departing figure. Then he turned towards the city, which had gone quite pink in the approaching dawn. 'Dear God, what a thing is man,' repeated Karol, 'dear God, what a pitiful creature! How did Oedipus put it? He goes on four legs in the morning, two legs at noon and three in the evening … man, pitiful man … O God, O God!' He swiftly set off for his flat.

On waking from a very heavy sleep, full of painful reminiscences, he realised how very drunk he had been. And yet the tormenting sense of pity for mankind did not leave him along with the fumes of alcohol, nor later, when the fresh June day had blown his hangover away. His visit to the brown, very businesslike office of the lawyer did not improve matters. On the contrary, he was ready to weep with pity for the lawyer who, convinced of the greatness and importance of his insignificant person, ruffled his ashen hair and goggled with his ashen eyes, and with immense precision shook the ash from his cigar into the shining ashtray carefully positioned on his large brown desk. The matter in hand was very clear and simple to the intellect of the common man. But the lawyer stacked up unforeseen complications, then demolished them with a single sweep of his masterful hand, only to contrive complex new explanations of the simple old truth that two times two is four. It never entered his head that the unassuming but well-built young man sitting opposite him had a heart filled with sympathy for him and was thinking about his wretched little life, which to the lawyer seemed the epitome of equilibrium and good sense. He was only surprised when Karol interrupted him in mid-sentence and said, 'No doubt you'll do as you think right, that'll be the best.' Then he got up and took his leave in a rather distracted way.

What was to be done? Karol left the lawyer's office and sloped off for a coffee, then found himself on Ujazdowskie Avenue again, at the hour when large street lamps came on among the dense blue trees. He got drunk again in very jolly company, played poker at a private club with a balcony overlooking the garden, won, and went home at dawn, with a feeling of emptiness – and a certain sense of dread. Instead of making himself tea on the gas stove he had a compelling urge to turn on the gas tap and not light it. With a complete effort of will power he managed to set the lighted match to the device. Terror and anxiety swept over him, so he opened a window which gave him a view of the metal roofs next door, and it felt as if he were living in a grey, metallic world, where shadowy figures battered out of metal were pretending that the current of life flowed through them. A grey and white sky opened up before him, artificial and unreal. He gazed at it. Suddenly the kettle whistled. This sign that the water had boiled seemed ironical. He switched off the gas, checked that the tap was properly turned off, and without touching his tea lay down on the comfortable bed. The morning, full of sunlight, brought him peace again.

Meanwhile Father Górski had paid a most ill-timed visit to Krzywizna. Hopfer wasn't at home, Zdanowski was hiding in the copse and only Desmond King appeared to receive the priest. It turned out Father Górski had spent more than a decade working in the United States and spoke English with a strong Polish accent and in a very American manner, but he was fluent, so they could communicate. The conversation was more like a catechism, with Father Górski asking the questions and Desmond answering them.

The small, thin, delicate figure of 'the Blackamoor', as he was popularly known at Krzywizna, could not sit still in his large armchair. He was constantly moving about on the red and white poppy-patterned covers, gesticulating animatedly. His favourite gesture, which had nothing to do with the thread of the conversation, was to raise his right arm, point a finger skywards and waggle it about, as if to give force and emphasis to his argument. Combined with some story, of his birthplace or his schooldays, for example, the inappropriacy of this gesture had a comical effect.

'I was born in Puerto Rico,' he was saying politely, leaning towards Father Górski and at the same time wagging his finger as if preaching. 'I am a Catholic, my mother was Spanish.' And he shook his hand again, as if to say, 'yes siree!'

Father Górski wore a smile of indulgence on his face while staring at 'the Blackamoor' as if he were a monkey. He was amazed every time Desmond answered, raising his eyebrows above his glasses, his puffy eyes sinking into the creases of a smile, as if by talking Desmond were performing an incredibly difficult trick, as if he had learned how to talk, like a magpie or a parrot. Every time he spoke the priest's face reflected the thought, 'Just look at that – black as your hat but he can chatter like a person!'

Without taking his eyes off him, he stared at the diminutive figure, a redundant stray, strangely out of place in this Krzywizna drawing room, which was so very Polish and provincial. Desmond's spidery fingers were toying with the fringe of the old-fashioned sofa as he gave copious answers to all the clergyman's questions, as if he had long since had the answers ready in his head and was reciting them for an exam.

At one point Desmond suddenly sat up straight, and in describing a Negro play featuring the Lord God and all the angels, he stood up and in a flat, rasping tone began to declare that the Negroes can see the glory of the Lord God of Hosts, and how the might of Heaven appears to their simple hearts. There he stood, finger raised, hoarsely stammering out his speech; meanwhile Father Górski went on staring at him with an indulgent smile, like that of a highly cultivated person watching someone who doesn't know how to use a knife and fork.

Just then Julek came in and the conversation moved on to other themes. Julek spoke English poorly, so they had to talk in Polish, leaving Desmond for the most part silent. Julek was feeling nervous; his anxious mood had intensified, which he ascribed to the frequent storms. The priest's visit irritated him, and the Negro's behaviour annoyed him even more, the black buffoon. He made an effort to sound polite, but Father Górski soon noticed that his smile was forced, and sighed.

Jarosław Iwaszkiewicz

The conversation passed on to matters of great importance to the priest. They spoke of the borderlines between poetry and sainthood, religion and art. Here Julek took the floor, very confidently, so it would seem. But after each claim he made he immediately broke off and seemed to fall silent inside, so that each of his platitudes, once initiated, had to labour on all the way to its meaningless conclusion.

Finally they gave up on that subject, which Julek was finding painful. Instead, Desmond told them about Iceland, another place where fate had cast him up in the past, and then about Denmark, where he used to work for Danish radio. At Father Górski's request for an example of the Danish language he rattled off a couple of verses:

'... *Jord, min Moder, Jord, min Moder,*
södt af Sol og Maane tvunget,
du har Floder, du har Floder,
som for mig har aldrig sunget,
löndomsdybe Vandringsvande,
Maanehulk mod Siv og Sande
gennem farefulde Lande ...'*

Julek pricked up his ears. In the poetry he caught the sound of the magic spells he seemed to need, and he remembered how Longfellow's poetry had suddenly

---

* ... Earth, my Mother, Earth, my Mother,
sweetly steered by Sun and Moon
you have rivers, you have rivers
which for me have never sung,
mystery-deep migration waters,
moon sobs rocking roads and sands
through the distant fearful lands ...
(Translated by Erik Stinus)

210

aroused and hastened such a vivid experience. As soon as Father Górski had gone, he asked Desmond to repeat the rhythmic verses; Desmond gave him a volume of Thøger Larsen's poetry, pointing out the work that interested him and translating one word in three of it for him. The rhythm of this poetry appealed to Julek. He tried to translate it into Polish, but he could only manage every other line, and not even that very well, for he couldn't catch the ballad's rolling, sing-song tone.

> '*In a dream the sea speaks loudly*
> *singing of its journeys far,*
> *telling of its fish-filled rivers,*
> *praising high our aqueous star,*
> *briny days and depths sunk deeply,*
> *oval-sided fishes fleetly*
> *dart with youthful massive eye …*'

In spite of not coming out as they should, these lines sank deep into his consciousness. As he wandered aimlessly about the house he kept repeating them, although they didn't really match his mood, or the season, or the situation. And yet he could hear the themes of some other, completely inaccessible reality threading their way through that melody. He had the constant feeling of standing in front of a locked gate, and it was this very feeling that filled him with such anxiety, growing by the hour.

> '*… briny days and depths sunk deeply,*
> *oval-sided fishes fleetly*
> *dart with youthful massive eye …*'

Once again he found himself by the pond, in more or less the same spot as a couple of days ago; once again he

watched from afar as Desmond cast his rod into the green
duckweed-coated water. There was even a storm or some
bad weather approaching, just as before, and yet the feeling
inside him was completely different. He couldn't summon
up the strength to concentrate on anything, his thoughts
went flashing through his head at an unusual, elusive speed;
he couldn't make any decisions. At times he found himself
piling up resolutions but without involving his conscious
mind at all, which began to worry him, although they only
concerned trivial matters. The rolling metre of the Danish
verses failed to draw this trepidation into any stronger
rhythm. Everything was spinning like the chaotic eddies of
a river flowing by in no particular direction.

And so it went on for several days, his anxiety never
ceasing to grow, while an inability to relax became ever
more apparent. He had stopped praying and even found it
hard to do his prescribed penance; he did repeat the
words of the Communion of Saints three times, but so
formally that heaven knows if it brought any benefit to
the Holy Church.

He saw Desmond with his rod and couldn't help
thinking of his funny gesture, and yet he did have some
admiration for him. There was a committed, inner ardour
radiating from the black vagabond: his faith in the fact
that poetry and religion were one, which was met with a
polite but abnegatory smile from the priest, and Julek's
misshapen words, '*Jor, min mór, jor, min mór,*' as he transposed the Danish expression into Polish, 'O Earth, my
Mother!' Only towards evening did he feel some relief
from the unbearable stifling sensation, when dense, heavy
rain fell. The change of weather was forecast to last for
some time.

Next day he awoke full of vigour. Thin streams of rain kept pouring incessantly. Karol arrived, appeared at breakfast in his pyjamas and then went back to bed to sleep off the past few days that he had spent in Warsaw. Suddenly a storm erupted in the kitchen, and such a fierce one that its echoes carried around the house. It was Friday, and Mr Kletkie needed fish for supper and flour to bake the Sunday pastry; someone was supposed to have fetched them first thing but Mrs Sikorska had forgotten to make the arrangements, so there was quite a commotion. Kletkie said it was the last time anything like this was going to happen, that he would quit, and he ranted so loud that Julek was afraid Karol would wake up and the row would get even worse. So he went to the kitchen to calm the troubled elements. He didn't have much success, because Mr Kletkie kept harping on the same string, while Mrs Sikorska insisted that there was no one in the yard, everyone had already been given jobs to do, on top of which the cart had been sent off in the opposite direction. In short, there was no one to go for the provisions.

'Good God, what a lot of fuss,' said Julek, getting impatient. 'I'll go myself. Please have the one-horse chaise harnessed for me. Where am I to go?'

'To the mill, to Tarnice,' said Mrs Sikorska. 'You know the way, sir, don't you?'

'All right, but what about the rain?' said Kletkie.

'It doesn't bother me,' said Julek, already calm again. 'I love driving in the rain.'

And he wasn't bluffing – he really did like driving in heavy rain, lashing down on all sides as he sheltered beneath an expansive hooded cape. The horse trotted along the rain-clogged sand, water streamed off the reins and the cover, and through pure contrast Julek felt an inner comfort, warm and snug inside. So, without even thinking about where he was going, he steered the horse towards the meadows calmly and happily. Only as he passed Sulistrzyce, the little church and the priest's house that looked like a Russian villa, did he remember that he was going to Tarnice, to Mrs Rygielowa and Mrs Łowiecka. He found both ladies in the room above the mill, and in the mill itself Mrs Łowiecka's sons and the handsome mill hand, Zdzisio Zdyb, were bustling about all covered in flour. The mill was running, shuddering with every turn of the great wheel and the millstones, water was splashing through the floodgates and flour was pouring from little wooden spouts into large sacks, to be tied by Zdzisio. Upstairs he was treated to sloe gin again, and Mrs Rygielowa gave a detailed account of her late husband, who appeared to have been famed throughout the district. Apparently, old Rygiela was a drunkard and a great glutton, but he was pious too. It was he who, at his own personal cost, had built the new presbytery at Sulistrzyce, on the site of the old one, which had sunk so far into the ground that no priest was willing to live in it any more.

Julek couldn't remember how he responded to all this. The rain pouring outside, the rhythmic clatter of the mill and the splashing of the waterfall, the dripping wheels, Zdzisio and the boys shouting – it all blended into a single melody. And the sweet delight he was experiencing here at the mill was unfamiliar to him. Mrs Łowiecka hardly spoke at all; dressed in black, she was as common as ever, and as she set the plates on the table she let her heavy lids drop over her small eyes, black as sloes. They arranged that Julek would come to the mill on Sunday for the entire afternoon. The mill didn't work on Sundays, so the ladies would have more free time, and if it were fine they could all go out for a drive together. This plan appealed to Julek.

He even boasted of it to Karol. To his surprise, Karol rebuked him and shouted, 'What are you doing gadding about with those miller women?'

Julek didn't understand. Nor did he understand his own behaviour either. It had all started after his last visit to Tarnice – the anxiety, the worries and regret. Suddenly he felt carefree and happy. Sensing that Desmond was sad (maybe because he hadn't had a letter from Copenhagen for so long?) and as the rain was still pouring and it was damp and chilly outside, he persuaded Karol to order some wine. They drank two bottles of a fine Bordeaux, and once again ended up reciting poetry. After dinner in the ill-lit drawing room Desmond declaimed verse after verse. Karol kept laughing at him, but 'the Blackamoor' had no concern but his poems.

'You are a poet,' he said to Julek, hopping about like a cockerel in full feather, 'so you know! In poetry there is a moment when suddenly, in the blinking of an eye, you perceive another world. And you can also see that everything around you is just a shadow of that other, real world. Just like in a prayer. You can say the simplest words on earth, like the wonderful "*All night have the roses heard the flute, violin, bassoon* ..." and all of a sudden you feel a shudder, and you can see roses, not the ones growing under the window, but real ones, you can hear flutes and bassoons, but real ones, just like in Giotto's paintings. Yes, yes, what I'm saying is banal, but it's true, banal but true.'

'It's neither banal nor true,' said Karol, laughing, but in fact his mind was elsewhere. The day before in Warsaw he had dropped in to a church at dawn. He had been on

his way back from a drinking party and hadn't been fully
in command of his senses. In the church stood a crowd of
believers, both fat and thin, but with an early morning
stench of unwashed human being about them. His heart
was full of love, but he felt that wasn't enough, that some
other, extreme action was needed. And the word 'man'
was still causing him some inner commotion, which was
certainly far more intense than Desmond's excitement
while reciting poetry. But he couldn't help feeling a sort
of kinship between his own sense of pity and Desmond's
ecstatic reaction to the English words as they revealed the
horizons of the real world.

Meanwhile Julek couldn't recognise himself. Only
yesterday everything the jumping Blackamoor was saying
would have thrilled and absorbed him. He had been on
the same wavelength then. Today it wasn't just that he
was thinking in a different way, but that he was thinking
about something else entirely. The mystery of poetry left
him completely cold. He didn't feel like thinking about
poetry, or anything else. The wine had made him feel
drowsy. Finally the stream of Desmond's words went
pouring into his ears in a steady cascade, like water onto
the mill wheel – and he fell asleep.

On Sunday the weather was fine. Julek didn't go to
church, giving himself the lame excuse that 'the horses
will be needed after lunch'.

In short, he neglected the practice that he had observed
so strictly until now. He paced anxiously about the house,
went out in front where the 'unreal' roses bloomed,
and made a large bouquet of them. He got very angry
when lunch was a quarter of an hour late, twenty minutes
even, because Mr Kletkie wanted to make some special

entrecôtes. Julek went so far as to peer through the kitchen window. Kletkie, in a white chef's hat and unbuttoned tunic, which didn't cover his goitre, was standing in the middle of the huge room, arms akimbo and fists clenched, spitting on the floor and talking heatedly. Most likely he had already had an encounter with the bottle today.

'If they want entrecôtes, let them have entrecôtes! And let them wait. Countess Branicka of Biała Cerkwa herself had to wait for my entrecôtes. They're no ordinary entrecôtes, you know … entrecôtes like these weren't even served at the Tsar's court. And who have we got here? Mr Hopfer, well, he's the master, that I understand. But the rest of them? What about that Zdanowski? He's just a student, my dear Mrs Sikorska, nothing but a student. And as for that Blackamoor, if you please, where on earth has he sprung from? He's not a man, he's just a stray dog … a wretched little specimen, hands like a monkey – I ask you! and he goes lording it about among the gentlemen, guzzling my entrecôtes – damn it, but he's a greedy beggar … I hate him,' he snorted, and broke off abruptly.

Julek was greatly amazed when, at the belated lunch, Desmond, usually so mild, let out a great tirade against the cook, maintaining that he demoralised the entire staff, was overpaid and was altogether unbearable. The more heated he became on the subject, the more Karol was amused, until finally he said, 'Do give it a rest, Mr King, it's really none of your business.'

How he regretted those words! Desmond was very embarrassed, gulped a few times and fixed his eyes on his plate. He didn't say a word for the rest of the meal, though Karol addressed him more than once. Nothing could distract him or catch his interest. He had taken offence in the same childish way as he had lost his temper.

217

Jarosław Iwaszkiewicz

After lunch Julek was surprised and annoyed when Karol announced that he would go to Tarnice with him. Julek was very unhappy about it, but once they were there he decided it was a good thing Karol had come. Karol was cheerful and chatty, never letting Mrs Rygielowa get a word in edgeways, and drinking a lot of vodka. He spoke for everyone, since Julek and Mrs Łowiecka were both very reticent.

After tea the three of them went sailing on the pond, while Mrs Rygielowa and the boys drove the horses around it, to meet up with them in 'the wood'. Past the pond stood a dozen or so black pine trees with some shrubbery beyond. In everyday parlance at the mill this place was called 'the wood'. Once they had all met up, Karol kept old mother Rygielowa and the boys company. They sat down beneath a tree and gazed at the view, holding an instructive conversation about the depth of the pond, the income from the mill and the industriousness of the faithful Zdzisio, etcetera. Meanwhile Mrs Łowiecka, or Jadwisia, as she was called, set off with Julek to gather flowers in the bushes. She was wearing a cheap cream and red patterned dress. She looked worse and older than ever in it, her eyes were lost beneath her drooping lids, and her unshapely nose, clumsily powdered, disfigured her sincere expression. Julek chatted with her cheerfully, but he couldn't help thinking how ugly she was. Only her mouth was fairly fresh and wide, with pretty teeth. The moment he looked at her mouth, she leaned over to him and said, 'Why don't you kiss me?'

Julek hesitated and felt himself go pale. But at once he got a grip on himself, firmly grasped her by the shoulders and kissed her passionately. He felt a violent shudder, and at the moment when she wanted to break away he held onto her and kissed her again.

They went straight back to the company, without looking at each other and hardly speaking. Jadwisia was waving a large spray of flowers, as if dusting the trees with it; she swayed gently as she went, confident and satisfied. In Julek everything had changed so quickly that he couldn't tell what was happening to him. He could still taste the woman's lips, the first kiss he had ever placed on anybody's lips.

This kiss had changed the colour of the entire land-scape. The pines, the pond, the mill, even Karol's face looked different. Karol noticed Julek's confusion and al-most divined the cause. Redoubling his loquacity, he told a funny story, now and then casting an anxious glance at his friend's face. Julek was sitting with his knees up, star-ing blankly at the shining surface of the pond, and chew-ing on a thin blade of dry grass, tickling his nose with the tip of it. He was holding his chin high, with a typically stubborn, passionate expression on his face. Deep in his bright blue eyes some cares went flashing by.

They returned to the mill in the same formation: Jadwisia, Karol and Julek in the boat, and Mrs Rygielowa and the boys in the carriage. Kazik and Staś begged to be allowed to go in the boat but their grandmother wouldn't let them. 'You'll capsize the gentlemen. You always get up to such tricks in that boat.'

'But Granny, the boat can't capsize – it has a flat bot-tom,' Kazik solemnly insisted.

'And Karol's an excellent swimmer,' said Julek.

But these assurances were of no use, and the boys went back in the carriage. In the boat, conversation was not animated.

Towards evening the two friends set off for home. It was a warm twilight, the skyline melting in a bluish haze into the horizon. Over the meadows, where huge storks were standing, a cool, enigmatic breeze was wafting, as if cold air were seeping out in narrow, branching currents. There was a strong scent of clover, with vast armies of crickets chirruping among it, coating the fields in a thin layer of sound. At the point where the blurred haze of the horizon changed into a solid, greenish dome, there hung a small moon, like a fingernail clipping. Then they entered the garden, in among the beans, stocks and roses.

The friends were silent, with Karol at the reins. They had nothing to say to each other; they knew all too well what had happened. At last Julek spoke.

'I've invited Mrs Łowiecka to Krzywizna on Thursday.'

'I'm awfully sorry,' replied Karol calmly, 'but I have to be in Warsaw that day. Why didn't you fix another day with her? Should I order a special supper?'

'As you wish,' said Julek.

That evening, as Julek was pacing up and down the drawing room, Karol was sitting on the apricot-coloured sofa again. This time his stare was fixed not on a potential plaything, but on his friend's anxious pacing. Finally he spoke.

'My dear Julek, I would advise you to drop this matter. Let it rest, that'd be best.'

In his impatient state Julek knew it was already too late for him to 'let it rest'. 'What matter? I don't go poking my nose into all your endless affairs in Warsaw, do I?'

'That's only *because* they're endless.'

Julek gave Karol a look. There he sat with those black, knitted brows of his, staring rather painfully into space.

'Why are you so concerned?' asked Julek, standing in front of him.

'Why am I concerned? It's obvious. I asked myself exactly the same question. I'm concerned about your integrity, your unique personality. It's undeniable – I was talking to Desmond about it only the other day – you really are an unusual person, you're an original, and I wouldn't like to see you turn into someone ordinary.'

'So you call being in love being ordinary?'

'In love?' said Karol, laughing. 'No one's talking about being in love!'

'I am,' said Julek firmly. 'I'm in love with Mrs Łowiecka.'

He was surprised to hear himself say this, yet he was speaking the truth. But Karol wasn't shocked; Julek's confession, so sudden and unexpected, highly amused him. He snorted with irrepressible laughter, resting his head against the apricot silk of the sofa. But he soon stopped laughing – standing in front of him, with teeth clenched, Julek seized him roughly by the arms of his jacket and, pale with rage, gave him several hard shakes. 'If you ever laugh at Mrs Łowiecka again …' he said through gritted teeth.

Karol fell silent, and stared for a moment at Julek in pure amazement; then he removed Julek's hands from his arms and calmly pushed his friend away. He stood up, shook off some invisible crumbs, and slowly made his way towards the door. 'I think we'll talk about this later,' he whispered, but slammed the door shut with a bang as he went out.

Wild rage had taken hold of him. He could see Łowiecka's plebeian face before him. 'For an old hag like that to take such a man away from us!' he thought. He went upstairs to find Desmond, but he wasn't there. Next to Desmond's little room there was a door leading onto the balcony above the front porch. Too enraged to know

221

what he was doing, Karol went out onto the balcony. On the point of sunset, half the sky had suddenly gone red, purple streaks were flying across a grey background, and everything in front of the porch – the elms, bushes and two red farm buildings – stood immobile in the glow. The stables and barn, like silted-up aisles in a green canal, stood sunken into the brushwood. And in this ordinary, everyday view Karol perceived some motion, or something about to move. Concealed by the buildings, in the slope of the elder bushes, he could sense a sort of anticipation. He was lost for words as he gazed out at the red sunlight, and for a fleeting moment it seemed as if the landscape were revealing its mystery to him in a single utterance. But the moment of anticipation passed, the question which Karol was suppressing deep in his soul did not float up to the surface, nor did it receive an answer. Maia's veil seemed to shudder, then at once fell still.

Karol looked out at the courtyard again and saw nothing but a perfectly ordinary courtyard. Someone touched his arm; Desmond was standing behind him. He looked at his still, sad face, but it was the Negro's usual facial expression.

'Julek has fallen in love with that woman from the mill,' said Karol.

Desmond didn't answer but seemed to nod. Karol could hardly see him; the red glow was dying in his eyes and on the buildings. Evening had set in.

From that evening onwards events unfolded at a catastrophic rate. The next day Karol left for Warsaw. Desmond was only to be seen at mealtimes, or by the pond. That Thursday, when Mrs Łowiecka arrived in a peasant cart harnessed to a small pony driven by Zdzisio, was like a festival in miniature. There were flowers everywhere, the house smelled of floor polish, and on the beautifully laid dining table coloured candles were burning. Mrs Łowiecka came in a modest black dress; the celebratory atmosphere, the scent of roses and the live flames of party candles seemed to alter her outward appearance. She had become altogether pretty – the perfect atmosphere had effaced her common look.

Mr Kletkie not only prepared a splendid supper, but like the *maître d'hôtel* in a Parisian restaurant he came in to ask how they had liked it. He raised his leucoma-scarred eye and held a hand to his chest beneath the goitre. He deemed it appropriate to entertain the company for a while. He was wearing his white chef's tunic and linen hat, but he had a silver watch in his fob pocket, with a silver horseshoe hanging on the chain. As he chatted he fiddled, or rather toyed with the silver horseshoe, which tinkled gently. He told a few anecdotes about various dishes he had cooked, such as Chateaubriands and fieldfares for Princess Bichette, then for a change he talked about the cemeteries on the Riviera, where 'every tomb is like a chocolate box', and finally about Burgundy and its various flavours. Sensing that he had made enough of an impression on the impoverished student and the forester's wife, with a few fancy dance steps he withdrew into the wings.

Once they were left alone in the drawing room there was a strong scent of roses. Julek said nothing, but only because he felt nothing. He knew his whole life was in ruins. Then he took Mrs Łowiecka to his room, and there beneath the portrait of Pius IX, their conjugal life began. Julek had absolutely no idea how it had come to this. The only reason why Jadwisia did not stay the night was that Zdzisio was waiting for her outside.

*

When, after a long absence, Karol returned to Krzywizna, he found out that Julek had already moved to Tarnice.

As the result of an immediate conference with Karol, Desmond went to see Father Górski and then brought him back to Krzywizna. Father Górski was 'horrified', as Desmond put it. He paced up and down the drawing room, wringing his hands like an old woman. 'I must admit, sir,' he lamented, 'that on the day of his confession he looked quite simply a saint ...'

'Ho ho ho,' Karol hooted with laughter. 'Did you really go that far, Reverend Father? I'm afraid we're all rather far from being saints. How does Léon Bloy put it? "Man's only real tragedy is his inability to be a saint ..."'

These words stopped Father Górski in his tracks. 'How did you put it? What was that you said?'

'It wasn't me that said it,' laughed Karol, 'it was a French writer called Léon Bloy.' And he repeated the maxim.

'Almighty God, man's only real tragedy ... And I've been so deluded! When he was sitting there after communion, so childlike, I really thought ... That woman was at church then too ...'

'Was she?'

'Yes, she was. That was where they met.'

'Yes, that's right.'

'You see what a short step it is from the ascent to the fall, Father.'

'O my God, O my God,' intoned the priest, at a complete loss.

A suggestion was made that he should go to the mill and speak to Julek, but he didn't want to do it at all. He excused himself as best he could, saying, quite rightly, that he didn't know Julek well enough to interfere in such a personal matter. Finally it was decided that Karol would go to the mill.

He put off the visit for a few days. He had news of what was happening at Tarnice from Kletkie, who went there for fish and flour. Outwardly nothing had changed, but after some days the cook reported that Mrs Rygielowa had gone to her sister's, taking both grandsons with her. This event, behind which much evidently lay hidden, filled Karol with concern. At last he resolved to go.

The situation was not a pleasant one. His heart was pounding a bit, but he whistled a tune to give himself courage. As soon as the horses pulled up at the mill, Zdzisio leaped out of the woodwork, covered in flour, but smiling so broadly that all his gums were on show, making him look very ugly. He said that Sir and Madam had gone for a walk but would be back at any moment. He sent a lad out to meet them, and then went back into the mill as he had a lot to do. Drucik, the little black mongrel that belonged to the mill, kept running after Karol and jumping up playfully at his legs. Karol stood on the weir, leaned against the tall millstone and stared at the pond. It looked like a fine afternoon. An opaque, round blue and grey cloud stood on the horizon, casting a reflection in the pond; set against the vivid golden blue of the sky its dove-coloured shade created a subtle contrast.

Along they came from the direction of the wood, smiling and beaming. As before, Jadwisia was holding a bunch of flowers, and Karol thought she looked radiant, quite handsome even. Julek looked like a child beside her, especially as he was wearing casual trousers; he was smiling, but there was some confusion in his smile. All three went upstairs and sat in a corner of the large room. Jad-

wisia sat opposite Julek without taking her eyes off him.
Even while speaking of the most down-to-earth matters
(they began, for example, with spiders, which were nest-
ing in the mill in great abundance), Julek cast frequent
glances at her, as if seeking her approval. As his hosts
were rather reticent, Karol started telling them about
Warsaw and his adventures. He noticed that Łowiecka
listened keenly to these stories, although the restaurant
and gaming house atmosphere was completely foreign to
her. He got the impression that she would willingly have
plunged herself into that lively jungle. It represented a
sharp contrast to her situation, and to the indigent envi-
ronment of the mill. Julek smoked a lot, but behaved
exactly like the master of the house, treating Karol to
food and drink. Zdzisio brought in some tea, and Jadwisia
laid the table without once leaving the room. With a
somewhat ceremonial gesture Julek, as host, invited
him to table. Karol felt very awkward, waiting for the
moment when Jadwisia would leave them alone.
Unfortunately this moment never came, and Karol realised that Jadwisia didn't want to let them be alone
together. So he resolved on a bold advance and said,
'Do excuse me, please, Madam, but I was hoping to
have a word with Julek in private.'

Jadwisia laughed out loud, but her pique showed
through her laughter. 'Do you have such big secrets?' she
said.

At this Karol was annoyed. He frowned and answered
her quite sternly, 'Yes, Madam, it just so happens that
we do!'

He and Julek left the mill and walked along the narrow
path leading around the water to disappear among the
meadows. A strong scent of hay blended with the heady

226

odour of lime trees in bloom, or rather at the end of their blooming, somewhere nearby. For a while, of course, both of them were silent.

Karol was the first to speak. 'You know perfectly well, my dear Julek, that I have no right at all to interfere in your personal affairs, nor do I have any intention of moralising; let he who is without sin cast the first stone, I'm certainly no moralist ... and I don't want, nor do I have the right ... I just wanted to ask you ... to help you, maybe ... How do you imagine the near future?'

Julek stared at the ground for a while, saying nothing. Then he ran up onto a grassy slope. He pointed out a dissolving cloud that was tinged with pink. Karol sat down on a rock beside him.

'You know what,' said Julek suddenly, chewing on a blade of grass, 'you know what ... I can't imagine it at all. I can't see anything ahead of me ... and there's nothing I want. For the time being the mill provides some income.'

'Yes, but how will you manage without Mrs Rygielowa? The whole show relied on her experience, didn't it? And as she's not there any more ...'

'Zdzisio is an excellent worker.'

'He might cheat you.'

'There's never any guarantee against that sort of thing ...'

'So what if Mrs Łowiecka's mother doesn't come back?'

'You know, I would prefer you not to call her Mrs Łowiecka.'

For a while Karol fell silent. 'I can't call her Mrs Zdanowska,' he said.

'Why not?'

'That's not the point. Is Mrs Rygielowa coming back?'

'Certainly not for the moment. And I wouldn't want her to come back right now.'

'Is it irrevocable? Did you have a quarrel?'

'Oh, no, it's just that Jadwisia doesn't like having her mother around. The old lady said something about the boys being unaware of my role here … something of the kind …' As he said this he tossed away the chewed-up blade of grass. 'What do I care?'

'You don't seem to care about anything.'

'Not much.'

'Do you know, Father Górski came to see me. It was he who asked me to come here. He wanted me to talk to you.'

Karol wasn't looking at Julek as he said these words, so he couldn't see the expression on his face. What a pity! Julek looked horror-stricken, but not for long – he quickly regained his composure. A new dull, dove-grey cloud dune had appeared on the horizon, while above it rose pink round-capped Himalayas. Every time Julek looked up at them they were brighter and brighter blue, as if dense pink liquid were leaking from their glassy blue shell. Finally they turned an icy shade of purple.

'You see,' said Julek after a long silence, 'you see it's like this. I was a bit too self-confident, so it all slipped away from me. I am aware of everything – I know what I have lost, and at what price. But please don't torture me. It's just that it couldn't withstand the test of happiness.'

'My dear Julek, isn't happiness rather overstating it?' said Karol.

'Call it what you like. It couldn't withstand this woman. Now that I have the certainty for the time being that she is mine, that there is something which wholly and finally belongs to me, that I have her beside me and can turn to her at any moment of the day ... it doesn't matter what she's like – she's mine. That's enough for me, that's everything. I have renounced all the Aquinases and Assisis, everything that's unnecessary compared with our true love, so do and say what you like, it doesn't bother me at all, it passes me by, it doesn't even touch me. So, whether it's hunger or poverty, even if it's hell, if that's what Father Górski wants, it's all the same to me. I couldn't care less ...'

Karol waited a moment, then added, 'Father Górski took you for a saint.'

'That's real madness,' said Julek indignantly. 'Why are you telling me that? I'm sorry to have disappointed the old chap ...'

'Desmond thought better of you too.'

'Well, now he can think the worst of me. But what about you, Karol?'

'What do I think? You know what I'm like. I don't give much thought to anything. I'm not a tranquil person. Now I'll be even more anxious, because you know, in the middle of all that racketing about in cafés, offices and night clubs, travelling around and getting drunk, sometimes in the most unusual circumstances, don't laugh, but I often think of you. Wherever Julek is, there's equilibrium and tranquillity. He's truly alive, but what about me? I only just exist, like a mayfly hovering above the swamp.'

'Now you can think, wherever Jadwisia and Julek are.'

Karol burst out with impudent laughter. 'But that's not the same,' he said. 'The old Julek meant it really is possible to attain peace on earth, instead of this awful anxiety and transient fear of mine. Real peace. You have never turned your back on the night, like Desmond, you have never even seen the night! But now, Julek, now tell me, for God's sake, do you have peace, that old peace of yours?'

Julek glanced up at the sky again, but the clouds were going purple, melting into the darkening firmament. The stars were out. 'Now,' he said slowly, 'she and I look out together at the eternal night before us. That is real peace too.'

'Julek, Julek,' cried Karol, jumping to his feet and tugging at Julek's sleeve, 'don't say that, don't ...'

Julek smiled. For a moment Karol could see the old, self-confident Julek; he caught a fleeting glimpse of his smile of forbearance for everyone and everything, but then an alien element flooded Julek's face, changing it into something different, unfamiliar and dead-looking. Only his deep blue eyes were burning, suddenly growing huge, as if they really were fixed on the shadow of eternal night.

Without another word they stood up and walked towards the mill. As they came near the building, Julek stopped, turned to face his friend and in the most matter-of-fact tone, as if asking to be passed the salt, said, 'And there's one more thing. Jadwisia doesn't want us to see each other any more. You'll do that for her, won't you? All right?'

For a moment Karol was dumbstruck, and then he calmly replied, 'But of course.'

And they went on their way.

Then for several months Julek saw no one. He was always and everywhere with Jadwisia. Yet whenever he was left alone for a moment in the fields or in the house he immediately felt a sense of loneliness, as sharp as pain, which lasted until the moment she came back again. He realised what was at the root of her charm: her presence gave him the illusion of being able to overcome the irrevocable loneliness that burdens mankind. He had to kiss her, touch her, hear her rather rasping voice, and at once night turned into day, her smile was mirrored in his, her eyes in his. They gazed at each other incessantly, they hung on each other's every word, they spoke in a single vocabulary, using the same expressions, almost in a single voice. The rhythm of the mill works and Zdzisio's shouts stimulated all this improbable happiness, all this passionate frenzy. And Julek, reflecting on eternal bliss, hardly regretted having given it up for his present experience.

, The nights were worse, especially towards autumn when they began to get longer. He would wake up and listen to the frail woman's even breathing as she slept. At these moments he would be overcome with fear of responsibility for her and for himself. He would sit up in bed, throwing off old Mrs Rygielowa's heavy eiderdowns, and the sense of desperate loneliness would return. There was no way out, and it was all dreadful: the mill, Jadwisia, Zdzisio, the pond – quite simply life itself. He felt as if he could not so much as raise a hand, that tomorrow he would be unable to step outside the mill, that he would bay at the moon like a dog – he was beset by worries about anything and everything, but never about the most important thing, his lost confidence in existence. God had set, like the sun, and had not risen again, had not reappeared in a flash of light in the sky, and the whole world was as cold as the ground before dawn.

Sometimes when he felt like this he would wake Jadwisia. He would touch her breast, breathing regularly as she slept, and shudder as the physical contact brought him straight back to reality: the mill, the spiders, tranquillity. At dawn the millstones began to whirr, set in motion by the heedful workman. But sometimes dawn was a long way off, and just placing his hand on her heaving breast was not enough, and he would wake her, heavy with sleep, to disturb her with meaningless, unrelated questions, just to hear her sleepy voice saying, 'Don't worry about it ... go to sleep ...'

And then like a child he would turn to face the wall and, like a child drawing patterns and letters on it, he would fall asleep and not wake until morning, for she had told him to. It reminded him of times when he was ill in childhood, when his mother, long dead now, would watch over him; when he broke into a fever and wanted to fly, to run, to flee, a cold hand would touch his brow and almost the same voice would tell him, 'Go to sleep.'

He spent days on end telling Jadwisia about his life, heedless of the fact that she seemed to find it boring. There was nothing interesting about his life, not a single adventure, not a single journey – nowadays his inner adventures were unimportant to him because they struck no corresponding chord in her – so he spoke of the most ordinary, mundane things, such as his nannies, his mother's dresses, his schools and teachers, his first poems – such pitiful, everyday things that were only brought to life by two points of brilliance: his religious and poetic experiences.

Jadwisia had a strange attitude to Julek's poetry. She regarded it as a way of making money, of rising in the world and gaining importance – and at the same time she was rather jealous of it. She didn't like it when he wrote too ostentatiously, withdrawing from her, she didn't like it when he read her his more recent or his older work, dismissing all of it with the comment, 'How nice, how nice.'

But for him that was enough. Only now did he feel that he had never before had anyone to read his poems to. He and Karol had got to know each other long ago, as the sons of two old friends, but Karol's subtle, rational opinion of his literary works was nothing compared with Jadwisia's comments – because Jadwisia was a woman, and because she made him happy.

For, in spite of all his worries and fears at night, his present experience was the closest thing in the world to an understanding of earthly happiness, and the world, which he scorned, was only claiming its rights along faraway, leisurely paths. He did not miss Warsaw, or the company of the permanently drunken poets of his generation, with whom he had associated for so long. He was alone, both in Warsaw and at Tarnice.

But then came short days, and endless evenings. The mill worked less and less. To begin with, everyone in the neighbourhood had brought grain to Tarnice, simply to be able to go and see the extraordinary lovers. But as they turned out to be quite ordinary people, who didn't even put in much of an appearance, the mill's popularity waned very quickly. The reaction was to be scandalised: an older woman who had left her husband and children to live with such a young pup! 'Stop them from earning' went the slogan, broadcast most likely by Kletkie, whom the mill's inhabitants disdainfully referred to as 'that unsavoury element'. In any case, in the heat of his diatribes he often didn't know what he was saying. In short, less and less corn was coming into the mill.

At first, when business was going fairly well, they had spent too much money, fooling themselves with the hope that this state of affairs would last for ever. They had regularly sent money to Mrs Rygielowa for the boys, who were attending school but were very poor learners. But now it was becoming harder and harder to send even a tiny sum.

A particularly rainy autumn set in, and the spiders were unusually tenacious. The whole upper floor was dusted every day, but they kept coming through from the mill area below, where naturally there was no question of dusting, and where heavy silken spider's webs hung in every corner and from the ceiling.

On the rainy days, which he used to love so much, Julek simply couldn't cope at all. He would wander up and down the entire mill, visiting all its nooks and corners, starting with the small, damp cellar, dug out of the weir itself by those who had erected the building many years ago. He would walk around and around the millstones, watching the flour fly through tubes and strainers before streaming out of wooden pipes. He would stare at the cogs and gears, and sift through the bran, wholemeal and corn stored in boxes and meal chests.

As the situation became ever harder and money ever scarcer, Zdzisio was a real comfort. He managed to get by, he went to people for corn, he parleyed with the Jews. It was damp and wet in the mill; Julek was more willing to forgo his lunch than a fire in the great oven. Zdzisio supplied the wood, but Mrs Łowiecka didn't have the nerve to ask him where it came from. At some point in November came days when there wasn't enough for lunch. There was nothing but potatoes, supplied for free by Zdzisio from his parents' three-acre farm a mile beyond Sulistrzyce. Zdzisio had got up at dawn and gone home on a drizzling morning, when on air swollen with moisture the first snowflakes were flying by in streams of rain, and had come back with half a sack of potatoes, extorted from his mother, who still had three starving brats to feed. Finally, while out stealing wood in the forest, Zdzisio fell into the hands of the gamekeeper and was put under arrest for a week.

Mrs Łowiecka simply couldn't manage, so Julek put on Zdzisio's apron and set to work in the mill. Moisture continued to seep in, whenever the door was opened rain poured in, and anyone who entered the mill brought large cakes of mud on their hobnailed boots, which at once got mixed in with the omnipresent flour dust. Finally something broke in the gearing, which Julek wasn't capable of investigating, and the mill stopped running. Trying to raise the floodgates, Mrs Łowiecka caught cold and sprained her hand. She took to her bed. The rain kept falling incessantly.

Their living quarters consisted of the large room with windows overlooking the pond, and four small rooms set around it, one of which was their bedroom, while the rest were unoccupied. In a dismal mood Julek wandered from one empty room to another, whistling. Then he put on Zdzisio's sheepskin coat (he hadn't even fetched his winter things from Warsaw) and went for a turn about the pond. Everything looked different now from in the summer. The green water seemed thick and viscous. Raindrops were leaping over its surface, but in spite of this dance the water was languid and dormant. The banks of the pond were slippery and Julek had to take care not to fall. He walked to 'the wood', where the wind was restlessly stirring the branches of the pines and rain was lashing their blackened trunks. Now they were like great underwater plants, set in motion by slippery currents. As he walked home he gazed at the sunset, red as a weeping wound despite the clouds and rain.

As he wiped the mud from his feet he was aware of coating them in flour, but that was his only conscious thought. He could feel life trickling through him, nothing more. He had no regrets – he wouldn't allow himself that, just cold-blooded insistence on sticking to his guns. As he went upstairs, the sick woman called out from the bed-room. 'Is that you, Julek?'

And at once a sense of security was rekindled inside him.

'Could you light the burner and make me some tea, please?' she asked.

'There's some paraffin, but no sugar.'

'Never mind, I'd just like something hot.'

'I'll make it right away, my darling.'

Soon after he came into her room with a mug of hot tea. Feverish, Jadwisia sat up on one elbow. She was old and ugly, Julek could see that. Yet the one and only time when Jadwisia had reflected on what had happened, and had expressed her regret, saying, 'Now look what I've brought you to!', he had replied on the instant, 'But Jadwisia, how can you say that? You've brought me happiness!'

And it was true: no sooner was he by her side than a sense of tranquillity and happiness filled him to the brim. He could feel nothing else, and only when left alone did he pay for this tranquillity with terrible nights of anxiety.

Towards Christmas the boys had to be taken out of school, because there was nothing left to pay for their education. Despite the objections of their grandmother, they came to live at Tarnice, and Julek's morning hours were now occupied in giving laborious lessons to the two harebrains. The older boy, Kazik, was a proper little scamp, yet Zdzisio, whose short-term arrest had given him a sort of martyr's conceit, found in him an able helper at the mill. Kazik dealt with all sorts of errands, went to town to see the Jews, bartered with the peasants for leftover grain and even, horror of horrors! drank vodka with them. Now Zdzisio could spend all his time on the spot, seeing to the business. Staś, the younger boy, was more placid, more attached to his mother, and more jealous over her, so he hated Julek, whom he was told to address as 'Uncle'. He was also more aware of his mother's adultery and never laughed, as his older brother did, at the nasty, coarse remarks of the peasants, who, after a swig or two, came to unload corn at the infamous mill.

Through artful publicity and price reductions, Zdzisio somehow managed to lure a few customers back to the mill. For a while business picked up again. The winter was mild, and there were fish to be caught. Occasionally Mr Kletkie drove by for some, and even came over to chat with Julek, who fobbed him off with monosyllabic answers. Indeed, the cook was not very busy because Karol was away from Krzywizna for the entire autumn.

At the end of August it had occurred to Karol that it was a long time since he had been abroad. Desmond encouraged him to go to the Salzburg festival. It was a tempting idea, so he got his hands on some money and a passport. He wanted Desmond to come with him, but Desmond was feeling tired and preferred to sit it out at Krzywizna. He had become friendly with Father Górski now, and could never extract himself from the presbytery at Sulistrzyce. Later on he was due to go to Denmark again.

Getting hold of some money and a passport, trying to persuade Desmond, and making his own mind up all took so long that by the time he reached Salzburg the festival was already over, and the clean, bright little back streets along the green river Salzach were empty, shining in the sunlight like virgin asphalt. Though preoccupied with his own petty cares, and not very sensitive to the charms of nature, Karol suddenly felt moved by the beauty of this place.

It was September, and the entire Salzburg district was gathering in the second harvest of hay, so there was a smell of hay and manure, spread over the meadows the length and breadth of the countryside. There were no crop fields to be seen, just meadows. Amid these green expanses stood grey mountains and glassy lakes, dotted about at random.

He took the tram to Berchtesgaden, went swimming in the Koenigsee, the most beautiful lake in Europe, attended a jolly country fair, drank beer in a vast wooden hall, and saw Lionella, the 'Lion-Woman', who had seven toes on one foot and twelve on the other.

'Lionella, *sage mir*,' boomed the dusky impresario in a declamatory tone, '*wo bist du jetzt*?'

'*Ich bin in Salzburg*,' affirmed the Lion-Woman in a childish voice, drawling in a mannered way.

'*Wo bist du jetzt*?' – in the authoritative tone of the brutal exploiter of human frailty and human folly – became the *leitmotif* of this journey.

Karol went on foot from Salzburg to Innsbruck along an enchanting road between cliffs and meadows. On the mossy, deep green underlay of the Alpine meadows masses of pink autumn crocuses were shooting up. A boundless blue sky hung low over the mountains, which looked as if they were made of spun wool or heavy silken cloth. He went through the unforgettable Lueg Pass, full of legends and soaring trees. He had an equally memorable night on the road to Werfen. Evening fell early, and it was very dark. Heated air drew a veil across the streets of the little town, carrying an intoxicating scent of autumn hay. Large golden stars shone in the distance. He walked down the main street and back again, his nostrils filled with the pungent odours of autumn in the mountains. The place was full of fusiliers, girls and children playing, and the evening had a celebratory atmosphere to it, but it was just a celebration of the fine weather.

'*Wo bist du jetzt?*' he said to himself, and found out that he knew neither who he was nor where. He couldn't answer that abrupt question. He was as ignorant as Lionella, and would never be any the wiser – he knew nothing.

He stopped in his tracks in the middle of the street. Nothing! What a dreadful word. Even though the golden stars and the warm black wings of the Tyrolean night were spread above him, he knew they weren't there for him. He could find no meaning whatever in that wondrous, staggeringly beautiful world. And once again he thought of Julek – Julek had it all, he thought, he knew everything, it was all clear as day to him – what the world is, what a man is, and what it all means. He used to answer our questions with an obstinate, proud and disdainful smile, a smile of confidence and self-possession. And he had given it all up for that common woman's smile, for autumn in the mill, amid cold draughts and spiders' webs, for the crude innuendo of the peasants bringing grain for milling.

'And what if one could take Julek's smile and secret away from him?' he thought to himself. Now he was

standing at the window of a hotel, redolent with the va-
nilla odour of pine wood. Before him, against the starry
sky, loomed a mountain, the same shade as the sky but
starless, covered in spruce forest, and a towering robber
barons' castle. The entire village was gradually settling
down; the hotel resounded with thuds as hobnailed boots
were cast off, worn out with rambling, while the Salzach
murmured below, endlessly telling the night about its past
day's labour. Karol stood at the window and wondered
how to extract his friend's secret from him.

But it wasn't easy; the sky, whether over Werfen or
over Krzywizna, was empty – though full of worlds he
couldn't interpret. Was it Thrones, Principalities and
Powers shining up there in the heavens? Or white
dwarves and red giants? What, where, how? *Wo bin ich*?
What was the meaning of it all?

He felt as if everything he could see was just a veil
before his eyes. Never before had he felt so acutely that
everything that his reason told him was outside himself
was actually inside, and that as soon as he closed his eyes
the entire world would vanish.

He closed his eyes. Just then a warm, fragrant breath
of wind blew in from the meadows along the river below,
and although Karol had closed his eyes and the world
outside had ceased to exist, it flowed over his brow,
his lips, and then his entire body in a tangible caress. Sur-
prisingly, this breath of wind, which he might have
interpreted as equally unreal, seemed instead to be a
confirmation of the world existing outside him, and at the
same time a promise of a better, more tangible existence
than the one in which 'shadows dream of shadows'.

Next he went to Genoa, where he wandered the
amphitheatre of streets, saw window displays filled with

yellow peaches, spent baking hot days listening to countless singers in shady alleyways, ate golden-green figs, pouring white wine over them, as a kindly old American lady he met at the Palazzo Rosso had taught him. He looked down from on high at the blue harbour, and had no idea what on earth it all meant to him.

Later in the autumn he spent some time in Munich, that absurd, affected, thrilling and enchanting city. At the feet of the 'Bavaria' statue, a fat, disproportionate figure of a woman, he attended the Oktoberfest, where he saw a whole ox being turned on a spit, hundreds of gigantic barrels of beer being emptied, crowds of people stopping to stare at the tents of fake Red Indians, and a little monkey freezing in a tiny wire cage, put out on display in the October sun. He rediscovered his own sorrow. In the park at Nymphenburg the leaves were turning golden and falling, hundreds of ducks were swimming on the canal, and the pavilion windows were exhibiting porcelain birds and fruit. The opera opened its season with *Die Meistersinger von Nürnberg*. It was the first time he had heard it, and not until the quintet in the third act, the tune intoned by Eva, seeming to filter through from heights unknown, did 'the fountain of tears' of Wagner's music reveal itself to him.

In late autumn, not long before Christmas, he went back to Warsaw without even looking in at Krzywizna. All his own, as well as his friends' business, all sorts of small but tedious matters seemed to have been just waiting for his return to erupt with new, unanticipated force, to catch him in their net, intoxicate and stun him. He had never known anything like that winter. It was one endless whirl of engagements and meetings, with not a single free moment. All the thoughts and emotions he had gained in

241

Jarosław Iwaszkiewicz

the green Tyrol were blown away in an instant. Desmond had come back from Denmark feeling unwell and very downhearted. Karol suspected that he was in love with a Polish woman who lived in Copenhagen, hence his affection for Poland. Then he had fallen ill for real, and Karol had had to put him in the care of a hospital, keep an eye on him and confer with the doctors. In short, Karol was as breathless as a greyhound. On the other hand his business affairs had improved greatly. His estate was cleared of debt and finally in the black. This was when he thought of making a will, naming as his primary heir Juliusz Zdanowski, writer, resident of the mill at Tarnice. And so time went by until March.

One morning, when Karol was still asleep after a wild night out with the lawyers who had won him a case, there was a ring at the doorbell. He was in no hurry to answer it, but the bell rang again, once, twice, then a third time. So he tumbled out of bed, shaking off heavy sleep – and found himself face to face with a rustic fellow. The face seemed familiar, but he couldn't think where from. The fellow bowed.

'You don't recognise me, sir, I'm Zdyb, Zdzisio Zdyb … from the mill.' With these words he smiled, showing his gums and a fine set of teeth. At this smile Karol remembered who he was.

'Ah, Zdzisio,' he said, 'come in.'

He went back into his room and sat sleepily on the bed. Zdzisio stopped meekly on the threshold. In Karol's small bachelor room he looked a great hulk of a man, with his soft, fair thatch and teeth like a Thoroughbred horse. Only now did Karol notice how very handsome he was.

'Well then, have you come from Tarnice?' he asked.

'Yes, squire, from Tarnice.'

'From Tarnice,' repeated Karol, rather reluctantly. 'How are things there? Are they well?'

'Yes, sir.'

'Did they ask you to pay their respects?' said Karol, trying to make it easier for Zdzisio.

'No, sir, Mrs Łowiecka and Mr Julek don't know I'm in Warsaw. I was only meant to go and see Gryc in Grodzisko.' Gryc in Grodzisko was well known to the entire neighbourhood as the biggest dealer in grain and fish.

'So why have you come?'

'If you please, sir, they've nothing to eat at the mill.'

'What do you mean, nothing to eat?'

'There ain't a farthing in the house. The mill ain't been working for a long time now, I were even fetching potatoes from home, but my mother won't give me no more ...' – at this point he faltered – ' ... because she's none left. So there ain't no potatoes, let alone bread and dumplings.'

'What about Mr Julek?'

'Oh, Mr Julek is just a youngster. He sits and writes to all and sundry, and the stamps cost money to boot – more than twenty-five groshys a day goes on those stamps, at least until yesterday, when even that ran out.'

'He hasn't written to me, has he?'

'No, squire, he ain't.'

'Wait, I'll give you something right now, but I haven't got much on me. You should have gone to Krzywizna for some supplies – Mrs Sikorska would have given you something.'

'I did,' said Zdyb calmly, 'but Kletkie wouldn't let me in. He said a lot of nonsense and refused to give me a single tin.'

243

'And why is it you that's doing all the thinking?' asked Karol, scratching his head dozily.

'Who else is to take charge? I'm the only one there with a head on my shoulders,' he said proudly, but blushed so deeply that his pale blue eyes looked even paler. In an effort to conceal his blush he turned to face the wall in a deeply naïve manner.

Karol smiled. 'A fine head you've got! You should have come to see me ages ago.'

'I didn't dare.'

Karol gave him some money, told him to come and see him whenever there were lean days at Tarnice, and sent him off, clapping him on the shoulder. At the same time he decided to leave for Krzywizna. On the one hand this would curtail his present way of life in Warsaw, but on the other it would bring him closer to the countryside. He wanted to be near his friend, who was so badly off; he also reckoned that on empty stomachs the idyll was doomed to disaster. Desmond, too, now well again, came hurrying after him, back to his little garret room, where he spent his convalescence. Kletkie finally had someone to cook for, but he was drinking so much now that there was not much comfort to be had from him.

It was a long time since Karol had been in the country so early in the spring. Where he had admired the vast, expansive landscape in autumn, the range of impressions had greatly diminished now, and yet on a smaller scale he went on discovering the same moving sights, the same wonders. His discovery of nature, which had started in Salzburg, had not faded or vanished in this hard, smoky, windy spring.

Every day he went for an early morning walk in the fields or the garden. Skylarks were twittering and soaring upwards, and the notes of their song were like the first pale leaves on the graceful birch trees. There in the morning rain, stirred by a cold wind, stood wild pear trees covered in buds, just waiting for the first ray of sunlight to burst open. A roadside cross, with four hawthorn bushes around it, stood silhouetted against the damp air, drying in the wind, like a living thing.

He kept watch on these phenomena like the motion of the hands of a clock that was soon to strike a new and joyful hour. He couldn't help feeling a sense of anticipation of some great and beautiful event. He was waiting for the trees to bloom and for the birds to come back.

One evening when it was already dark, he was on his way back from the sodden, pungent black fields. Overhead, dense, low, revitalising clouds were passing by. And suddenly amid the clouds a piercing scream rang out, plangent and vernal – it was the call of wild geese. They were passing overhead, flying low and fast. Soon their cries were nothing but a distant echo.

'You'll never catch up with them, Karol, you never will,' he said aloud to himself, and his heart ached with a sharp pang of grief.

Desmond, haggard as a corpse, was walking along behind him, reciting all the English, French and Danish poetry he could remember; he had added Polish to his repertoire as well now. Meanwhile, the spring was overcast, chilly and wan. Time at Krzywizna was wearing on, but there was no news from Tarnice.

Around this time there was an unexpected incident at Krzywizna. That day Kletkie had drunk himself into a stupor and was lying unconscious in his room; the entire house was asleep, and Karol and Desmond were just about to retire for the night when suddenly Mrs Sikorska burst in like a thunderbolt with the news that Genowefa was giving birth.

Someone would have to go to Sulistrzyce at once to fetch the midwife, so Mrs Sikorska herself set off, as she was the only one who knew where the old lady lived, and it was a matter of urgency. Shocked and worried, Karol went to see the patient. She was lying alone in a cramped little cubbyhole at the back of Mrs Sikorska's room, sweating profusely and clutching at the bed rail. She was emitting regular, feeble groans, but she turned her dull, semi-conscious gaze on him.

'It's Kletkie's fault,' she said, although he hadn't asked her any questions.

He stood over her for a while, and as she didn't seem to be in any imminent danger, he turned to go, but she seized him by the hand and in a state of terror begged him not to leave.

Karol thought the delivery was still a long way off, so he wasn't overly concerned at this, when suddenly Genowefa let out a very loud scream, followed by a long howl of strain and suffering, and her little daughter came into the world before Karol's very eyes. He caught a glimpse of the tiny creature, red and frightful with its fat umbilical cord, lying between Genowefa's legs in a pool of blood and mucus. All of a sudden the creature began to snort like a little foal, but much more daintily, and soon after a thin, pitiful squeal rang out from under the legs of the moaning Genowefa.

Shaken to the core, Karol held tightly onto Geno-wefa's hand; in a daze of shame and joy she was still moaning and crying. He leaned over the child; it looked hideous, and so pitiful that he felt like crying too.

'What a thing is man,' he thought of his old refrain.

Just then Mrs Sikorska appeared with the old lady, and laughing sent him into the other room. But Karol couldn't laugh. He was shocked by the pitiful, wretched birth of human kind.

'They're all, all of them born like that,' he told Desmond.

'I think you were probably born like that too, weren't you?' said Desmond.

There couldn't be any news from Tarnice, because there was nothing going on there. Beset with material cares and concern about the health of Jadwisia, who had become feverish, Julek had fallen into more and more of a trance, which might at first sight have been taken for selfishness. Mindlessly he took the boys through their lessons, which had become an extremely burdensome chore, then he would go to the mill, where Jadwisia had told him to check on Zdyb's work. But it didn't take long, as there was less and less work to do, and in the run-up to the new harvest it had ceased entirely. Zdzisio had brought in some money, claiming it was dues extracted from the peasants and the Jews. It never entered Julek's head to have the faintest doubt about the source of this income. Jadwisia knew it came from Hopfer, Julek's friend who had been driven away from the mill.

One day towards the end of March there was a painful scene between the lovers. For lunch there was potato soup and dumplings again, which Julek ate in silence, then asked for some tea. At that moment Łowiecka's misery and exasperation exploded in an unexpected attack, and all her complaints and invective landed on Julek's head. She insisted that all because of Julek she was wasting her life and her children's lives at the mill, that they

247

were in such dire straits because of him, and that it was his fault she was living in terrible sin. Łowiecka wasn't religious. She had spent her life in the wilds of the Carpathians, which was just as primitive as a mill outside Warsaw – in short, all the reproaches she cast at Julek were quite unjustified and groundless. It surprised him greatly; he thought maybe he hadn't really known this woman until now, but it made him feel unspeakably sorry for her, and he tried to calm her tears, which were streaming copiously down her haggard face.

He embraced her warmly, sat her down, kissed her brow and stroked her hair. Gradually she calmed down. 'So come on then, little one, tell me,' he said gently, 'tell me, and don't cry, tell me you're happy, aren't you, you're happy, right? Remember the words of the prayer, "I regret, O lord, my dark desires … A flower does not desire, it does not weep … no thought occurs to it … but Thou didst not want me to live in ignorance of being alive." It's a joy to know that, isn't it? So tell me, are you happy?'

'Yes, I am,' replied Łowiecka rather uncertainly.

'So you see, one has to make certain sacrifices for the sake of happiness. It's worth suffering a lot of things in exchange for one brief moment of happiness.'

'What if it isn't worth it?' said Łowiecka through her tears.

At these words Julek caught a glimpse of the abyss of his own self-deprivation in exchange for a brief moment of happiness – a vast, refulgent chasm, with only a fence as frail as a floodgate separating him from it. Not even the tiniest drop of water was seeping through from that chasm – and he could feel that his lips were parched.

Since then he had returned to his solitary strolls, although the early spring was very nasty, and cold gusts of wind shot through his threadbare coat. It was chilly and gloomy. Sometimes on his walks he reached the corner at the top of the meadows, from where he could see the church at Sulistrzyce. Its blue painted tower stuck out among the bare grey trees in the shadow of its rusty roof. The wind-tossed trees in the cemetery sloped westwards, their branches swaying pitifully; the sky was grey, covered in thick, dull clouds.

More than once he thought of carrying on, going past the church and then dropping in at Krzywizna. At such moments Hopfer's manor house seemed a refuge, the cretonne-covered furniture a garden of rest, and Desmond as refreshing as a cool mountain spring. But he knew he couldn't go there – it would mean having to walk past the church and raise his cap to the cross he had betrayed, and there was no place for him at Krzywizna any more. Whenever he thought how impossible it was to go further, he found justification in the simple fact that 'besides, it would be so unpleasant for Jadwisia!'

One day, he was on his way back from one of these solitary walks, frozen to the core and thinking of having a glass of vodka. Before the mill stood some unfamiliar horses, but he took no notice, as so many carters came here with grain or for flour. But on his way through the mill he noticed a strange look on Zdzisio's face; he was chewing his lip as he untied a sack of wholemeal from the pipe. He nodded knowingly.

'What's up?' asked Julek.

'Mr Łowiecki's here,' whispered Zdzisio into Julek's ear.

Julek's heart sank. But without a moment's hesitation he confidently climbed the stairs and entered the main room. Jadwisia and Łowiecki stood up from the table.

Jarosław Iwaszkiewicz

Łowiecki was a tall, greying man with a large moustache. Jadwisia had traces of tears on her face, yet she said calmly, 'Mr Zdanowski, Mr Łowiecki.'

The gentlemen exchanged greetings, and then they all sat down at table. Gesturing in the manner of host, Łowiecki invited Julek to share the food that was laid out on the table. Łowiecki went on eating, drank some vodka, then asked for tea. As he brought in the kettle, Zdzisio cast a rather superior, even mildly ironical glance at the assembled company. Julek's ears burned with shame.

He and Jadwisia remained silent. Łowiecki spoke a lot, but only on trivial matters.

'You must be surprised to see me here,' he finally addressed Julek. 'I myself was not expecting to visit the mill again.'

His voice was flat but firm and manly, with an eastern borderlands accent. He was altogether stronger and more resourceful than Julek. As he sat opposite, his bulging blue eyes stared straight into Julek's. The whites of his eyes were shot with small red veins, and his fair but greying crew cut accentuated his rural appearance.

'I came to see my sons,' he went on, noisily stirring his tea and chewing the bread and sausage, which he must have brought himself, as there was nothing to eat in the house. 'I haven't seen them for a long time and I was missing them. And I won't have far to come any more – I'm living in Warsaw now, I've been transferred to the state forestry administration. I've got a nice flat in a coop-erative in Żoliborz. I'll take the boys to my place in the autumn. I think you'll let me have them, won't you? No? As you think best.'

He said all this calmly and sincerely, looking at Julek in a kindly way as if he were a younger brother, and through his conversation he created a cosy family atmosphere. The room was warm, and Julek was glad of the hot tea.

Łowiecki had a straightforward way of accepting *faits accomplis* without any drama. At the same time he was unnervingly sure of himself. It was as if he regarded his wife's Tarnice episode as something transient and impermanent; his self-confidence sent shivers down Julek's spine.

Łowiecki did not dally at the mill for long. He gave the boys some sweets he had brought for them, and when in answer to the question of who was teaching them now they said 'Uncle Julek' he didn't wince at all; he merely looked over their books and exercises. For the entire duration of his visit Jadwisia studiedly avoided Julek's gaze. With eyelids lowered and a weak smile on her lips, she was silent, seeming subdued and apprehensive. Her personality seemed to have faded into the shadows of the March evening.

By the time Łowiecki left it was getting dark. Together they saw him off from the threshold; the forester leaned and kissed Jadwisia on both cheeks in a perfunctory, ritual way, as if he were off to town for a couple of days. Julek felt more strongly than ever that Jadwisia was another man's property, that she belonged to another world, to a different generation, and that the fact that she was married was an insurmountable obstacle.

As he seated himself in the carriage Łowiecki said to his wife, 'If you are ever in Warsaw, drop by, come and see how I live. You could even stay the night – I've got three rooms now.'

The carriage moved off with a loud whirring of wheels. Łowiecki turned and waved, then vanished among

251

the chilly shadows. In silence they turned towards each other.

⸜ In the short time they had spent outside, Julek sensed a change in the nature of the harsh spring wind. It was cold, but at the same time there was a distant breath of melting snows on the breeze. In the blue twilight the whistling of the gale was no longer playing an autumnal tune.

They sat down at table again. The green lampshade cast a dull shadow on Jadwisia's long face as she drummed her fingers on the table.

'Well I never,' she said suddenly, 'he's living in Warsaw!'

Julek knew that a flat in Warsaw had long since been her ideal home and that she would have given a lot to live in the capital.

But instead of appreciating the degree of her sacrifice, and that she stayed on in this wilderness and poverty for his sake, he felt envious. Not of Łowiecki, the strong, older man, but of the city.

Darkness fell as they sat there opposite each other, quietly mulling over the thoughts that the unexpected visit had prompted. At last, Julek stood up and went out onto the balcony. Beyond the pond, to the east, way up on high a weak moon was glowing, dead still among the violent gusts of wind. The lights of Warsaw reflected in the black sky, so very near, and yet so impossibly far away.

Just then Julek had the most bitter feeling – not of regret or despair any more, but simply that Jadwisia's love, her real, true love, meant very, very little.

He went back to her, kissed her and embraced her simply and sincerely. He could see in her eyes that he had

driven away not only all thought of her former husband –
who had brutalised and beaten her – but also of Warsaw,
and everything else in life. At the same time he felt that
the life ahead, breezing in on the first breath of melted
snow, was a vast desert, devoid of achievement. He had
felt this once before, in the mountains, when just before
reaching the very top, an easy one to climb, he had given
way to the persuasions of idleness and turned back in view
of the summit. That night he fell asleep with the same
sense of something missing in his soul, and the next few
weeks, chilly and cloudy, brought neither relief nor remedy for his permanent feeling of sorrow.

One day he was awoken at dawn by something prick-
ing his hand; a spider had bitten him, then run across
his body and disappeared behind the bedstead. Julek
inspected the tiny wound at the bottom of his middle
finger, where he found a double bite mark. Then he
tried to go back to sleep, but couldn't. He tossed and
turned, and felt thirsty, so he went into the main room
for some water. The sun was rising behind the misty
pond. He opened the door and went out onto the
balcony. It was chilly, so he went back in, threw on his
coat and stood out on the balcony again.

Water, bushes, trees – all blended into one, like a face
steeped in a veil of mist. For a long time Julek stood and
stared at that face, trying to find a meaning in it, but he
knew it was in vain. He wanted to tear the mist apart and
see God behind it, but he couldn't. Never before had his
frightened soul felt such deep terror at the world's obscurity. He clasped his hands to his brow and repeated
that name, now nothing but a hollow sound, 'O God, O
God, O God! What does it all mean?' And as if something depended on it, he pressed the question, he made it

insistent, urgent and compelling, 'O God, what does it all mean? where is the meaning of it all?'

But the lifeless landscape gave no answer. The bushes around the mill stood colourless, as if lying in wait, jealously guarding their secret, as if ever so slightly removed into the depths of eternity. The grey water lay beyond them still and flat as a metal plate. Seized with cold, he retreated. A fearful cold, that shot through him like a sharp, slender lancet, sought out his once ardent heart to strike it numb. The emptiness of the world was like the emptiness of a mirror where he couldn't see his own face.

He fell into deep, heavy sleep. Jadwisia awoke him, happy, younger somehow; as he opened his eyes and saw her leaning over him in a red and black dressing gown, well rested and smiling, once again he felt that sense of security, of being alive in her presence.

'Get up,' she cried. 'Get up. The blackthorn is in bloom!'

He jumped out of bed. The early morning mist had lifted and it was a beautiful spring day. He went out onto the balcony. The bushes, which at dawn had looked dead and grey, now stood out against the bright blue water and the bright blue sky, all covered in a white snow of flowers. He bolted down his breakfast.

'Let's go and look at the blackthorn,' said Mrs Łowiecka.

'Guess what,' complained Julek, 'a spider bit me on the hand … last night … there, look …' and he showed her the scratch mark. 'It still hurts, you know.'

'It's nothing,' said Łowiecka dismissively. 'I'll wash it for you.'

She fetched some peroxide and wiped the wound with cotton wool.

, 'There you are. It's nothing, I tell you.' Catching a note of concern in her voice, Julek wondered.

They went out to see the blackthorn. The bushes stretched far along the water. They weren't at all remarkable – summer and winter long they were inconspicuous. Only now, and only for a few days, did they appear in their full glory. Snowy plumes fell like ostrich feathers from the leafless grey branches, light as a breath of wind. At one point the bushes formed a dense thicket, great fountains of fluffy, snowy whiteness growing taller than a man's height. They tried to go through this thicket, but became entangled in it. Finally, Jadwisia got through along a side path and Julek could hear her calling from over by the pond. 'Julek, Julek, come and see how lovely it is by the water!'

Meanwhile he couldn't force his way through to her. For a moment he felt as if he were dreaming. Surrounded by dense, prickly blackthorn, he had lost the path and was fighting his way blindly through the bushes. He drew aside two branches, overgrown with white lichen, and caught sight of the pond, vivid and blue, with Jadwisia standing pensively by the water, hands folded behind her head. Her figure stood out in relief against the sky-blue background. The first spring clouds were rising towards Krzywizna. A vast white fortress – the domain of the angels – stood motionless, triangular, tooled out of thistledown, the colour of mountain snow, a tower of Babel of the celestial sphere. The cloud was just starting to cast its reflection in the water.

Jadwisia's presence gave some sense to this landscape; though foggy and blurred, her figure was at least palpable.

'I love you,' he said aloud, though she couldn't hear him. And in his elation he grasped the two wands of

255

blackthorn that he was holding apart. It pricked his left hand. He looked at the wound – a long sharp thorn had stabbed into him an inch away from the spider's bite. A fat, red drop of blood appeared, its dark purple colour contrasting sharply with the deep blue of the sky and water, the whiteness of the clouds and flowers, and the blackness of the woman's silhouette.

Ignoring the stab wound, Julek walked over to Jadwisia. He removed her hands from above her head and kissed them. They sat down by the waterside in an embrace, and drew into their nostrils the fresh scent of moisture and flowers, the scent of spring.

'Don't worry, Jadwisia,' said Julek, 'don't worry. We're happy, and we're going to stay happy.' Leaning towards her he gazed into her eyes. But in her plain, black pupils there lay a twinkle, a distance, as if she were avoiding an answer, as if she had shut the door on Julek and walked away from him in her thoughts. Like an echo she repeated, 'We're going to stay happy.'

Once again Julek had a sharp sense of his own isolation. The illusion of contact with another person afforded him by Jadwisia's presence had dissolved, and in spite of being together they were both alone, just two lonely people sitting by the lonely water.

Up ran Drucik, who had sought them out in the bushes. The little dog pawed at them in excitement, but this canine enthusiasm only served to heighten the sadness of the moment.

Towards evening Julek began to complain of a growing pain in his hand. It had swelled up a lot, and at the height of the swelling two marks showed, the spider's bite and the blackthorn wound. Jadwisia sent Zdyb to the chemist's for Burow's solution, but he didn't come back for ages. Apparently he had run into Kletkie, and they had slung such abuse at each other that they had to be forced apart. Evidently, they had had to drown their agreement or lack of it at old Stukułka's, because Zdyb returned late, extremely cock-eyed, and responded to Mrs Łowiecka's rebukes by standing up for himself most high-handedly.

During the night Julek struggled in his sleep, and was clearly quite feverish. He dreamed of a spider, scuttling off into the blackthorn thicket, first tiny, then becoming huge. At daybreak the fierce pain in his hand awoke him and wouldn't let him go back to sleep. His whole fore-arm had swollen up, and long red streaks had appeared along the muscles. Jadwisia took fright and sent for the doctor. Towards evening the district doctor came, exam-ined the hand, prescribed a very tight hot compress, and left. Next day in the afternoon Julek fell into a heavy doze, interrupted by shivering. Kazik helped Zdzisio in the mill, where there was a little grain again. Łowiecka left Staś by Julek's bedside and set off on foot for Krzywizna to borrow a thermometer, as she had to take his temperature.

That fine evening Karol was sitting on the balcony overlooking the garden, waiting for the sun to set. He had had a fruitless talk with Kletkie, who had refused to admit paternity of Genowefa's baby daughter. He had stood in an inspired pose in the middle of the kitchen, waving his fist as he not only cast doubt on the poor girl's claim but even swore vengeance and all kind of misfortune upon her. The final result was his dismissal.

Later, as he packed up his goods and chattels, he foamed at the mouth, cursing Krzywizna and its owner, while summoning up all the great families and all the magnificent residences which had enjoyed his entrecôtes and Kraków buckwheat kasha.

Compared with these splendours, Krzywizna shrank into obscurity, and its inhabitants along with it. But to reduce them to utter ignominy, he went on to give details of all the menus of all the great parties and wedding feasts he had ever prepared. Mrs Sikorska simply collapsed beneath their great weight, while there stood Kletkie in his chequered trousers, brandishing a riding crop ornamented with a rusted dog's head, as he spat forth the names of all those dishes and ingredients, which to the poor housekeeper sounded like all kind of foreign devilry.

Only Desmond was left now, wandering about the drawing room, putting on record after record. On the still air of the spring evening the blaring of saxophones and the plangent tones of the Hawaiian guitar sounded odd, more suited to a crowded, stuffy night club. The stream of jazz made no impression on the silent countryside as it waited for the close of day. The red sun failed to imbibe these sounds, their aimlessness rendering them even more plaintive amid the sky-blue expanse enveloping the manor house. The guitars jangled in time with the first cicadas of evening.

Desmond was feeling better. He and Karol did a lot of talking about the spring, and about Genowefa's new-born child. Desmond had become the baby's godfather; he wanted to name her 'Night', but Polish custom wouldn't allow it, so she was called Natalcia. Karol's cloud of gloom had passed over now, giving way to a reborn, slightly easier world. These days were beautiful.

... All night have the roses heard ...

Then suddenly there stood Łowiecka before him, the last person he had been expecting. Her dress was crumpled and her hair unkempt. She had come in a hurry and was plainly exhausted. At once she began asking for a thermometer, saying Julek was ill.

At first Karol was worried; he realised something was wrong. However, he calmed down considerably once he had found out what was the matter – just a silly scratch. But Łowiecka told her story so incoherently that he couldn't tell whether the infection was from the spider's bite or the blackthorn; she never did give a precise answer to that question. She stayed longer than was necessary for borrowing a thermometer. Karol could see that she was anguished, and that there was something else she wanted to tell him, but he didn't prompt her to pour out her heart, for fear of an apology for turning her back on his house.

Karol thought she was exaggerating Julek's illness, merely using it as an excuse for her visit. As he had to be in Warsaw for a few hours the next day, he promised to bring a doctor, a friend of his, who happened to be a famous surgeon.

Łowiecka kept putting off her departure, as if afraid to go back to the mill. Karol sensed that there was something she wanted to say or ask. But all she said was that Julek was asking for Desmond. Finally, without airing perhaps the most important things, she took the thermometer and left.

Next day at first light Desmond drove to the mill. Karol did not get back from Warsaw until the afternoon; the doctor was to come in the evening. Karol ordered the carriage to take him straight to Tarnice from the railway station. The mill stood idle, and no one came out to meet him. He ran through the gloomy ground floor and up the dusty stairs. In the large room he came upon a prostrate figure lying on the floor. To his great dismay he found it was Father Górski.

'Good God! What are you doing here, Father? What's the matter?' he said, almost forcing the old man to his feet. The priest was in tears.

'Would you believe it?' he said in a strangled tone, 'he refused the confession, he didn't want it … he turned his back on the Holy Communion … he turned his face to the wall … he clamped his mouth shut.'

'What has happened?' said Karol as he led the tearful old man as quickly as he could to the corner furthest from Julek's bedroom and sat him down on a chair. 'What has happened, Father? Is it really that bad?'

'Łowiecka sent for me, so I came at once. But he refused me, he refused! What a man he is!'

'Is it that bad?'

'It's very bad.'

Karol left the priest leaning against the window frame, shaking with violent but soundless sobbing. He gently opened the door and went into Julek's bedroom, where semi-darkness reigned. Her hair loose, Łowiecka was standing over the bed; Desmond was sitting beside the invalid, holding his healthy hand. Julek was lying on his back in a terrible fever, breathing heavily. The whites of his eyes were shining beneath half-closed lids. His entire left arm was swathed in bandages, swollen thick as a log. Red streaks of infection ran from under the bandage across his shoulder and chest.

Łowiecka turned and looked at Karol. Desmond, too, cast him an outwardly blank, yet very painful look, then went on staring fixedly at Julek's face.

Karol took Łowiecka into the other room. 'What's going on?' he asked. 'Is it much worse?'

Łowiecka gave no answer. Her lips were trembling with stifled tears as she absently stroked the lapels of Karol's jacket. Seeing that she would burst into tears at any moment he led her off into the little room opposite, where her sons were standing at the window. Karol told them to leave and they slunk off down to the mill.

But Jadwisia did not start crying. She told him that Julek hadn't slept all night, and that she had stayed up too; he had been conscious, but saying the strangest things, half of it incomprehensible, and he was longing to see Karol. He had a tremendous fever, his heart was growing weaker and she had sent for the priest. She confirmed that Julek had refused even to look at the priest and had rejected the sacrament, turning his face to the wall with his mouth shut tight. In fear of profanity, the priest had consumed the Host himself.

Karol left Jadwisia in the boys' room and asked her to make some tea for Father Górski, who was now sitting quietly in the dining room, resting his head in his hands. Karol went back to Julek.

Julek had opened his eyes but didn't see Karol enter. Desmond was muttering poetry and whenever he stopped Julek whispered, 'Go on, Desmond, go on'.

Casting another fleeting glance of despair at Karol, Desmond started up again: *'It was the schooner Hesperus, that sailed the wintry sea …'* And so he went on to the end of his ballad, but as soon as he stopped Julek opened his eyes and again said firmly, 'Go on, Desmond, go on'.

At once Desmond repeated the final stanza:

'Such was the wreck of the Hesperus, in the midnight and the snow …
Christ save us all from a death like this …'

261

The doctor came, examined the patient and went with Karol into the dining room. Father Górski was sitting in an armchair with a large breviary, praying almost out loud. 'Yesterday there would still have been a chance to amputate the arm,' said the doctor in a matter-of-fact way.

As Karol was seeing the doctor out, he noticed Zdzisio in the bowels of the mill, flushed and agitated as he raised his hand to hit little Kazik; illuminated by the reddish light from Zdzisio's cubbyhole, the group moved into the shadows and disappeared from sight. Once he had seen the doctor to his horses, on his way back through the darkness he came across Zdyb.

'Why did you hit the child?' he snapped at him, his mind elsewhere.

'If you please sir, he was telling filthy tales about his mother.'

'Telling filthy tales? About his mother?'

'That he was, sir. The little swine!'

Julek was feeling better now. As Karol entered his room, Łowiecka was kneeling by the bed and Desmond had stopped his recitation; Julek recognised his friend and smiled.

'Julek,' said Łowiecka suddenly at the top of her voice, as if determined to say something, 'Julek, listen to me.'

Karol froze. Julek smiled again weakly, less conscious now. With a great effort he said, 'Jadwisia, what is it, Jadwisia?'

'There's something I have to tell you. I want you to know everything.' She sat down on the edge of the bed and grasped Julek's healthy hand in both her own; he withdrew it from her grip.

'Listen to me ...'

Karol realised it was his turn to act. Briskly he stepped up to the bed and put his arm around Mrs Łowiecka's shoulder. 'Jadwiga,' he whispered firmly, 'Jadwiga, please bear in mind that Julek is very ill.'

She turned her vacant gaze on him, not taking in a word he was saying.

'He can't go like that,' she said, abruptly loud, 'he can't go like that, I must tell him the whole truth.'

Karol quickly took control of the situation. He seized Łowiecka by the arms as tight as he could and wrenched her off the bed; he noticed Julek open his eyes wide in dismay at the sight of their struggle. In his fevered state his eyes looked almost black and deep as wells.

Almost by force Karol dragged Łowiecka out of the room. In the dining room she hung on his neck, shrieking hysterically. 'Yes, yes, I must tell him. He mustn't go like that, he mustn't!'

Karol dragged her over to the stairs. 'Let him die in peace,' he said.

They all but fell downstairs into the mill, where they reeled about in the darkness and came to rest against some sacks. Łowiecka tugged at her dress.

'He must know, he must know, I must tell him …'

'Calm down!' Karol shouted angrily. 'What have you got to tell him? Why can't you let him die in peace?'

'The truth, the truth … I want to tell him the truth!'

'To hell with your truth!'

'I've been unfaithful to him ever since he has lived here. I've been unfaithful to him with Zdzisio.'

A loud, rustic hawking resounded in the darkness. Zdzisio was somewhere nearby. Karol gave Łowiecka a violent push in that direction. 'Zdzisio, look after her,' he said.

263

Almost out of his senses, he ran upstairs. Here it was quiet. Father Górski was whispering prayer after prayer. In Julek's room Desmond stood leaning against the bedstead with his cold, black, simian hand on the dying man's burning brow, his nimble lips still whispering, '*Christ save us all from a death like this ...*'

'Go on, go on,' Julek tried to say, as Desmond's words fell silent.

And Desmond started up again: '*All night have the roses heard ...*'

And so it went on, until the next day at four in the afternoon, when Julek's heart stopped beating. Mrs Łowiecka came in when he was already completely unconscious.

As Karol and Desmond were on their way home the Negro said, 'Maybe those poems were his communion?'

That evening Karol changed his will in favour of Desmond King.

A couple of weeks after Julek's funeral, in spite of everything Karol set off for Tarnice to visit Mrs Łowiecka. He found her with her mother, who had been at the mill since Julek's death.

It was a fine day in May and very warm. The sky was full of large clouds; they stood high, lit up by the sun like the templates for some unearthly mountains. White and ethereal, they kept changing shape, drifting about the dull blue sky. The mill pond was shimmering, pure and blue. As Karol drove up to the mill he saw Mrs Łowiecka's sons fooling about with the boat which last year had served for rides on the pond. He left Desmond with the horses.

Mrs Łowiecka was calm and looking better. When she was out of the room for a moment her mother informed Karol that her daughter had had a letter from her husband, so kind and so sincere that she had been very moved by it and had cried all night. Mrs Rygielowa was expecting the Łowieckis to be reconciled and her husband to forgive her everything.

Karol gazed out of the window at the bright blue pond and thought how Mrs Łowiecka herself may have a thing or two to forgive her husband. And it also occurred to him that it hadn't been worth so much fuss and bother only to end like this. But how else could it have ended? Swollen rivers return to their course, lost souls find peace, youth turns into old age. Right now he might even envy Julek for being over on the other side so soon. He would remain young and restless for ever. Never in his life would he come to know composure.

In reverent tones, Łowiecka told him everything Julek had said and wished for, in rather too much detail at that. In her voice he could detect an element of pleasure in her own anguish. She gave copious detail, reminding him of her mother's conversational style. There was no question of any dramatic confession. The person of Zdzisio had been once again demoted to the level of mill hand.

Karol gazed in silence at the woman's face, as on and on she talked.

It was very hot in the room, as usual, with the stove blazing, although it was warm outside. As before, a large white cloud was slowly drifting out from behind the pond; small, slanting violet streaks ran across its white background, like the whiteness of certain flowers. When Jadwisia stopped talking for a moment, they could hear the boys' shrieks coming from the pond, and another voice too: it was Desmond calling out in his awful Polish.

Karol stared hard at the face that was his friend's grave. Just as on a grave, the lines and wrinkles of regret

were fading, but ever so much faster. When Julek was
alive, Łowiecka seemed unable to live without him, but
now he was dead a newer life brought colour to her
cheeks; she was more natural, more confident, and more
ordinary. She had become common again, just as the first
time Karol had seen her.

. The tides of life, ruffled by Julek's disappearance, were
settling down again. A couple of periodicals would go on
to publish his final poems, then a small volume would appear, and that would be it. This woman would go back to
her husband; Mrs Rygielowa would run the mill again;
Zdzisio would relinquish his claim, with no regrets; the
wheel would slowly start to turn, the grain would begin to
whirr, the wholemeal would be milled, and irises and
buttercups would bloom yellow on the Utrata.

Just then they heard a violent shriek and a clatter of
feet on the wooden stairs. In rushed Desmond, hands
aloft and clucking like a hen, 'Mister Charles, Mister
Charles, Charles, Charles ...'

Everyone leaped from their seats.

'It's Kazik, Kazik, he's drowned,' cried Desmond, 'he's
drowned!'

The women rushed onto the balcony, but Karol lost
no time at all. Down the stairs and through the mill he
flew, casting off his jacket and waistcoat in one go. Desmond went running after him, squealing like a puppy and
tugging at his sleeves as he snatched up his discarded
clothing. Once they had reached the edge of the water,
they found Staś running to and fro, in floods of tears,
jumping frantically into the shallow water, pointing and
shouting, 'There! He's there!'

The boat was lying upside down in the deepest part of
the still blue pond. Something was moving and sending

up bubbles beside it. Karol threw off his shoes and trousers and leaped into the water. It was icy cold, and for an instant it took his breath away. But with strong, confident strokes he swam towards the boat. At the deepest point in particular the water was very cold. He could feel himself shivering and was afraid of getting cramp. Swiftly he swam across the short stretch. He had no trouble in feeling his way to Kazik, who was moving about in the water; he seized him by the hair and leaned against the boat, which yielded obligingly to his endeavours. Kazik was down to his shirt and had now lost consciousness. Karol seized him by the shoulder pleats and pulled him to the surface. With an enormous effort he laid him on the upturned boat, which had a flat bottom. He turned the boy face up, and water poured from his mouth and nostrils. People were already on their way from the mill in another boat.

Karol got back into the water, and grasping the back of the boat, gave it a mighty push towards the approaching vessel, kicking his legs hard as he did so. But at the same time he could feel the slimy boards of the boat slipping from his hands. He felt a sharp, impossible pain in his chest, water flooded into his mouth and his legs refused to do his bidding.

With a final effort he turned onto his back, and there above him he saw the high white cloud, and the slanting lilac wisps against it, then fathomless, boundless sky, melting into azure. Hardly a split second went by, yet suddenly he could feel and understand everything that had eluded him his whole life long, especially that night in Werfen. The veil before the world had been drawn aside, rent apart and vanished, and he could see – no, not just see, but touch, as the clear water streamed through his fingers he could touch the secret of life, at last no longer a secret. He was filled with pure bliss and a sense of peace so great that death alone can divulge.

And as he was leaving this world without regret, its meaning finally revealed to him, for a last moment he could still see Desmond standing on the shore, one hand raised skywards. And he thought he saw the man rising into infinity, rising towards the peaceful clouds, like a great black angel pointing towards the fading summit of the celestial firmament.

July 1936

Central European Classics

This series presents nineteenth- and twentieth-century fiction from Central Europe. Introductions by leading contemporary Central European writers explain why the chosen titles have become classics in their own countries. New or newly revised English translations ensure that the writing can be appreciated by readers here and now.

The selection of titles is the result of extensive discussion with critics, writers and scholars in the field. However, it can not and does not aim to be comprehensive. Many books highly prized in their own countries are too difficult, specific or allusive to work in translation. Much good modern Central European fiction is already available. Thus, for example the contemporary Czech novelists Kundera, Hrabal, Klíma and Škvorecký can all be read in English. Could one as easily name four well-known French, Dutch or Spanish novelists?

Yet, if one reaches back a little further into the past, one finds that it is the Central European literature written in German which has been most translated – whether Kafka, Musil or Joseph Roth. We therefore start this series with books originally written in Czech, Hungarian and Polish.